STRIKE OF THE STINGRAY

ALSO BY DAVID DELEE

Brice Bannon Seacoast Adventures
Crimson Storm
Siege at Tiamat Bluff
The Yakuza Gambit
Strike of the Stingray
The Oceanic Princess
Facing the Storm

Parker Quinn Archaeological Thrillers
The Scarlet Death

Dark Justice Thrillers

Between Truth & Lies	Out of the Game
Cold Cases	With Intent
Too Far	Moral Misconduct
Stare at the Moon	Pin Money
While the City Burns	Crystal White
Takedown	Fatal Destiny

Runners

STRIKE OF THE STINGRAY

A BRICE BANNON
SEACOAST ADVENTURE

DAVID DELEE

COPYRIGHT

For more information about new releases, special events, and exclusive content only available to subscribers, sign up to get David's newsletter.

https://www.subscribepage.com/daviddelee

Thank you for purchasing this book. We hope you enjoy it.

Dedicated to the brave men and women who serve in the U.S. Coast Guard, past and present. Thank you for your service.

Semper Paratus
"Always Ready"

STRIKE OF THE STINGRAY

Five Years Earlier
Outside Kandahar, Afghanistan

THE SUN BURNED HIGH in the bleached-out sky, a white orb searing a stretch of paved road running through the barren landscape south of the NATO-controlled Kandahar Airport. The arid desert rolled out on either side of the road like a lumpy brown dirt carpet. Scattered patches of sagebrush and brushwood broke up the dreary monotony of bumps and berms.

Nothing moved in the hot desert until a tan, high-mobility multipurpose wheeled vehicle—commonly called a Humvee—sped along the highway, traveling at a steady thirty-five miles per hour. Camouflaged in a desert sand pattern, the military transport vehicle was armed with an M2 Browning .50-caliber machine gun. It crewed with four personnel. The gunner was in position, wearing a dark ballistic vest, a tan camouflage helmet, and large, orange-shaded goggles. The vehicle provided security for the close-column convoy that followed.

Traveling forty meters behind their security escort, a light-armored vehicle served as convoy lead to three medium tactical vehicles and one M925 five-ton cargo truck. The trail vehicle was a second Humvee.

Sergeant Josh Starling drove the trail vehicle with Specialist Jon LaRosa riding shotgun—literally. Born in Sedona, Arizona, Starling was no stranger to temperatures that could reach a hundred and four degrees Fahrenheit and to an unrelenting barren desert that offered no relief from the broiling sun and searing heat. Beside him, LaRosa, an olive-skinned Puerto Rican kid who'd lived his whole life in Miami—complained nonstop about the heat, as if his whining could change it.

"How ain't you hot, Sarge?" he asked again, wiping a rolling drop of sweat from his temple.

"Used to it." Starling sped the Humvee up, closing the gap between them and the last tactical vehicle, the M925. A blunt-nosed truck capable of transporting ten thousand pounds of cargo in its seven-by-fourteen-foot bed, it had a hinged tailgate and side racks, troop seats, and a tan canvas cover that sagged between its wobbling supporting ribs as the truck barreled down the road.

"They say it's different," LaRosa said, making conversation.

"What's that?" Starling asked, not caring what LaRosa had to say.

"Dry heat versus tropical heat," LaRosa replied. "It's all friggin' hot, you ask me."

Starling didn't respond, but that didn't stop LaRosa.

"Least where I'm from," he said, "you've got lots of water to jump into. Cool yourself off, you know what I mean?"

Before Starling could reply, he heard the split-second whine of an RPG and saw the streak of a white contrail flare across the barren landscape ahead of them. A thunderous explosion of sound followed. The blast obliterated the lead Humvee. Both their company commander and their platoon leader were in it. Its windows were blown out. Flames licked the roof. Oily black smoke billowed into the sky—a clear indicator to Starling there'd be no survivors.

Small arms fire opened up on the convoy from the low desert berms.

The radio crackled with frantic voices, calls for assistance, and airstrikes. Curses were shouted over the static as some convoy vehicles moved forward while others went in reverse, each driver indecisive as to whether to push ahead out of the kill zone or back up.

A second shoulder-fired anti-tank missile struck one of the tactical vehicles up ahead.

The impact lifted the truck onto two wheels before it slammed down again, righting itself. Two soldiers leaped from the cab. They ran for cover away from the burning truck and dove into a low gully beside the road.

An exchange of small and medium arms gunfire raged up ahead. Over it, Starling heard the rapid spitfire of a .50 caliber machine gun.

If there was Hell on Earth, this was it.

Starling threw his Humvee in reverse as the five-ton ahead of them barreled backward, desperate to get out of the kill zone. Starling slammed on the brakes and spun the Humvee around. The roadway behind them exploded in a geyser of macadam, dirt, and smoke.

"Get out!" he shouted to LaRosa. "Get out!"

The overly talkative specialist did as he was ordered, taking his M16 with him. They ran for the gully beside the road and dove for cover.

The five-ton truck struck Starling's abandoned Humvee, upending it a split second before another RPG-launched missile destroyed its cab, engulfing the vehicle in fire and smoke. From inside it, Starling and LaRosa could hear the dying men scream.

The engine compartment burned. The flames inside the cab roared out through the shattered windows, reached the canvas cover stretched over the ribs of the truck's cargo compartment, and soon it was burning hot, too.

From the bed of the truck, voices cried out.

Starling scampered out from the gully. "Cover me!" He raced for the vehicle, providing his own cover fire as he ran.

"Sarge! Josh! What the hell are you doing?"

Starling ignored LaRosa. He reached the back of the truck.

Tipped over at an angle, it crushed the Humvee beneath its two tires on one side of the rear tandem dual axle. He climbed up on the hood of his crumpled vehicle and unhinged the tailgate of the five-ton. It slammed open. He jumped back as the Middle Eastern men trapped inside the cargo space leaped and scrambled off the Humvee to escape the burning truck.

They tumbled to the ground and ducked as bullets pinged off metal and chewed chunks out of the macadam, spitting dark pebbles around them like shrapnel. The men were dressed in drab green and brown baggy clothes. Most wore a taqiyah. All were handcuffed behind their backs with black zip ties. In all, two dozen men fled from the back of the truck.

Ahead of them, another vehicle in the convoy exploded. More rocks and shrapnel rain down, pelting them. Starling ducked and covered his head.

One of the men from the back of the truck—a tall, dark-skinned man with a scraggly black beard and a soiled turban—stumbled over to Starling. He turned his back. The sergeant cut off the zip-tie restraints with his Ka-Bar knife.

The others gathered around him. Starling cut off all their zip ties, too.

When all the prisoners were freed, the tall man in the turban reached out and covered Starling's hands with both of his, cupping them, shaking them. "You saved our lives. You saved my life. You have been a good friend to me through troubling times, Josh Starling. Your compassion shall not go unrewarded."

The sound of approaching attack helicopters filled the air as the fighting around them grew fierce. The cries of the dying echoed over the barren emptiness of the desert. More RPG munitions landed and exploded around them.

"You must go, Ghaazi!" Starling shouted over the latest explosion. "Run! Now!"

Ghaazi Alvi nodded and took off running, joining the other escapees as they ran low and fast, quickly disappearing behind the rolling berms of desert and rocky ridges.

Starling watched them go with a grim but satisfied smile. He heard the roar of enemy vehicles and saw a cloud of dust billow up from behind their well-placed concealment. He nodded once and ran back to where LaRosa anxiously waited.

Starling slid back into the safety of their dusty, ad hoc foxhole.

"Christ, Sarge. What'd you do? You aided those prisoners in escaping."

Starling stared at him for a moment and then said, "I did."

He aimed his Beretta M9 at LaRosa's forehead and pulled the trigger, killing him. To the corpse, he said, "Let me know, Jon. Does Hell have a dry or tropical heat?"

FRIDAY

CHAPTER ONE

DRESSED IN TAN SLACKS, a short-sleeve polo shirt, and boat shoes, Brice Bannon walked through the kitchen of his seaside tavern, the Keel Haul. A hole-in-the-wall dive bar on the main strip in Hampton Beach, a coastal jewel on the eighteen-mile New Hampshire seacoast.

The Keel Haul was Bannon's pride and joy.

At least, it had been until three weeks earlier, when a group of terrorists attacked the bar in the middle of the night, shooting up the place with automatic small-arms fire and grenades. Fire, smoke, and a lot of bodies later, the resulting damage had made a soup-to-nuts renovation all but unavoidable.

A process the Keel Haul was currently undergoing.

Paint-splattered metal scaffolding was pressed against one wall near the front of the bar. A worker in painter's overalls was taping and plastering the ceiling. Sawhorses, open gang boxes, ladders, and big rubber garbage cans with brooms and shovels stuck in them were all around the place. Sawdust covered the floor. Painters, carpenters, electricians, and laborers filled the bar with more people than Bannon typically served on a Saturday night.

He stepped through the propped-open kitchen door just as a table saw buzzed to life behind him. The noise vibrated his back teeth. He flipped back and forth through papers on a clipboard as hammer guns and power drills added to the cornucopia of construction sounds. Tables and chairs were stacked in one corner—a canvas tarp draped over them. Plastic sheets covered the booths, taped down with duct tape. He walked toward the bar, greeted by more banging and the colorful shouting of construction workers with Garth Brooks singing about his friends in low places from the jukebox.

Bannon glanced up from his clipboard in time to see his best friend, John "Skyjack" McMurphy, step through the open front door. It was open because there was no longer a door there.

Before the attack, the door had been a conversation piece. Salvaged by Bannon from an 18th-century British frigate, he'd discovered it during a dive off the coast of Rye Beach, just a few miles north of Hampton Beach. He'd restored the door to near-pristine condition and even installed an authentic brass porthole, complete with dog ears and nuts. To gain entry into the bar, the terrorists had blown the door to smithereens. What little was left was in the thirty-yard dumpster out back.

McMurphy paused in the doorway and looked around. His expression was one of amused bewilderment as he made his way to the bar. He wore gray running shoes, blue jeans, and a plaid work shirt—open and untucked. Underneath it, a black T-shirt that read: *603 Live Free or Die*. The state's area code and motto.

At six feet tall, McMurphy was as wide as a linebacker and could be twice as mean when angered. His unprovoked demeanor was jovial and as self-deprecating as they come. A career officer with the Coast Guard until his retirement a few years back. He had dark red hair, worn longer now that he was out of the service. As was usually the case, he puffed on a thick stogie jammed into the corner of his mouth.

The stools along the bar were all covered with plastic except for one.

There sat Captain Floyd, an ancient regular with rounded shoulders who, as near as anyone could tell, came with the bar when Bannon bought it. Floyd was never seen without his sea captain's hat. He looked to everyone like those carved wooden statues of a sea captain sold in every seaside novelty shop throughout the New England seacoast.

When he wasn't drinking, Floyd covered his beer mug with a liver-spotted hand to keep the dust from it.

McMurphy grinned. "Should've known you'd be here, Floyd."

"That's Cap'n to you, young man, and you can't smoke in here. It's against regulation."

McMurphy gave the old man a mock salute, ignoring his request regarding the cigar. "Aye, aye, Cap'n, sir."

Floyd grinned approvingly. "More like it."

Bannon stepped behind the bar and dropped the clipboard next to a stack of tumblers, also under plastic.

"Some mess you've got here, brother," McMurphy said.

"Tell me about it. These change orders are costing a fortune, and they keep rolling in."

Bannon was a ruggedly handsome man in his mid-thirties. As tall as McMurphy, he had a trimmer physique. One tailor-made for surfing, running, and swimming, which Bannon did a lot of in his younger days. Like McMurphy, a former commander in the Coast Guard, he remained in the reserve, but he no longer cut his dark, wavy hair to strict military regulation either.

A fine coating of sawdust covered it presently.

McMurphy leaned his elbows on the bar, planted a foot on the brass foot rail, and looked around. He reminded Bannon of a cowboy in the old West.

"When do you expect to be done with all this?"

"A couple or three days, according to my contractor, who I just met with." He looked around the bar, too. "Yeah, color me skeptical. Beer?"

"Thought you'd never ask."

Bannon reached under the counter and dug through a cooler full of ice, coming up with two chilled bottles of Coors Light. Bannon handed one to McMurphy.

"Gracias, sir." He tipped the bottle toward Bannon and then sucked half of it dry.

"What're ya thanking 'im for?" Floyd asked. "Service in this joint's been crap for weeks now."

"That's because we're closed, Cap'n. For renovations."

"Didn't ya notice all the construction going on around ya?" McMurphy asked.

Floyd looked around as if seeing it all for the first time, a sour expression on his face. He shook his head. "Naw. Ain't that."

Bannon gave the old man a bittersweet smile. "I miss Tara, too, Floyd."

"What?" The old man furrowed his forehead. His thick white eyebrows bunched over his nose. "Ya mean that girl hangs around here pretending to be a bartender?" He harrumphed. "Don't make me laugh. She's a pain in my—"

"Speaking of Blades, you hear from her lately?" McMurphy asked, drinking his beer.

"No. She's ghosted me." Bannon leaned on the counter and used his thumbnail to tear a rip in the silver label. "Learning her brother was alive after all this time thinking he wasn't. It hit her pretty hard."

"Not to mention finding out he's the evil terrorist mastermind who tried to kill nearly six thousand people." McMurphy shook his head. "That'd mess with anybody's head."

"Yeah, then there's that."

Bannon had dealt with devastating betrayals before. But he didn't have a brother or any siblings, so he'd never experienced the hurt that kind of betrayal would cause, not from a blood relative. His parents had been killed when he was very young. He had no memories of them. He'd grown up in the system. His earliest memories were of being bounced from foster home to foster home until he turned eighteen. That day, he joined the Coast Guard. There, he'd found a family at last.

"She went to go find him, didn't she?" McMurphy asked.

"That'd be my guess."

"I would've helped if she'd asked."

"That's why she didn't ask. She thinks this is her problem to fix."

McMurphy nodded. "You worried?"

Bannon gave the idea some thought. He shrugged. "Tara can take care of herself."

McMurphy nodded. "Yeah. Me, too."

The three of them were brothers and a sister-in-arms. That made them closer than family. So, of course, he was concerned for her. "Tell you the truth, though. It's Ghaazi Alvi's well-being I'd worry about more once Tara catches up to him."

"Amen to that, brother." McMurphy finished his beer. "You ask me, the little weasel deserves everything she gives him."

"Want another?" Bannon asked, indicating his empty beer bottle.

McMurphy slapped the bar. "No. Thanks. I've gotta run." He stepped back. "But the reason I stopped by. The Seacoast Penguins, we've got a game tonight... Six o'clock. Wondered if you wanted to tag along? We're going up against the Saltwater River Cats. The division leaders. We're gonna crush 'em."

McMurphy coached a Little League baseball team in the Hampton Beach organized youth league. He'd done it for years, and Bannon often went along and helped out. It was fun. He loved baseball, and the kids were great. A lot of them were sons and daughters of deployed servicemen and women. As such, much of the coaching came down to consoling the broken hearts of those missing their loved ones.

"Would love to but can't." Bannon held up his cell phone. "Grayson. I've got a meeting with her later in Boston."

Elizabeth Grayson, the former U.S. Army Four-Star General and current Secretary of the Department of Homeland Security, for whom they worked. Covertly. The two men and Tarakesh 'Blades' Sardana formed the core members of a small team of specially trained, highly skilled operatives she'd brought together for unique, sensitive, and, when necessary, secret missions outside the normal channels of either Homeland Security or the Department of Defense.

When she'd first approached him, Bannon called it black ops, and Grayson had bristled at the term.

"Secret, yes, but not black ops," she'd insisted. "A single unit that's small, efficient, and nimble enough to respond to and investigate specific, targeted threats to the homeland, threats that can't be effectively handled by standard operating means or a normal military response."

In other words, she said, a chance to make an actual difference in this scary world. To get things done when the lumbering, behemoth-sized political bureaucracy couldn't or wouldn't.

The three of them had agreed to her terms. And she to theirs. A few hiccups notwithstanding, the arrangement had worked well so far, going on nearly five years.

"Lucky you," McMurphy said. "What's she want?"

"Didn't say, specifically," Bannon said. "I'm hoping there's been some progress in locating the other railguns."

Three weeks earlier, Bannon and his team had tracked down a group of terrorists led by a zealot named Aziza Faaid. He and his cell had gotten their hands on a scaled-down, portable version of a devastating weapon called a railgun. Usually, the size of a battleship-mounted sixteen-inch, 50-caliber naval gun, the sort that weighs two hundred sixty-seven thousand pounds, with a sixty-six-foot-long barrel length.

Faaid's scaled-down railgun had fit on the bow of a thirty-five-foot-long Bowrider.

Based on state-of-the-art technology, the weapon could deliver a seven-pound projectile at seven times the speed of sound, generating muzzle energies of nearly fifty megajoules. Put in perspective, that was the kinetic energy equal to the impact of a five-ton bus traveling at over three hundred miles per hour.

Faaid had planned to use the railgun against a passenger cruise ship called the *Oceanic Princess,* under sail with over six thousand guests and crew onboard. Bannon and his team defeated Faaid, but not before his attack killed twenty-eight people and injured a hundred more. Two FBI agents and a Coast Guardsman named Troy O'Neil were among those killed trying to put a stop to the horrific plan.

Only after the weapon was destroyed and the terrorists were either killed or captured did Bannon and his team learn the railgun they'd sent to the bottom of the Atlantic Ocean was only a prototype. One of four. And the attack on the *Oceanic Princess* had simply been a test run. Three more operational railguns were out in the wild, somewhere in the United States. Waiting to be used. And no one had a clue where they were.

McMurphy handed Bannon his empty bottle. "Better you than me. Maybe ask her again why she benched us rather than have us help in the search. After all, it was us—we—who saved the day, as I recall." He slapped the bar and turned for the door. "Just saying. Have a good one. You, too, Captain Floyd."

Floyd held up a single finger.

McMurphy laughed. "You're a hoot, old-timer. Always good for a laugh, Cap'n."

When he reached the door, where there was no door, McMurphy turned. He pulled a Seacoast Penguins baseball cap from his back pocket and mashed it down on his head. He mimed opening an imaginary door, stepping through it, and then closing it again. Once on the imaginary other side, he leaned in, calling out over the construction noise. "Might wanna see about getting a door *before* you try and lock up tonight. Just a suggestion."

"It's being delivered in an hour, wise guy," Bannon shouted back. "Good luck. I've seen your kids play. I love 'em, but you're gonna need it."

McMurphy feigned horror and placed a hand over his heart. "Ouch!"

Bannon waved him away with a smile. "Get out of here."

CHAPTER **TWO**

THE LITTLE LEAGUE FIELD was in the neighboring town of Seabrook, in the Governor Weare Park. The field wasn't anything fancy. Had a nicely maintained diamond with a chain-link backstop and a four-foot-high chain-link fence running along the first and third base lines. Parents and friends lined the low chain-link fence on either side. The air felt thick and warm. The humidity was off the charts and about what one would expect in August in New Hampshire. The sky had turned purple. Overcast with thick clouds slowly drifting by, bringing with them the threat of a late afternoon thunderstorm.

McMurphy predicted the rain would hold off long enough for them to finish the game. Still, he crossed his fingers.

He removed his cap and wiped a bead of sweat from his forehead as he returned from breaking up a squabble between two players over how close the catcher was getting to the batter.

The umpire called out, "Play ball!"

Well into the early innings, the River Cats were up over the Penguins 3-2. So far, McMurphy thought with a wry grin. He had confidence in his boys—and girls, he reminded himself. The Penguins were in the twelve-year-old division, and two of his best players were girls—Sally Mumford, their pitcher, and Narwa Nour in left field.

He stepped back behind the backstop, wearing his cap and a pair of Ray-Bans, wishing he had a cigar. He never smoked around the kids, never even chewed on an unlit one around them. He clutched the links and shouted, "Come on, Tommy."

Mary Pawlowski, Tommy's mother, stood beside him. She had dark brown hair and was in her early thirties. A pretty woman, but she had the look of someone carrying the weight of the world on her shoulders. Life had not been kind to her so far, and it showed.

McMurphy knew because her husband was a friend. He'd also saved McMurphy's big redheaded butt while they were both in Afghanistan, not so affectionately known by those who'd served there as the sandbox.

Andy Pawlowski was a local boy born and raised there on the seacoast, like McMurphy, but they didn't know each other. Not until they met ten years ago, when Andy, a member of an armored brigade combat team, pulled McMurphy from a burning MH-65 Dolphin search and rescue helicopter he'd managed to crash in the eastern province of Nuristan, Afghanistan, saving his life.

They both returned from the sandbox physically whole, but re-entry into civilian life for Andy had been rough. He suffered from PTSD, had trouble sleeping, and had developed debilitating paranoia. As a result, he had trouble holding his temper, keeping a job, barely functioning day to day.

There had even been an incident of battery against Mary. Just the one time, she insisted.

"Hey, Mary," McMurphy said, shaking loose the cobwebs of the past. "Tommy's looking good at the plate."

She watched the skinny kid in the blue jersey at bat. Her son. She reached her fingers through the chain links, gripping the backstop like she was holding it for dear life. "Andy's been taking him to the batting cages on the weekends."

"That's good. It's helping. He's seeing the ball much better today."

The pitcher pitched. Tommy checked his swing. The ump called a ball as the baseball slapped into the catcher's glove.

McMurphy cupped his hands around his mouth. "Good eye, Tommy. Good eye." He looked at Mary. "Speaking of… Where is Andy? He knew there was a game today, didn't he?"

"He picked up a job. Last minute," Mary said.

"That's great," McMurphy said. "Doing what?"

At the sound of the ball smacking into the catcher's mitt—Tommy had swung at a pitch and missed—McMurphy called out. "That's okay, Tommy. You've got this."

"Driving," Mary said. "He's been hired to pick up a shipment from a warehouse somewhere up in the Lakes Region. Deliver it to Boston."

McMurphy gives her a sideways glance from behind his Ray-Bans. Andy's MOS was 19 Kilo, an M1 Armor crewman, meaning he learned how to drive and shoot tanks in the Army. With little civilian demand for such a skill, Andy had been training to get his CDL license. He'd learned to run big rigs overseas, but the last time they spoke, he'd told McMurphy he hadn't yet taken the test.

"Legit?" McMurphy asked about the work.

Mary shrugged. "It's a job."

Before McMurphy could make his feelings about that known, they were interrupted by the crack of an aluminum bat smacking a baseball hard. Tommy had hit a blistering line shot up the middle. The crowd cheered. Two outfielders and the second baseman were chasing the ball all the way to the fence.

McMurphy waved his arms, yelling, "Take two! Take two! Go, Tommy."

Mary bounced on her feet and clapped.

McMurphy charged out from the backstop and ran to the third base line as Tommy reached second. The outfielders were still scrambling to pick up the ball.

McMurphy shouted, "Third, Tommy. Take third!"

Tommy glanced over his shoulder to the outfield, then took off running again.

The left fielder picked up the ball and fired it in.

"Go! Go! Go!" McMurphy shouted.

The throw came in.

Tommy chugged along, losing his helmet along the way.

"Slide!" McMurphy shouted. "Hit the dirt!"

Tommy slid.

The throw was wide. Safe at third.

McMurphy reached third base as the boy came to his feet, dusting off his pants. He patted a meaty hand down on the boy's shoulder. "A triple! Holy cow, you smoked that ball, Tommy. Great job. Really great."

Tommy beamed. The shortstop from the other team handed him his helmet.

"Nice hit," the kid said.

"Thanks." Tommy put his helmet on. He looked up at McMurphy but frowned. "Sure wish my dad was here to see it."

McMurphy looked over at Mary. Not the first time Andy had disappointed the boy.

CHAPTER **THREE**

AS THE SECRETARY OF the Department of Homeland Security, retired general and one-term senator from the great state of Louisiana, Elizabeth Grayson oversaw a large number of federal agencies, including ICE, FEMA, TSA, the Secret Service, Border Patrol, and the U.S. Coast Guard, among others.

The U.S. Marshals Service wasn't one of them.

That tickled Bannon's internal warning systems when Grayson's chief of staff told him to meet her at the Federal Marshals Office on Courthouse Way in downtown Boston.

He arrived ten minutes early and was directed to a small conference room overlooking Boston Harbor. He declined an offer of coffee while he waited and opted instead to watch the sailboats entering and leaving via the channel. A one-hour harbor cruise ship motored past, returning its passengers to the landing at Long Wharf.

Just in time, Bannon thought. The sky over the water had turned threatening. A low ceiling of purple clouds had grown thicker and more menacing since Bannon left the Keel Haul on the forty-five-minute drive south. It wouldn't be long before the first splatter of rain began to fall.

Before leaving the bar, he's showered and changed into fresh clothes—a dark polo shirt this time, clean khakis, and a less worn pair of boat shoes. It was the dressiest he got unless the situation required his Coast Guard dress blues or, God forbid, the one dark suit he owned. Fortunately, this wasn't one of those situations. He'd left the light shell jacket in his truck, along with his .45. The gun he'd locked in the glove box.

Elizabeth Grayson strolled into the conference room. She had on a dark pantsuit and carried a leather briefcase bag. A thin woman in her late fifties with narrow, sharp features, she'd let her hair go naturally gray and looked all the more distinguished for it.

"Brice, you're here. Good. We can get started." She sat at the head of the conference table.

The young woman who'd escorted Bannon up from the lobby came in and placed a cup of coffee on the table for Grayson. She looked over at Bannon and smiled. "Are you sure I can't bring you anything, Commander?"

He returned her smile. "I'm fine. Thanks."

Once the woman was gone, Grayson asked Bannon how the repairs were going on the Keel Haul.

"Coming along," he said. "We should be ready to open in a few days."

"That's good."

It hadn't been until after Bannon resigned his commission and retired from the Coast Guard full-time that Grayson approached him with the idea of heading up her little strike force. He'd agreed on several conditions. One had been that when they weren't on assignment, he, McMurphy, and Tara would be free to live their lives, not sit around bases on standby waiting to be called into service or endlessly running drills for the sake of keeping them busy. In other words, he wanted them to be civilians, untethered to either the military or the bureaucracy, until the homeland needed them.

An unconventional idea that Bannon never thought would fly. Instead, Grayson agreed instantly. She'd even joked and said the arrangement would keep them out of her hair, with one caveat. They'd stay out of trouble. For the most part, they did.

Thus, the Keel Haul had been bought and renovated. A lifelong dream of Bannon's was to own and run a seaside bar. Nothing fancy. And sure, the place wasn't much, but it was his. A place he could call home, which he'd never had before in his life.

"So, what's up?" he asked, sounding casual, but his curiosity was piqued.

"There's been some developments." She pulled a stack of folders from her large leather briefcase bag and plopped them on the table.

"Regarding the loose railguns?"

"Yes."

After Bannon and his team had neutralized the threat to the *Oceanic Princess,* the task of locating the remaining railguns believed to be somewhere on U.S. soil fell to the Department of Justice, led by the FBI's anti-terrorism division and with assistance from Homeland Security as needed.

Bannon and his team had been, as McMurphy put it, benched.

That suited Bannon fine. They were a strategic strike force with neither the manpower nor the resources to conduct a nationwide search for the super weapons. They got called in when action, not investigation, was required.

That decision did not sit well with Tara, however.

But, of course, she had a personal stake in the situation.

She angrily vowed to make it her mission to find and stop her brother, Ghaazi Alvi. The man believed to have masterminded the attack against the *Princess*. They had it on pretty good authority he also had plans to use the remaining three railguns in additional attacks against the United States.

A race against the clock they dare not lose.

Against Elizabeth Grayson's official explicit orders not to go after Ghaazi, Tara soon disappeared without a word. She had gone out on her own to protect Bannon and McMurphy from any blowback her actions might cause.

Unofficially…

"Before we get into that," Bannon said. "Tell me about Tara. You are keeping tabs on her, aren't you?"

Grayson frowned. "We were."

He didn't like the sound of that.

She went on to explain. "We tracked her movements through Saudi Arabia, Tunisia, and even parts of Afghanistan and Iraq. We lost her crossing the border at Khorramshahr. The last we knew, she was still somewhere in Iran."

"Iran. What is she doing there?"

Grayson shrugged. "It would help if we had more information about Ghaazi Alvi. You knew him, yes?"

"Briefly. He was part of the mercenary group Tara was running with at the time. They freed me from the Taliban camp I was being held at. They operated under different aliases at the time. After that, we ran a few ops together. He was intense, focused, skilled. Not long after, he and Tara had a falling out of sorts, and he left."

"What did they fight about?"

"Not something we talked about much. I got the sense they had a difference of opinion about how to achieve their goals."

"Which were?"

"Revenge for their parents. Avenging their deaths." Bannon wiped at his brow. "Ghaazi wanted to take a scorched earth approach to dealing with their enemies."

"Which were who exactly?" Grayson asked. "They'd already dealt with those individuals specifically responsible for the bombing."

"That, I think, was part of the problem. The enemy kept changing. It was *Al-Jamā'ah al-Islāmīyah* at first. Then, Al Qaeda, the Taliban, ISIL. When Ghaazi left, most of the team went with him. Tara took it pretty hard. She and her brother were close. They'd fought together since their parents were killed. Those of the group that were left disbanded and went their separate ways. Tara joined up with us."

"Did she really believe Ghaazi was dead?"

Bannon took his time before he answered. When she'd gotten word her brother had been killed in a NATO airstrike in the northeast province of Panjshir, she'd gone a little crazy. She drank heavily, and twice, he and Skyjack had had to bring her back from what amounted to angry, revenge-seeking suicide missions. They'd rotated back to the United States soon after. It had taken a lot for Bannon to convince her to come with them to the States. Bannon never reported the incidents, nor were they ever spoken of again. Nor would he now.

"No doubt in my mind," he said in answer to Grayson's question. "I'm assuming you still have no idea where he is, either."

Grayson frowned. "If anyone's better at getting off the grid and staying off it than Tarakesh Sardana, it seems it would be her brother. Honestly, we have no idea where either of them are. And I don't mind telling you, it's frustrating as hell."

"Then be thankful Tara's doing what she's doing," Bannon said. "Because if anyone can find him, it'll be her."

"What worries me is what she'll do when she finds him."

Bannon had had the same thought earlier while talking with McMurphy. He kept those concerns to himself and changed the subject. "Tell me about the guns."

"We've located and secured one of the railguns."

"That's great. Two down," he said. He and his team had sent one to the bottom of the Atlantic Ocean. That left two more to go. "Where'd you find it?"

"In an abandoned warehousing facility upriver from Lake Erie, in Monroe, Michigan."

"Michigan? That's unexpected."

"Yes and no. Michigan has the largest Muslim population in the United States. A good place for Islamic fundamentalists to hide in plain sight."

"And radicalize and recruit."

"That, too." Grayson opened one of the files in front of her. "It also gives us our first clue as to how they smuggled the weapons into the country. We believe they were shipped in through the St. Lawrence Seaway."

The seaway was a three-hundred-seventy-mile waterway consisting of a series of locks, canals, and channels between the United States and Canada that allowed cargo ships and other maritime vessels access to ports in both countries and to travel from the Atlantic Ocean to the Great Lakes, reaching as far inward as the western end of Lake Superior.

"They were smuggled in? Not built here?"

"Broken down into various parts, shipped, and then reassembled here in the States is our best guess. With the first one on the bottom of the ocean floor, this is DARPA's first chance to examine one. They're reverse-engineering the thing now. What we've learned so far? It's the Frankenstein Monster of weapons creation. A hodgepodge of technology and retrofitted design specs from Russia, China, North Korea, and Iran. It's even got a fair amount of allied countries' tech, including designs stolen from us."

"Doesn't say much for the security of our intellectual properties."

"Tell me about it, but rest assured, that issue's being addressed."

He grinned, pitying the people who would eventually be on the receiving end of Grayson's wrath over it. "Do we know who actually constructed the damn thing?"

"Not yet, but that's not our concern at the moment. The remaining loose railguns are. Faaid and Zayd left how-to instruction videos behind before they died. Those guns can be made operational at any moment. It's like a time bomb ticking down—"

"And we have no idea how much time is left on the clock."

"Exactly. That's where you come in. You and Ms. Barnes."

Bridget Barnes, the radicalized American woman who threw in with Aziza Faaid and Safiyyah Zayd, their Middle East specialist in electromagnetic rail technology, and who'd acted as muscle and enforcer of their terrorist plan. She was also responsible for the death of Seaman Troy O'Neil, a member of a Coast Guard Maritime Safety and Security Team assigned to work with Bannon during the mission. It was

Barnes who'd led the attack on the Keel Haul that destroyed the bar and left O'Neil dead.

The only one of the three masterminds of the attack to survive, she'd cut a deal with Grayson upon her capture. She'd agreed to provide information against the terror cells she'd worked with in exchange for immunity from prosecution, which had carried with it the death penalty. Now, she enjoyed the all-expense-paid hospitality of the U.S. Marshals Service as a protected witness and probably would soon be granted a new identity and be lost in their famed Witness Relocation Program.

"Oh, you can't be serious." Bannon jumped to his feet. "No way."

There was a soft knock on the conference room door. Without waiting for a response, the door opened. In strolled Bridget Barnes. Followed by a young man in a dark suit, he nodded to Grayson before retreating from the room, closing the door behind him.

A federal marshal, Bannon reasoned.

Barnes wore her bright red hair pulled back and tied in a ponytail, dressed in tight, stonewashed blue jeans and a navy plaid flannel shirt. The sleeves were rolled partway up her arms, revealing her heavily freckled forearms. Her fingernails were manicured and painted blood red.

She sure didn't look much like a prisoner to him.

Bannon pressed his lips together and felt a vein pulse in his neck. O'Neil was dead. Twenty-eight passengers and crew from the *Oceanic Princess* were dead. Hundreds more were injured because of her. And she's getting manicures for crying out loud.

It was all he could do to keep from leaping over the table and wringing the woman's neck. He looked at Grayson and shook his head. "No way," he said. "No way in hell am I working with her."

CHAPTER **FOUR**

THE WOMAN BRICE BANNON and his friends knew as Tarakesh Sardana, who Skyjack McMurphy had lovingly nicknamed Blades all those years ago, wasn't in Iran. Not any longer.

While Secretary Grayson was briefing Bannon, Tara stepped smartly along a jetway in New York City's LaGuardia Airport, entering the international terminal. Deplaning Air Emirates Flight EK219, arriving from Dubai International Airport at Gate C28.

She strolled purposefully into the waiting area.

Kamal Chandra, the Deputy Director General of the India DIA, the Defence Intelligence Agency, stood wearing a dark suit and carrying a cup of coffee in one hand. He watched Tara emerge from the jetway wearing a wide, floppy-brimmed, pecan-colored sun hat, solid-heeled black boots, slim-fitting slacks, and a cream-colored blouse under a dark leather jacket. She carried a single overnight bag. Her full black hair was loose and bouncy. With her dark, exotic skin, sharp features, and trim physique, she turned heads as she always did.

She saw Chandra and acknowledged him with a nod.

As she got closer, he smiled and handed her the coffee cup in exchange for her carry-on. She leaned in, letting him kiss her cheek. They walked toward the exit but slowed as the crowd bottlenecked, trying to get through the security checkpoint.

She didn't ask Kamal Chandra how he'd gotten past security to be waiting at the gate. She'd known him for so many years she'd stopped being amazed a long time ago at his ability to do what others could not. They'd fought side by side in the same mercenary company during the war in Afghanistan. They'd been friends then and at one time had become something more intimate.

But that had been a long time ago.

"How was the flight?" Chandra asked to make conversation.

"Long."

"Nice hat," he said.

"Hides my face from the security cameras. The mustache," she said. It was new, pencil-thin, and barely visible on his dark face. It made him look like an Indian Inspector Clouseau. "I don't like it."

He grinned. "I'll shave it off right away."

"Good." She smiled. For the first time in weeks, it seemed. "He's here?"

"Straight to business." They bypassed baggage claim. Tara traveled light. "Good to see you haven't changed, *mushkil ek*."

She frowned but loved that he'd called her that. It was a pet name he'd given her years ago during a fight they were having. It meant *difficult one*. They exited the terminal. They each slipped on dark sunglasses. Not really necessary on the overcast day, but after years of hiding in the shadows and operating under disguise, doing so just felt natural, like wearing a mask.

"My car is this way." He pointed to the left, steering her toward a black town car waiting at the curb.

The driver got out. A large, Middle Eastern man wearing a dark chauffeur's uniform. Tara knew the man would be much more than that. In simplest terms, he was a bodyguard.

Chandra was that important. The man opened the back door and took Tara's bag from Chandra. Tara slipped into the backseat, and Chandra followed. The chauffeur climbed into the front seat.

"Varma, you know where to go," Chandra said.

"Yes, sir," he replied and then raised the partition between the front and back seats with the push of a button.

All sound deadened around them. The interior had a rich leather scent and that nice, new car smell. After so many hours in coach, the seats were like heaven. She took off her floppy hat and dropped it on her knee, then fluffed her thick black hair out.

"We can speak freely now." Chandra offered Tara a drink.

"You didn't answer me," she said.

Her old friend sighed. "Yes, Tara, he's here."

"You're sure? It's him?"

He gave her a patient smile. "I did not become Deputy Director General of the DIA by being bad at my job. It's him. I'm sure."

Tara sighed, visibly relieved. "You're right. I'm sorry." She patted his hand. "It's just this is very important."

"As one might imagine. Your brother, back from the dead."

"It's more than that, Kamal. Much more."

"That I also gathered, which is why I agreed to help you. Off the books, as the Americans put it."

"And your superiors know nothing about this?"

"Sealed lips, as you requested. And a prudent precaution, as it turns out."

"How so?"

"Your brother," Chandra said. "Clever devil that he is, he has slipped into yet another identity. The man is like a chameleon."

"Which is why I've had such a difficult time tracking him down," Tara said. "I thought I had him once in Saudi Arabia, in Buraydah, and then again in Jafariyah."

"In the Qom Province? In Iran?" Chandra asked, sounding both impressed and concerned.

"Yes. Both times, he slipped through my fingers." Tara reached out and squeezed his hand. "Thank you for your help, Kamal. It means so much to me. Now tell me. Where is my brother?"

The career intelligence man turned his head and pointed out the side window. They had driven across the Borough of Queens and under the East River through the Queens Midtown Tunnel into Manhattan. The city appeared almost gothic under dark, low-hanging clouds that looked ready to open up and dump a deluge of water down on it.

Varma turned north on 1st Avenue.

In response to Tara's question, Chandra pointed out the window. "There."

She leaned forward and looked out, surprised—no, shocked—to see Chandra pointing at the prominent and instantly recognizable Secretariat and General Assembly buildings of the United Nations.

"You're joking."

Chandra frowned. "I wish I were, *mushkil ek*. I wish I were."

The town car continued driving past the complex and showed no signs of slowing down.

"Where are we going?" Tara sat forward, watching the buildings slip past.

"To our hotel," Chandra said simply.

"No! I want to see him. I need to confront him."

Chandra sighed and turned toward her. He gave her a patient look.

"You think charging into the U.N., an international territory, I might add, and making some kind of scene in the middle of an assembly meeting is your best move? It is not going to happen, Tara. I have helped you this far, operating on blind faith and loyalty because of our... friendship, but now, you must tell me what this is all about.

"I know your... " He hesitated to find the right words. "Obsession with finding your brother is fueled by more than his Lazarus-like rise from the dead."

"I cannot say, Kamal. It's... classified."

"Does it have to do with your continued association with Brice Bannon and the Homeland Security Secretary?"

Tara didn't know how to respond. Her work with Bannon, for Grayson, was... well, classified. That her old friend, a spymaster of the first order, knew of it didn't surprise her. Still, she worried about how much she could—or should—say.

"I am well aware of the work you do for Secretary Grayson," he said. "I would not say it's common knowledge in the intelligence community, but your activities of late have attracted attention." He smiled. "If I may add, Bannon's probably the worst person in the world Grayson could have called on to fly missions under the radar. Subtle isn't in the man's vocabulary."

Tara shrugged. Chandra had a point. He had worked briefly with Bannon and McMurphy, as well as with her brother, in Afghanistan before Ghaazi Alvi splintered their group and disappeared, only to be later reported dead.

"The *Oceanic Princess*. Can I assume that was the three of you?"

Tara nodded.

"I thought so. Well done, from what I hear. What does your brother have to do with it? That is really why you're after him, is it not?"

"Yes," Tara admitted. "Did you know he was alive?"

Her old friend turned and looked out the window. She watched his reflection in the window as the city rolled past, their town car driving north through Lenox Hill to the Upper East Side.

After her parents' deaths, Tara and her brother, under assumed identities, joined the Algerian Navy. They had trained and were stationed in *Mers El Kébir* for most of their service. Both had applied for a cooperative exchange program to attend the Marine Commando Force School, the Indian Navy's elite Special Forces training program. Tara was one of only a few women ever to attend such training. A privilege denied most Indian women who served. She graduated in the top five percent of the program.

It was there she and Ghaazi met Kamal Chandra, an instructor at the time.

Not long after graduating from the MARCOS program, Ghaazi and Tara grew disillusioned. They feared they were not doing enough to strike back against the terrorist organizations, like *Al-Jamā'ah al-Islāmīyah,* the group that had killed their parents. A private contractor recruited them to join a mercenary outfit. Being freelance could make a real difference, they were told. And it paid very, very well.

They abandoned their Algerian identities and were officially classified as AWOL, away without leave. Those people disappeared to reemerge as Tara Sardana and Ghaazi Alvi.

Once recruited, they could handpick their targets—not for the money, but so they could fight the fight their way. Work for those they wanted to work for. Refuse to do the bidding of those they didn't want anything more to do with. And it had worked for a while.

Over the next few years, they'd struck at the hearts of *Al Qaeda* and the Taliban, fighting alongside the coalition allies and sometimes independently of them in Iran, Pakistan, and Afghanistan. They'd done good work.

During that time, they'd run into Chandra, sometimes on the battlefield, often in the green zones, where they'd catch up over a smuggled bottle of Kouroum of the Nile or Amrut single malt whiskey. He and Tara became romantically involved for a spell. Neither of them pretended it would amount to more than a wartime fling as Chandra rose quickly through the ranks of India's Defence Intelligence Agency and Tara descended deeper and deeper into the dark mercenary world she'd chosen. Still, they kept in touch.

Of course, always the spy, he kept their secrets.

While her brother, Ghaazi, remained disillusioned. He didn't believe they were accomplishing enough. He wanted to do more. Strike faster, hit harder. He began to think they were fighting the wrong enemy altogether. It was easy to understand. Confusion ran high as the wars raging in the Middle East continued, shifting, morphing, until who was friend and who was enemy blurred, seemingly daily, making the old adage 'the enemy of my enemy is my friend' truer than ever, until it perverted into 'the enemy of my enemy is my enemy, too, unless they could do something for you.'

Chandra remained silent.

Tara asked again, "Answer me. Did you know?"

"I had heard rumors, yes. Reported, unconfirmed sightings."

"And you didn't think to tell me?"

He shrugged. "There was nothing to tell. Ghost stories. Unsubstantiated snippets of maybe. I wanted to be certain before I... I raised your hopes."

"Don't give me that." She crossed her arms, angry, and turned away. She looked at her reflection in the smooth glass. "You were afraid if you'd told me, I'd have gone after him. You were afraid I'd go and kick his ass."

"Or worse." Chandra forced a smile. "There, you've wormed my dark secret from me. It's your turn."

Tara weighed her options. If she refused to give Chandra any more information, he'd withhold what he'd learned about Ghaazi. She couldn't allow that.

"The attack on the *Oceanic Princess*. Ghaazi was behind it. He orchestrated the whole thing. What's worse, the weapon that was used, there are three more like it still somewhere in the United States. Weapons Ghaazi plans to use against unknown targets, with nothing to stop him. Except me."

CHAPTER **FIVE**

THE GAME WRAPPED UP an hour later. Tommy scored the winning run from third on an RBI single by Narwa Nour, their Muslim left fielder. With the River Cats defeated—take that, Brice—the Penguins were only two games out of first place.

McMurphy smiled. They had a real shot at getting into the playoffs this year.

The River Cats' players had somberly packed up their gear with their heads down, but not before every Penguin player high-fived each of them, thanking them for a fantastic game. With that done, dozens of parents were now trying to herd their running-around offspring—wild horses would've been easier to corral—and get them into waiting cars. Excited, hungry, and with the days of summer dwindling down to just a few, the kids would soon be invading the local family-style restaurant chains, pizza places, and ice cream parlors like a pack of wild wolves. McMurphy silently wished the waiters and waitresses good luck.

The sun hung low in the west, turning the low ceiling of purple clouds red, with some yellow, granting them a brilliant sunset. A breeze had picked up. It swept away the heavy humidity of the day, turning what had been a sticky, uncomfortable day into the promise of a rather pleasant evening.

If the rain held off.

Over the sound of car doors opening and closing, trunks slamming shut, and kids and parents calling out their goodbyes and congratulations, McMurphy placed a hand on Tommy's head and rubbed his buzz-cut brown hair.

"Great job out there today, Tommy. A triple, outstanding base running, and that diving catch out by the warning track. Amazing. Good thing the Yankees didn't have a scout here. They'd have signed you up on the spot."

Tommy screwed up his face. "When I get to the big leagues, I'm only playing for the Sox."

"The *Red* Sox?" McMurphy rolled his eyes. "Oh lord, say it ain't so. You're a Red Sox fan?"

McMurphy grew up in Boston, but as an act of rebellion— one of many against his old man—McMurphy rooted for the Bronx Bombers his whole life.

"I live in New Hampshire. In the middle of Red Sox Nation. What else would I be?" He shoved the baseball bats into the Penguins' equipment bag.

"Be a rebel. Root for someone other than the home team."

"Who's your favorite team? Don't tell me the stinky, old Yankees."

"Heck, yeah. Best franchise in Major League history. Ever." McMurphy smiled down at the boy.

Tommy shook his head. "And I thought you knew about baseball."

McMurphy laughed. "We'll see what you've got to say after the Bombers crush 'em in the Bronx this weekend."

Excited, Tommy dropped the equipment bag. "Oh, shoot. That reminds me. My summer camp is going to the game on Saturday night for our end-of-the-season trip this year."

"The Yankees-Red Sox game?" McMurphy looked over at Mary. "It's in the Bronx, you know. In New York."

Mary leaned against the backstop. She watched the exchange with a smile, her handbag clutched over her shoulder. At his look of concern, she gave him a what-are-you-gonna-do shrug.

"I know. Cool, right?" Tommy went on. "We're taking a bus, and we're going in early and do the tour, you know, of Monument Park. I mean, I know it's Yankee Stadium, and the Yankees, blah, but still, that's gotta be cool, right?"

"Right," McMurphy agreed.

Tommy picked up the bag and shoved the rest of the bat and the catcher's gear into it before cinching it closed. When he was done, he shouldered the bag with a grunt.

"Put that in the back of my Hummer, would ya?"

By that time, everyone else had left. Besides his tricked-out, black Hummer H1, the only other car left in the lot was Mary's ten-year-old red Santa Fe.

As Tommy lugged the heavy bag over toward the Hummer, staggering to the left under its weight, Mary joined McMurphy at their team bench.

"New York City, huh? You think that's a great idea?"

"Look at him," she said. "You want to be the one to tell him he can't go? I don't think the kid can handle any more disappointment." McMurphy looked over at the boy. She had a point. "The camp does something like this every year. They have a lot of chaperones going. They'll be well supervised. It'll be fine."

"Are you or Andy going?"

"Andy. If he's back in time."

"You sound worried."

"He's got a track record, John. It's not good. He'll disappoint the boy again."

"He's a great kid, Mary."

"He is, isn't he?" She forced a smile. "Even after everything Andy's put him through."

"Kids are strong," McMurphy offered. "Resilient." They had to be, he thought, reflecting on his childhood. His own monster of a dad. Damn if that wasn't a story for another time.

She looked up at McMurphy. "John… "

Then she fell silent.

He chucked her under the chin, lifting her head so they were face to face. "You think something's wrong. What is it?" Before he could stop himself, his mind went to the darkest of places. "He didn't hit you again? Or Tommy?"

"No. No, nothing like that. If anything, it's the opposite. Andy's been good, really good, lately. Ever since I kicked… he moved out. He's been trying. He's still got his demons… "

McMurphy aimed his keyring fob at his Hummer and clicked it. The lights flashed, and the locks clicked open as Tommy approached it. He looked at the keys in his hand and fidgeted with them. "We all do, Mary."

"Sure. But some… you're handling them better than others. Better than Andy."

"He had a rough time of it over there. Mech Infantry. What those guys did, what they saw. He had a front-row seat. I flew over it most of the time."

Downplaying his activities in the sandbox, leaving it at that, but Mary didn't let it go. "You're full of it, John McMurphy. Andy told me some of the things you had to do, too."

"Whatever he said, he exaggerated. And he should learn to keep his big trap shut."

They started to head toward the cars. McMurphy pulled a Cuban cigar from his work shirt pocket but didn't light it.

"He came back different," Mary said. "You didn't know him before."

"I knew him then. I know him now. He's a good man, Mary. Don't give up on him."

"I'm not." She touched McMurphy's arm, stopping him. "I swear. I just hate what it's done to him. What being over there turned him into coming back home. And now they… just abandon… everyone. Leave our boys to fend for themselves."

McMurphy knew. The PTSD hit Andy hard. He had trouble finding a job, and when he did, he couldn't hold on to it. He reacted badly to sudden loud noises. He barely slept. Once the fatigue set in, he started to drink to blot out the memories and to dull the pain. When that didn't work, he'd moved on to pills, only making things worse.

McMurphy had intervened, getting him the help he needed. He set him up in a couple of twelve-step programs. He stayed with him for two and a half weeks while Andy detoxed. Then, he got him counseling that specialized in treating returning vets. Treatment McMurphy paid for out of his own pocket. "He hasn't relapsed, has he?"

"No. Nothing like that. Like I said, he's been good. But it… "

"Talk to me, Mary. What is it?"

"I wish you could have known the Andy I sent to war." She choked back tears.

McMurphy grabbed her and pulled her into a hug. She held onto him tightly and cried. Her body shuddered from the sobbing. After a minute, she pulled back and wiped tears from her eyes. They both looked over at Tommy, but he was leaning against the fender of McMurphy's Hummer with his head down, playing a video game on his smartphone.

"It makes me so mad he's like this, I could scream. I just wish they'd given me back the same Andy Pawlowski I sent them. It's just not fair."

"I know it's not. But it'll get better. He's doing the right things. Trust me, with time, it will get better."

"All done," Tommy called out, getting impatient. "You guys coming or what?"

McMurphy called back, "Coming, buddy." To Mary, he said, "You going to be okay?"

"Yeah," She sniffled and slipped on sunglasses to hide her wet, puffy eyes. "Yes. I… there is just one thing. I didn't say anything before the game. I didn't want you to worry, but… "

"Out with it, Mary. I can't help if you don't tell me."

"Andy. He was due back home yesterday. At first, I thought traffic. Or he got a late start, or he broke down on the highway… "

"He would've called you."

"That's what I figured. I didn't want to bother him. He was so happy to get this gig." She forced a worried smile. "I didn't want to be that badgering ex-wife, but when I couldn't stand it anymore, I called him."

"You did the right thing."

"A bunch of times. He hasn't answered me." She looked at him, but all McMurphy saw was his reflection in the lenses of her dark glasses. "I've been blowing up his phone since yesterday, John. It just goes right to voicemail. I left messages, but he hasn't called me back. I'm starting to worry now."

McMurphy gave her arm a reassuring squeeze.

"Don't sweat it," he assured her. "I'm sure he's fine. If anything's happened, we'd know it."

"How can you be so sure?"

"I'm listed in his emergency contacts. An accident or admittance into a hospital, I would've gotten a call from the police."

"I don't know if that makes me feel better or worse."

He held her by the shoulders and made her look into his eyes. "Trust me, we'll find him. Now, tell me everything you can about where he went. Who he's working for. I need to know everything."

She nodded. "Of course."

CHAPTER **SIX**

BANNON KNEW BRIDGET BARNES had made a deal with the government in exchange for her cooperation, immunity from prosecution, and relocation afterward. It galled him, but he understood it and hatefully admitted it was the right play. The information she had was too valuable to ignore. The lives that information could save were immeasurable.

Be that as it may, it didn't mean he had to see her. It didn't mean he had to be in the same room with her. And it certainly didn't mean he had to work with her. His stomach turned at the thought of that last one.

"Why is she here?" he demanded of Grayson as Bridget pulled a chair out and sat down. He took a perverse sense of satisfaction at seeing that the scratch marks on her face she'd sustained in a fight with Tara hadn't completely faded away.

"She's here to help us."

"That doesn't require me to be here." He pushed his chair under the table and took a step toward leaving.

"Sit down, Brice. Don't make me order you."

Bannon had the utmost respect for Elizabeth Grayson.

She'd served in and commanded combat theaters. She'd gone toe-to-toe with terrorists, enemy combatants, and politicians—the distinctions between the three were slight, in Bannon's opinion—and more than held her own. Respected and feared by both sides of the aisle, even considered one of the top five most influential people in Washington, and thus, the world.

Bannon sat back down. "You've got the FBI and Homeland Security scouring the country looking for the last two railguns." He squared Bridget with a hateful glare. "And you've got *her.* What do you need me for?"

"We want you to go to Monroe."

"Michigan? Me? Why?"

"We need you to look into the circumstances surrounding where and how the railgun was found," Grayson said.

"Which are?" Bannon asked.

"A homeless man. He used the warehouse for shelter on bad nights. Apparently, he stumbled across the railgun. Being a vet, he realized he'd stumbled onto something big. He reported it to the police," Grayson explained. "It was on pallets under a tarp. Luckily, local law enforcement had the wherewithal to contact the FBI. We moved in and seized the weapon, keeping its discovery as contained as possible. What we don't know and want you to find out is why the weapon was stored there and who was responsible for it being there."

"Send the FBI. They're better able to dig up something than I would be," Bannon protested. "I thought that was the game plan all along."

"To locate the guns, yes. But we've gone to a lot of trouble securing that weapon without fanfare, meaning without the press getting wind of it. After what happened with the *Oceanic Princess*, if the public learned these weapons were loose, we'd be facing widespread panic. We need you to make inquiries. Discreetly. You badgered me to let you get a private detective's license—go detect."

Bannon sighed. Go up there, nose around, ask a few questions. That he could do. Anything to get him out of this room, away from *that* woman. "Fine."

"You'll be taking Ms. Barnes along with you."

"Wait. What? Why?"

"Because she's lived up to her end of the bargain, she's been cooperating. Fully. She's had to," Grayson said, more for Barnes's benefit than Bannon's. "Not only does her freedom depend on it, but so does her life. The second she stops cooperating, she faces federal murder charges for her part in the deaths of the federal law enforcement officers killed as a result of her actions, as well as the murders of the passengers and crew aboard the *Oceanic Princess*—"

Barnes spoke up for the first time. "I get it. I stop helping—I'm screwed. Trust me, I'm all in."

"Trust you?" Bannon said. "That's a laugh."

"The second you step out of line, young lady," Grayson warned, "it's treason. A death sentence."

"That doesn't explain why she needs to go with me," Bannon complained.

"Brice, time is of the essence. The two remaining guns could be put into play any minute. Ms. Barnes knows how these cells operate. Anything you find, maybe she can tell us what it means, if anything, or nothing. She can keep you from chasing down rabbit holes."

"If she'll even tell us," Bannon said.

"I have no reason to conceal anything from you, Commander." She looked at Grayson. "As you've so emphatically stated, Madam Secretary, I have every incentive to be truthful and honest."

"Yeah, right," Bannon said, not buying it.

"Believe me or not, Commander, but my being there just may be the difference between you stopping those guns from going boom," she said. "Or not."

"I'd rather take my chances." Bannon stood up, looking at Grayson. "She's playing us. Playing you. She worked side by side with Faaid. She wouldn't know truth and honesty if they slapped her in the face. She had Ghaazi's ear. She knows where the guns are already. I'm sure of it. Keep her here and sweat it out of her."

"I don't," Barnes said, getting to her feet, too. "Faaid never trusted me. We were constantly at odds with each other. But that doesn't matter. He had no more idea where the guns were than you or I. It's Ghaazi who ran things above our pay grades. He's smart, cautious, and as paranoid as a double agent left out in the cold. You know that, Commander. You worked with him for a time."

"I knew him," Bannon countered. "Briefly."

"Long enough to kill Mullah Salam Nafez," Barnes countered. "A top Taliban commander in the mountain regions of Logar. His team and yours took out eight militant operatives in Helmand, where you captured three al-Qaeda agents. And the time you killed fifteen insurgents with him and your Ms. Sardana when they attacked a military patrol north of *Tarin Kowt*."

"Enough." Bannon glared at Grayson. Those were classified missions known to only a few. "It seems someone's been speaking out of school."

Grayson bristled. "I resent that implication, Commander."

"I know about those incidents," Barnes said, "because Ghaazi told me, not because anyone here has loose lips. Ghaazi told me those things so that I wouldn't underestimate you. He's cautious to a fault. He never spoke about where the other railguns were. I don't know why that gun was in Michigan, but I can help you find out."

Bannon didn't know what to make of her.

What he did know was he didn't trust her and wanted nothing to do with her. Yet, being a Coastie his entire adult life, in military service, he also knew how to follow orders. Even orders he vehemently disagreed with.

"Fine. When do we leave?"

"Now," Grayson said. "I have a Coast Guard C-37 Gulfstream fueled and standing by at Logan Airport." She stood up, concluding the meeting. "Godspeed. And try not to kill each other."

CHAPTER **SEVEN**

KAMAL CHANDRA'S DRIVER, VARMA, let them off at the front entrance of a four-star hotel in Lenox Hill, between 2nd and 3rd Avenues, across from the Bank of America Financial Center. Only late afternoon, the lobby was nearly empty. Chandra led Tara directly to the elevators. They rode to the top floor, where he produced a keycard and ushered her into a terrace suite with an outdoor patio.

The outdoor area was beautifully decorated with wicker chairs, a sofa, and loveseats, each with thick, comfortable padding and big, flowery pillows, potted plants, flowers, and small potted trees. There was a low table with a candle centerpiece and drinks set up beside a platter of cheeses, crackers, and fruit.

Tara took off her dark leather coat and draped it over the back of a nearby settee. She dropped her hat on the cushion, then crossed over to where two love seats were arranged, facing each other across the low table. Tired from the flight, she sat and sipped the single malt Scotch whiskey in front of her. The ice in the glass had barely melted despite the humid summer heat.

"I had Varma call ahead," Chandra explained. "He let them know we were on our way."

He sat opposite her. "How's the scotch?"

"It's great." She took another sip to make sure.

"Wonderful." He smiled. "The bottle cost two thousand dollars U.S. Such an expensive country you've chosen to live in, Tara."

"That's not typical, Kamal. You can get a bottle of twelve-year-old Johnnie Walker for around two hundred dollars."

He threw his hands up in the air in mock exasperation. Tara knew better. Kamal Chandra had been traveling back and forth from India to the U.S. for years. He was as familiar with America and what America had to offer as she was. He just liked to play the clueless foreigner. It was also a good weapon in his arsenal to use against his opponents. If they lied to him about things he knew, it told him not to trust them about things he didn't know.

"If I didn't know better, I'd think you were playing me, Kamal. Brought me up here," she waved an encompassing arm around, "with unscrupulous intentions." She added a smile and popped a grape into her mouth. "Like in the old days."

"My Riya would be most disappointed to hear you speak of such things."

"I mean no disrespect to your wife, Kamal, just ensuring your intentions remain pure." Tara stacked several crackers with chunks of sharp cheddar cheese and ate between sips of the delicious scotch. "How are Rija and your beautiful daughter, Kiara? She's what, seven now?"

"Eight going on eighteen." He sat back, crossed his legs, and stretched an arm casually across the back of the loveseat. "I brought you here for privacy, yes. The room and terrace have been swept for listening devices. Twice. We can speak freely and get down to the business at hand."

Tara sat forward. "Which is?"

"Ghaazi. Why he is here, and why you are after him?"

"I explained that. The railguns. You have no idea how devastating a weapon they are. If they were to shoot it at"—she didn't know—"a building, a plane, a concert hall. Hundreds, thousands, could be killed." She leaned forward. "These weapons have an effective range of fifty miles and can reach a maximum velocity of Mach 7. That's—"

"Seven times the speed of sound. After the attack on the *Oceanic Princess*, I read the intelligence briefings."

"Then you know we must stop Ghaazi."

"How does your brother fit into all of this? According to the briefing, Aziza Faaid was behind the attack. It was reported he was killed by Bannon, was he not?"

"Yes. But he was only the front man, working for Ghaazi." Tara poured herself a third drink. "The *Princess* was simply a test run. To make sure the weapon could operate as promised."

"How is it you know this?" Chandra asked.

Because of her work with Bannon and Homeland Security, Tara had top-secret clearance, including what is called category one Yankee White clearance, granted only to those who work within the inner circle of the Oval Office. It is the highest clearance granted by the U.S. government. As such, she had to tread carefully regarding what information she revealed when dealing with foreign dignitaries, even close friends like Kamal Chandra and allies like India.

"I was there. As for the rest, I'm not at liberty to say." She hated the dodge.

"Then perhaps I cannot help you after all."

"Seriously, Kamal? Lives are at stake, and you're going to play politics? With me?"

"You've become like the country you've aligned yourself with, Tara."

"I'm trying to stop a disaster, possibly three of them." She reached for the bottle, stopped, and left it untouched. She sat back in her chair. The soft cushions felt so comfortable she just wanted to curl up and nap.

She stared at Chandra, who remained motionless, like a rock. Frustrated, she blurted, "Fine. There's one person, I won't tell you their name, a member of Faaid's cell, who is in

U.S. custody. This person is cooperating with the authorities. This is how I know Ghaazi's involved."

"This person's information? It can be trusted?"

"What's been independently verified has panned out so far, yes."

In quiet contemplation, Chandra pursed his lips and ran his finger over his thin mustache. He dropped his hand into his lap and sat forward. "It was no easy task tracking him down."

"Tell me about it," Tara said. "For the last three weeks, I've been chasing rumors, dissecting aliases, tracking down reported sightings through half the Middle East and parts of Europe and Africa. I'm exhausted."

"And it was the information you continually provided me that ultimately led me to discover your brother's latest alias. Ghaazi has assumed a new identity. He goes by the name Fares Terzi."

"And he's here. In New York City."

"Yes."

"At the U.N. Why? What's he doing there?"

"Here is where it gets interesting." Chandra retrieved his drink from the table. The ice clicked in the glass. "Ghaazi—Fares Terzi—is operating as an envoy, here on a diplomatic mission."

"An envoy? For who?"

Chandra leaned in closer. "For a Russian delegation. Terzi is the personal assistant to Pyotr Denikin."

"The former Russian ambassador to the United States?"

The U.S. government had severed diplomatic relationships with several countries that supported the Syrian regime over the civil war raging there. While ties were not cut with Russia, many high-ranking officers were sanctioned by the U.S. in retaliation for Russia's support. As one of those sanctioned, Denikin was forced to resign his position as ambassador.

"What on Earth are they doing here?"

"They are here to make a presentation—a plea—to the World Security Council requesting concessions on behalf of the Syrian government and to demand an easing of U.S.

sanctions, all in the guise of seeking U.N. assistance for the refugee crisis."

"A humanitarian appeal," Tara said.

"Yes."

"All to cover up a terrorist operation here on U.S. soil."

"That is the news you bring, my dear. We thought it simply Pyotr's attempt at a GoFundMe campaign for their genocidal civil war."

"If only that were all it was." Tara squeezed her hand around her glass so hard she feared she might shatter it. She put the glass down on the table, harder than intended. This was the closest she'd gotten to finding her brother in over three weeks of chasing him halfway around the Middle East. She had him. "When can I get to him? I trust you have a plan?"

"I do." He smiled. "This evening, the ambassador is hosting a party—fundraiser would be the more accurate term—for his supporters and supporters of his cause. Hollywood A-listers, Washington insiders, lobbyists, movers and shakers from the private sector."

"Businesses that want the conflict in the region to end so they can return to making money in Syria."

Chandra nodded. "More than likely. And so the socialites might feel good about themselves."

"And Ghaazi. He'll be at this party?"

"Of course."

"You need to get me into that party."

Again, her old friend smiled. "That is the plan, *mushkil ek.*"

As if on cue, Varma came through the French doors that led back into the suite. He carried two dark garment bags over his arm. One had a Tincati Milano logo on it, a formal wear store on 67th Street. The other was from Carolina Herrera, a high-end women's clothing store on Madison Avenue.

"As you requested, sir." Varma held his arm out, presenting the two garment bags as if for inspection.

Chandra stood up and relieved the bodyguard of the garments, holding them high by the hooked hangers. "Thank you, Varma. Have the car brought around at eight."

Varma nodded, backed away, and turned, retreating from the terrace.

Tara came to her feet. She eyed the garment bag with suspicion. "What's this?"

Chandra held up the bag from Tincati. "This is my tux." He handed the other bag to her. "And this is for you. We cannot have you going to a ten-thousand-dollar-a-plate dinner as my plus one wearing," he surveyed her clothes, "like that."

Tara looked herself up and down. "Fair enough."

"I've taken the liberty of booking the suite," he said. "There are two bedrooms. I suggest you try and get some sleep. I suspect it is going to be a long night."

She grabbed her glass from the table and threw down the rest of her scotch. She swallowed, crunching the ice with her teeth. "This party, where is it?"

"On the *Morskoy Skat*."

"What's a *Morskoy Skat*?"

He smiled. "It's Russian for stingray. I can't wait for you to see. You're going to love it."

CHAPTER EIGHT

THIS IS A MISTAKE, McMurphy thought. He was at the wheel of his Hummer, driving north on Route 16. Dusk had begun to settle over the Northeast. He chewed on an unlit cigar stuck in the corner of his mouth, anxious. Going to check on his friend wasn't the mistake McMurphy meant. It was not going alone.

Mary sat in the passenger seat, having demanded she go along. When he'd said no, she'd refused to tell him where Andy had gone to get started on the driving gig he'd picked up. All McMurphy knew was that it was somewhere in the Lakes Region.

They'd wasted time arguing over it until McMurphy finally caved. They'd dropped off Tommy to spend the night with his best friend, Phillip something or other. Phillip was in the same summer camp with Tommy, and his parents were chaperoning the Yankees-Red Sox baseball trip into the city on Saturday evening.

With the sun riding low beside them to their left, McMurphy and Mary were making good time. Mary sat with her bare feet up on the dashboard. She picked at the chipped red paint peeling from her fingernails. All she would tell him was to drive north. When they were far enough he couldn't turn back to leave her behind; she'd give him specifics.

"Now will you tell where we're going?" McMurphy asked as he flipped on the Hummer's powerful halogen headlights to combat the gathering dusk.

"The Lakes Region. North of Winnipesaukee. Town called Center Harbor."

"What's at Center Harbor?"

"Andy, hopefully." She didn't look at McMurphy. "If not, Peter Lynch."

"Who's Peter Lynch?"

Mary didn't answer.

McMurphy looked at her in the gathering darkness. "Mary, what aren't you telling me?"

She dropped her feet to the floorboards and sat up. She twisted around to face him. "Okay. I didn't want to go into too much detail because I didn't want to get Andy in trouble."

"He's twenty-four hours late from a three-hour run. I think concern is in order."

"I meant in trouble with you."

"Me? Why?"

"He's hanging around with some new guys." She looked down at the console between the seats. "Vets, mostly. I'm afraid they're a little shady."

Trust your gut, McMurphy. Always. "Shady, how?"

Instead of answering, she said, "Andy's been doing good lately. Really good."

"You said. That's great to hear. What's that got to do with this Peter Lynch and these new friends of his?" McMurphy didn't like hearing about these new friends. Andy wasn't sober for very long, and that made him vulnerable to influence. What was worse, Andy had never mentioned these new friends. McMurphy spoke with Andy every couple or three days. They'd been getting together regularly every week or so, more, since Andy was helping him with coaching the Penguins.

Mary didn't answer.

"He never told me about them, Mary. I'm not his sponsor or anything, but that's not a good sign."

"I've only ever met Peter," she said. "He seems like a nice guy. Andy's been good since he met him. I thought it was good. Him making friends, hanging out with some guys he had something in common with."

"Tell me about him, this Pete. What do they have in common?"

"Like you. He was in the military, Army Ranger something or other. He served three tours. One in Iraq, two in Afghanistan."

"What else?"

"That's it, mostly."

"Say it, Mary."

"Say what?"

"You're holding back. What is it? You already said they were shady. Why?"

"It's probably nothing."

"Andy's unaccounted for. That's something." He took his eyes from the highway to steal a glance at her. In the dim glow of the dashboard lights, he could read the indecision in her eyes. "I need to know what I'm running into, Mary. Tell me everything."

"Okay. Fine. These guys, as I said, they're mostly all ex-military. Peter seems okay. But the others? They're a little rough. You know what I mean?"

"I thought you said Lynch was the only one you met."

"He is. From what Andy's been telling me. He's been hanging out with them. A lot."

"Up at Lake Winnipesaukee?"

"Yes. Camping and boating," Mary said. "Look, you know me. I've been around military people my whole life." Her father was a retired full-bird colonel, and her brother served in the Navy. "But these guys, John—they sound bitter. Angry. From what Andy's told me, a few of them are disabled, physically. Others are like him, suffering PTSD or worse. They talk a lot against the government."

"How do you mean? Like, it sucks how they don't take care of 'em after all we've done, or more like we ought to overthrow the government and run it right kind of talk."

In the dark, she shrugged. "I don't know, honestly. This is coming to me from Andy, peppered with his own anger, but yes, more overthrow is the sense I get. They've even got a name."

"A name? Like they're a club?"

She shrugged. "Call themselves the White Mountain Militia."

"Damn it." What the hell was Andy thinking, getting involved with knuckleheads like that? McMurphy asked, "Tell me Andy's not buying into all that crap?"

"Andy? No. He's angry. Rages a lot about why him, but he loves this country. He's all G.I. Joe, all the way. You know that, John."

"Yet he's thrown in with a bunch of government haters and agreed to transport who knows what for them. That part's still true, isn't it?"

"Yes. Of course. I would never lie to you, John. Not ever. He should have been back yesterday. When he wasn't, I figured he stayed longer, hanging out with his new buddies."

"Maybe drinking and partying."

"Maybe." Mary sounded sad saying it. "He needed money, John. He hasn't had meaningful work in eighteen months."

"I know it's been hard on him. And you."

Mary twisted back around, facing straight ahead. She put her bare feet on the seat and wrapped her arms around her bent legs, hugging them. McMurphy could feel the anger and the fear leeching off her. Through it all, she still loved Andy. McMurphy knew how hard that had been.

"You don't know the half of it. I'll tell you this. Those people have a right to be pissed off at the government. They train them to kill. Send them over to that hellhole on Earth. Then they do nothing for them when they return broken, physically and mentally. Thank you for your service." She saluted angrily. "Sir. Yes, sir."

McMurphy didn't take the bait. He concentrated on driving. They'd been at it for over an hour. According to his GPS, they had another half hour to go.

As they drove, McMurphy's cell phone rang. He dug it out of his pocket.

Mary jumped at the sound. *Semper Paratus,* the marching song of the Coast Guard. It was Latin for 'always ready.' "Who's that?"

McMurphy glanced at the screen. "My friend Brice. You've met him. He's been to a few of the Penguins' games."

"Don't answer it! Please."

McMurphy gave her a look.

"If Andy's done anything…wrong, I don't want to get him into trouble."

"Brice isn't like that."

Mary put a hand on his arm as the cell phone continued to play. "Please."

McMurphy hesitated and then shrugged as the phone went silent and the call went to voicemail. He pocketed the unanswered phone. Probably wanted to update him on how the meeting went with Grayson. Nothing that couldn't wait. He'd call him back when they stopped.

Thirty minutes later, they pulled into the small town square of Center Harbor, sandwiched between Winnipesaukee to the south and Squam Lake to the north. They drove past a lakefront park. It had a small gazebo. Already the broad leaves of the trees were beginning to change color.

Mary had curled up and leaned against the door. She'd napped the last leg of the trip. McMurphy gently shook her arm. "We're here. What now?"

Mary sat up with a start and blinked. "I… we need to find Peter Lynch. He's the one who offered Andy the job. I don't have an address or anything."

McMurphy slowed as they rolled through town. "Something's been bothering me," McMurphy said. "If there's like this whole group involved up here, why'd they need Andy to drive?"

"They don't have anyone who can drive a five-ton."

"A five-ton?" McMurphy didn't like the sound of that. Whatever they were moving had to be big to require a truck that size. But why were they using a military cargo truck in the first place? McMurphy didn't know, but he let it go for now. "Guess we'll start asking around. Small places like this, everybody should know everybody."

CHAPTER NINE

LESS THAN TWO HOURS after their meeting with Secretary Grayson, the Coast Guard C-37 Gulfstream touched down at the Custer Airport in Monroe, Michigan. Bannon hoped the airport's name wasn't an omen. The last thing he wanted was for this trip to end up like Little Big Horn, but with Bridget Barnes along for the ride, anything was possible.

A small regional airport, Custer consisted of a single runway, one corrugated metal hangar, and a small white building Bannon assumed served as a terminal. A chain-link fence with an open, unguarded gate surrounded the flat fields. He and Barnes deplaned on the tarmac, bypassed the terminal, and went straight to the parking lot.

A five-year-old Toyota Camry had been left in the lot for them. Pulled from the government's local forfeiture impound yard, which contained their inventory of seized vehicles, boats, RVs, and other properties, it was inconspicuous and had a full tank of fuel.

They got in. Barnes turned up her nose. "You'd think with access to all the vehicles seized from drug dealers and the like, we could do better than a beat-up, old, green Camry."

Bannon slipped behind the wheel. "What were you expecting? A Lamborghini?"

She brightened at the prospect. "Sure, that would work."

He slipped on a pair of Ray-Bans to combat the setting sun's strong glare and pulled out through the open gate. He aimed the car south. They drove until they picked up North Custer Road. There, he turned east and continued along the shores of the River Raisin. The further they drove, the more Bannon worried at the prospect this trip would end up being his last stand.

As they continued east, the sun dipped below the horizon behind them.

Not long after, they found what they came to see—the abandoned warehouse on Port Avenue. Bannon drove along a single-lane spur that led to the ambitiously named Port of Monroe. In truth, apart from a couple of storage structures, the port was a solitary building plopped down where the river bent to form a turning basin, a few miles upriver from Lake Erie.

Bannon pulled into the empty parking lot. Gravel crunched under the car's tires.

He eased the car to a stop facing an old timber railroad tie used as a bumper. Security lighting consisted of a single pole with a solar-activated bulb that had just started to illuminate as day turned into night. Around them were the closed-down port building, a crane and rigging company, and in the distance, the DTE Energy power plant, its two large stacks protruding into the darkening sky.

Barnes started to get out of the car, but Bannon said, "Hold on a sec."

He pulled his phone out and checked his texts and messages. There were none. He hit the speed dial on his list of contacts, put the phone to his ear, and listened. When McMurphy failed to pick up, Bannon hung up. He'd called earlier with the same result. This time, he sent his old friend a text requesting that he call back.

Bannon got out of the Camry, and they walked around the warehouse building.

Small, he estimated the building to be less than ten thousand square feet. It had an office complex and two overhead doors facing the dark river water. A rusted metal grill covered the main door, secured by a chain and a new, heavy-duty padlock. Bannon pulled out his set of lock picks and went to work. Less than five minutes later, the padlock snapped open.

He opened the gate. It squeaked noisily.

He was through the interior door lock in less than a minute.

"I didn't know burglary was a Coast Guard Academy-taught skill set," Barnes quipped.

Bannon opened the door and ushered her inside, giving the outside world a final once-over. "It's not. Blame it on my misspent youth. Besides, I didn't attend the academy. I got my commission through the officer candidate program."

"Either way, I'm impressed. Maybe you're not the Boy Scout I thought you were."

Bannon ignored her, not interested in the least in what impressed her. He snapped on a flashlight and played the beam around the empty dock area. The building had been abandoned for some time. Thick layers of dust and grit covered the floor. He crouched to examine tire track marks and footprints in the grit and dust.

"These look recent," he said.

Barnes, standing over him, looked down. "Forklift tires. Would need it to move the railgun in."

Bannon nodded, concurring as he stood up. "Probably two of them working in tandem. A lot of these footprints would be from the cops and whatever group Grayson sent in here to secure the gun. Let's take a look in the back."

"You don't really think there's anything here to find, do you?"

Bannon checked his anger. "No. But we're here, so we might as well make sure."

She rolled her eyes. "Fine, Boy Scout."

Bannon moved toward the back of the building. There were several closed doors along the back wall. Offices from when the warehouse was fully operational. "It beats sitting around the Marshals' offices, doesn't it?"

"Remains to be seen," she said. "They get great pastries from this bakery in downtown Boston—"

Bannon stopped and turned, aiming the flashlight beam in her face. "Tell me. How'd you get here?"

She stepped back and shielded her eyes with a raised arm. "I flew here. With you, remember?"

"Don't be a wiseass."

"Get the damn light out of my eyes."

Bannon panned the light away, resuming his search of the empty space. Reluctantly, he admitted, if only to himself, Barnes was probably right. There wasn't anything there to find.

"How'd you get mixed up with the likes of Faaid and Ghaazi Alvi? A redheaded southern girl like you doesn't exactly tick off all the boxes on the Middle Eastern terrorist profile checklist."

Barnes shrugged. "I'm an outlier. What can I say?"

"Clear up the mystery for me."

She sighed. "I went through all this with the FBI, Homeland Security, and Military Intelligence, and the list goes on."

"Now go through it with me. One more time."

She shook her head, her annoyance almost palpable. He didn't care.

"Fine. We've got nothing else to do. I'm just a small-town girl from Waynesville, Missouri, who met a boy and fell in love. He was from Arizona, attending the Military Police school out of Fort Wood. We met in an off-post bar. Seven years ago, I put the most important man in my life on a plane at Lambert International Airport. As he strolled through the security line that day, it was the start of a very long journey that would ultimately take him to Afghanistan and change both our lives forever. His name was Josh Starling."

"Was? He's dead?"

"Yes, but not in the way you'd think. Not over there. He did his duty, two tours with the 65th Military Police Company, 572nd MP Battalion, stationed in Kandahar."

Bannon listened as he poked under tarps covering paint supplies and looked behind ladders.

"Josh came home in one piece, physically." Barnes followed behind Bannon but did little to help in the search. "But you could tell he'd been affected by the crazy stuff he saw, some of the even crazier things he'd done."

"Like what?" Bannon asked.

"He never said, not in so many words—"

"He was discharged honorably?' Bannon asked, fishing.

"Oh, sure. Never anything like that, but when he came home—"

"Arizona or back to his gal in Missouri?" Bannon asked, deliberately interrupting her again. A technique that made it difficult for someone who's lying to keep their story straight if they're forced to mentally juggle details that way.

"To me, yes, but not Missouri or Arizona. A town called Pittsburg, on Lake Francis in New Hampshire, way up north near the Canadian border. A cabin he inherited from an uncle. After Sedona and Afghanistan, Josh had had it with hot climates and deserts." She smiled wistfully. "Things were good with us, with Josh, when he first got back. But he couldn't let it go. The experience, you know?"

Bannon nodded. He was familiar.

"He began obsessing over what was going on over there still. He couldn't put it behind him."

"What they did?"

"Sure," she said. "I guess. But it was more than that. Questioning what we were doing there, interfering where we had no right. A place we don't understand and have no right being."

"It's not that simple," Bannon said. "Especially over there."

"On that, we can agree. I didn't like it. Thought the wars were foolish. But Josh became obsessed. He felt like he needed to do something, to make a difference. He said a lot of guys felt the same way he did. That us being over there was wrong.

That this country needed to wake up to the real story, to what our people were really doing over there. Not just accept the lies the politicians and the media fed us, but to learn the truth. The real truth."

"Which was what?" Bannon asked.

"I told you, Josh was an MP, right? The CIA assigned his company to a prison called the Abyss. You know of such places, don't you?"

"I've heard rumors. Go on."

"Well. The conditions there were as horrendous as they've been described in reports that have surfaced over the years. Josh couldn't stand what he saw. The things being done to the prisoners. Inhuman was how he described it. Josh couldn't stomach what he'd seen."

"He tried to do something about it," Bannon guessed.

"No, he didn't. That's what haunted him when he got back. He befriended a number of the prisoners. Got to know them. He did his best to ease their time in captivity."

"Men who killed American soldiers," Bannon said. "Killed innocent people, hundreds of them, thousands."

"I'm not going to argue about that. You want to hear about this or not?"

"Go on."

"Josh felt he should've done more to help them. He only got one chance to do something worthwhile, he told me. Near the end of his last tour, they were assigned to escort two dozen prisoners from the Abyss. He wasn't told, but he suspected they were on their way to Guantanamo Bay. On the road to the airport, their convoy came under heavy enemy fire. RPGs destroyed several vehicles. Mortar fire, shelling, small arms fire. Five soldiers lost their lives that day. During the attack, Josh did the only humanitarian thing he could."

"Which was what, exactly?"

"He cut the prisoners loose. He saved their lives."

"He released dangerous POWs while five of his fellow soldiers lost their lives in a vicious attack. That doesn't make him a hero in my book."

"If you'd known what had been done to those men."

"There are channels for that sort of thing. Abu Ghraib, others, they were dealt with when they were discovered, properly. The prisoners weren't arbitrarily released to go out and kill who knows how many more allied fighters and innocent civilians."

"If people like Josh don't stand up, take a stand, where would we be?"

"If that's your justification for helping a terrorist group kill innocent civilians... Kill two FBI agents and a Coast Guardsman? You're crazier, or more evil, than I took you for."

"You should know," she said. "One of those men Josh released that day on that sunbaked, God-forsaken stretch of highway was Ghaazi Alvi. A man he'd come to know and like, even respect. He was a prisoner in the Abyss. Beaten, deprived of sleep, marched around naked to the constant blaring of rock music. Humiliated in who knew how many ways. It was under those conditions that Josh and he met. Where they became friends."

Bannon seethed. "Where they cooked up a plan to blow up a cruise ship and kill over six thousand people?"

"That came later."

Her casual dismissal irked Bannon, but before he could call her on it, he shushed her and snapped off his flashlight.

He'd heard the rusty gate open behind them.

Bannon glanced at the door they'd come through as a shaft of pale outside light lengthened across the floor. He held a hand out, signaling Barnes not to move. A shadow filled the narrow rectangle of light on the floor, a figure filling the doorway.

A voice called out, "Monroe Police. Don't anybody move."

CHAPTER TEN

THE *MORSKOY SKAT* TURNED out to be a luxury superyacht anchored in New York's Upper Bay where the Hudson and East Rivers converged at the southern tip of Manhattan Island between Governors Island and the Statue of Liberty.

"Built in a Danish shipyard fifteen years ago, it has a current market value of nearly two hundred million dollars," Chandra told Tara as they rode a ridged-hull water taxi out to the two-hundred-seventy-foot-long superyacht, privately owned by a Russian billionaire and on loan to former ambassador Pyotr Denikin for his humanitarian world tour. "The boat weighs forty-six hundred metric tons," he continued to read from a pamphlet given to them upon boarding the water taxi. "Has a cruising speed of fourteen knots and a top speed of twenty. It has four decks, twelve sleeping cabins, two ballrooms, and its own helipad."

The promised rain had held off, but the air remained warm and thick. A fine mist splashed over the small boat's bow as they raced toward the behemoth riding low in the dark water ahead. Behind it, the lights on the Verrazano-Narrows Bridge connecting Brooklyn and Staten Island blazed like diamonds and sparkled on the gently rippling water. The yacht was ablaze with light. Three rows of windows glowed radiantly from the interior lighting on each of the three passenger levels above deck. More lights were strung like Christmas decorations from the ship's bow to its bridge and back to the stern.

A six-passenger Bell 407 helicopter landed on the stern helipad as Tara watched. The yacht's lights reflected off the dark water, iridescent in their beauty. A nautical jewel in all its splendor. To its right, the Statue of Liberty, aglow with its yellow torch shining bright, kept a watchful eye on the ship and the harbor. Her torch held high and bright. Her stoic features unreadable, neither approving nor disapproving of what went on below her, simply a dispassionate observer.

Somewhere off in the distance, a police siren wailed. A reminder to Tara as they sped across the dark waters that no matter how serene and beautiful the setting, the situation she was heading into was fraught with danger.

The taxi slowed and eased in along the swimming platform across the yacht's stern. Tara accepted the hand of a guide as she stepped from the bobbing speedboat to the steady deck of the *Morskoy Skat*. Kamal Chandra quickly followed.

Arm in arm, they made their way toward the forward promenade deck at the ship's bow, following the crowd in the direction of their tuxedo-clad guides. Chandra had opted for a traditional black tuxedo with a bow tie, a white shirt with quarter-inch pleats, and French cuffs. He wore a pair of gold cufflinks that he said had been handed down to him from his father and had once belonged to his great-grandfather.

The dress he'd bought Tara was a stunning ivory, off-the-shoulder, backless gown with low-cut sides and a thigh-high slit. The dress beautifully contrasted with her dark, sun-bronzed skin. He'd accented the dress with a dramatic V-shaped diamond necklace, a matching bracelet, and strappy ivory sandals with four-inch heels. Tara couldn't remember the last time she'd worn heels. The breeze off the water, while warm, goosebumped her exposed flesh, of which there was a lot. But the thing that made her feel most underdressed was the absence of a gun or a knife of any kind.

They'd argued over that, but Chandra had been right. She'd never have gotten either past the two metal detectors they'd been put through or the hand wand they were going to be subject to before being allowed onto the promenade.

There, a tuxedoed bodyguard rechecked their invitation against photo identification. Tara presented her passport to the guard. It contained an alias, of course. The wand emitted a buzz, caused by the metal clasp of her necklace. Once cleared, they joined the cocktail hour already in full swing. A band played Middle Eastern music using traditional string, wind, and percussion instruments: an oud, a nay, a qanun, a tabla, and a violin.

The music stirred memories of her childhood, of her home, and of her brother.

"Security's tight," she said to Chandra as he handed her a flute of champagne. "And they're armed to the teeth."

"My guess," Chandra said, "they're a combination of Russia's Federal Security Service and Syria's National Defence Force."

"Still seems like a lot of muscle for a humanitarian boondoggle."

"Denikin is not a popular fellow. His humanitarian pleas for Syria's refugee problem have largely fallen on deaf ears in the political arena and on the world stage. Seen for what it is—a barely concealed attempt to circumvent the sanctions imposed on Syria for its outlandish behavior. As you can see from this evening's lavish festivities, it has become a cause championed by many human rights advocates, the press, and this nation's self-serving celebrity elite."

Tara and Chandra wandered around the large forward deck. They moved to the front of the yacht and shared a second flute of champagne. She looked over the bow at the city skyline. The Freedom Tower was aglow against the dark sky, prominent among the sparkling cluster of lower buildings around it, but not nearly as impressive a sight as the Twin Towers had been. Still, Tara thought, possibly even more meaningful in so many ways. A visible testament to the strength and character of the American people, of her adopted home.

Knocked down, they would never stay down.

Chandra asked Tara to dance. She agreed.

"I'm curious," he said. "Why have you chosen to continue to work for Bannon, for the Americans? There is plenty you could still do... at home."

She gave the question a lot of thought before answering. "I've made a lot of mistakes in my life, Kamal. I've done bad things for what I thought were the right reasons, only to learn I was wrong. I've done good things that only benefited bad people. Over there, home as you put it, everything shifts—loyalties, alliances, treaties—like the sands. There's no one, nothing, you can count on."

"Including me."

Tara forced a smile. "Present company excluded."

He smiled back. "Good to hear."

"Bannon's different," she said. "He saved me from going down a very dark path. He saved me from myself at a time when I needed it. He's a good man with a simple moral code. Good and bad. Right and wrong. I like that. I need that."

"Sounds naive," Chandra said. "The world's not that black and white, Tara."

Tara smiled at him. "Brice's world is."

They finished their dance, grabbed a couple more flutes of champagne, and proceeded down the side deck along the yacht's accommodation section, the four levels above the main deck midship. She wanted to get the yacht's layout.

There were many notable people on board. Celebrities, as Chandra had mentioned earlier, but also federal and local politicians, those who leaned socially left, including the mayor and the governor. The rest were mostly unknown to Tara: titans of business and members of humanitarian relief organizations, lower-level foreign dignitaries, and U.N. staffers. There was no press, but a commissioned photographer was snapping pictures that, once approved, would commemorate the evening and be used for press releases and propaganda purposes to sell Denikin's charade.

"I don't see Ghaazi." They'd returned to the promenade for another drink after their inspection of the yacht. They stood at the gunwale and leaned against the railing. "Are you sure he's aboard?"

"He's here," Chandra said. "I got a confirmation sighting before we boarded."

"Maybe he left."

"Doubtful. He needs to play his part."

Several tuxedoed personnel circulated through the crowd, informing people the ambassador was about to make a speech. Afterward, dinner would be served in the dining room one deck below.

A Middle Eastern man with dark features moved to the center of the promenade. He held a cordless microphone in his hand. After enduring a shrill feedback buzz, he said, "May I have your attention. If you'd be so kind. Turn your attention to the podium. This evening's festivities are about to start. We begin with a short message from our host, Ambassador Pyotr Denikin."

Chandra and Tara turned from the rail to face the podium set up at the front of the bow. The crowd circled tighter around the podium. The music stopped, and an anticipatory hush fell over the crowd.

Pyotr Denikin made his way through the crowd.

A short, balding man with a halo of dark hair, he stepped up on a box behind the podium holding a stack of index cards in his hand. He cleared his voice and began to speak. He worked without a microphone and never looked at his cards as he projected his message to the invited guests—mostly all like-minded individuals—while Tara listened.

She'd let herself get distracted by the deep baritone sound of Denikin's heavily accented voice until a firm hand seized her upper arm. She resisted the urge to lash out. Instead, she slowly turned toward the person beside her. In doing so, she came face to face with someone she had not seen in over seven years. Her brother.

"Hello, sister," Ghaazi Alvi said with an icy grin. "I heard you've been looking for me. This is as good a time for a family reunion as any, don't you think?"

CHAPTER ELEVEN

McMURPHY HADN'T EATEN SINCE lunch, so he insisted they stop and get a bite to eat.

He found a place called the Kayak Tavern, a relaxed family-style place that had a rustic, boathouse motif going for it. Overhead were wood timbers, a large comfortable bar ran along one wall, and the dining room in the back was lined with large picture windows, plank flooring, and maroon oriental carpets, all right on the spectacular shores of Lake Winnipesaukee.

He directed Mary to a table near the back. They arrived just before the kitchen closed for the night, so they had to order quickly. McMurphy had a bowl of clam chowder, the lobster, shrimp, and scallops stir-fry, and a side of Parmesan garlic fries. Mary went with the mozzarella and asparagus ravioli, giving two of her three jumbo shrimp to McMurphy to eat.

After dinner, he enjoyed a third Sam Adams summer ale while Mary indulged in a rare second glass of Sauvignon Blanc. He glanced through the divide into the bar. The Red Sox-Yankees game was playing on the TV. In the middle of the second inning, the Yanks were down two nothing. They'll make that up, McMurphy thought confidently.

When their after-dinner drinks arrived, he asked the waitress—Alice—about Peter Lynch. Local waitresses in small towns knew everybody. McMurphy said he was an old Army buddy of Lynch's and thought since they were up from Boston, they'd look him up.

"Oh, sure, hon. Pete. He lives out at the old summer camp off Avon Shores. Big, old piece of property. Six acres, I think, surrounded by woods and lakefront. Beautiful."

"A summer camp?" McMurphy asked.

"Camp Cove, they called it. Closed down about five, six years ago. Used to be really popular, but they couldn't attract the number of guests like they used to. The owners started having trouble keeping up with the costs. The county stepped in, bought the property dirt cheap, keeping it from foreclosure. Word around town was they intended to open it up as a camp for underprivileged kids, but that never got off the ground."

"Why not?" Mary asked.

"Way I hear it, the cost to renovate those old buildings and other equipment they'd need was too high. Then there's all the insurance issues. Guess it costs a lot to cover what could go wrong with a bunch of kids running around the woods and boating and all, not to mention any potential... Interpersonal problems might come up, you know what I mean?"

"How'd Pete end up out there?" McMurphy asked.

"Truth is, he and his buddies are squatting. It's kind of an open secret around here. Sheriff knows about it. County commissioners, too. Them ole boys all being vets, they turn a blind eye to it so long as they don't cause no trouble. Far as I know, they don't make a peep."

"And I'm guessing, if they did, you'd know." He gave her a big grin.

She smiled back and snapped her gum. "You know it, sweetie." She put the check on the table. "No rush on this. And if you're looking to make a run out there, it's west of here on Twenty-Five. When you come to Glidden, go left until you come up on Red Berm Road. It'll be on your right about a half mile in. Lake's on your right. Nice piece of property."

McMurphy handed her his credit card. "Know anything about his pals?"

Alice took the card. "They say they run a construction company." She leaned in, conspiratorially. "But between me, you, and the four walls, they're just a bunch of handymen getting hired out for day jobs here and there. Hanging out, drinking, and shooting off guns the rest of the time." She added quickly, "No offense, of course. They're sweet guys. And they did serve this great country. God bless 'em. Am I right?"

"Yes, Alice, you are." McMurphy thanked her.

He and Mary quietly finished their drinks. When McMurphy got his card and receipt back, he noticed she'd discounted their meal by ten percent. He wondered if that was for his own service to the country or to apologize for possibly offending his friends. He tripled the tip and left it for her.

They left, waving goodnight. Back in the Hummer, they headed out, following Alice's directions to Route Twenty-Five. Evening had turned into full-on night.

As they left the quaint town of Center Harbor behind in search of Camp Cove and Lake Kanasatka, the surrounding woods grew thicker and darker. Dark clouds shrouded the night sky, hiding the half-moon except for occasional gaps as the clouds tracked west to east.

The Hummer's bright halogen headlights blazed a lonely path along the dark strip of paved road until they found Glidden Road. The rusted road sign leaned at an angle, as if someone had run into it and not bothered to fix it. Barely legible, McMurphy almost missed it, but at the last minute, he made the turn. Filled with unrepaired potholes, the road deteriorated under them. He had to swerve violently to avoid the worst of them.

At six-tenths of a mile, Mary pointed. "There."

Off to the right, McMurphy saw a break in the thick trees where a wide dirt road intersected with Glidden Road. Set off the road was an old wooden sign that read *Camp Cove* and *Kanasatka Lake Reservation* in weathered, carved letters.

He slowed, switching off the headlights, and proceeded using only the Hummer's running lights to see by. He had no idea what sort of reception they'd receive, showing up late at night, uninvited. Vets tended to be a jumpy bunch, especially pissed off, anti-government, survivalist types. And armed, McMurphy thought, remembering Alice saying they'd sit around drinking and shooting all day.

He glanced down at the loaded Sig he kept in the door pocket beside his seat.

Off to the right, there was a break in the trees and a flicker of yellow light. He doused the running lights and further reduced his speed. He rolled down his window, listening as his big tires crunched over pebbles. The dirt road curved to the right.

He saw two squares of yellow light. Light cast from an upstairs window in a log cabin. It was too dark to see more detail than that. Off to the left, the flicker of yellow light he saw turned out to be the glow of a large bonfire. The fire crackled below a berm of mowed grass and on a sandy lakefront beach. Smoke and sparks drifted into the air. People were sitting around the campfire, black shadows. He heard the soft murmur of spirited conversation.

Barely driving at a crawl, McMurphy angled the Hummer to the right where several cars were parked. Recent tire tracks matted the grass flat. As he reached the edge of the clearing, a grassy slope of front lawn that led up to the large cabin, two figures silently emerged from the woods on either side of them. Sentries at a military dismount point.

They were dressed in dark clothes and armed with AR-15s, the civilian version of the military M16. They lacked the full automatic fire capability of the military version but were still plenty dangerous.

McMurphy slowed the Hummer to a full stop.

A third figure approached from the house. He strolled across the lawn wearing an old-style green Army field jacket.

His red hair cut to a steel-wool scrim. He carried a pistol in his right hand, held behind his leg.

McMurphy noticed anyway. He put the Hummer in park and opened his door. To Mary, he said, "Sit tight."

"Slowly," the sentry on his side said as McMurphy exited the vehicle.

"Hi, guys." McMurphy kept his hands wide but not high over his head.

He jerked his head around when he heard Mary's door open.

The sentry on that side—a Black guy—had pulled the door open. He growled, "Get out."

"Hey, there's no need for that," McMurphy said.

"Shut up." This sentry pointed the AR-15 at him. "We do the talking."

"There, there, Hector. No need for that," said the guy from the cabin. He raised a hand in the air—not the one carrying the gun behind his leg—like he was welcoming guests for dinner.

Hector glanced toward the man in the field jacket, looking away from McMurphy for an instant. It was all he needed. McMurphy grabbed his Sig 9mm from the door pocket and slipped it under his open work shirt, tucking it behind his belt at the small of his back without anyone noticing.

"Put your hands in the air," Hector said, returning his attention to McMurphy.

"We're not here for any trouble. We're just looking for a friend of ours."

The other sentry grabbed Mary by the arm and pulled her away from the Hummer.

McMurphy dropped back, spun, and drew his Sig. He pointed it at that sentry, then at Hector.

"Get your hands off her," he said. "Trust me, boys, I might not win this gunfight, but you'll know you've been in one."

Hector panicked. Demonstrating very poor trigger control, he fired off a shot at McMurphy. McMurphy ducked and fired back. One shot at Hector. A second one at the sentry holding Mary.

Mary got pulled from the Hummer and forced to the ground.

Her attacker fired at McMurphy, but he'd already crouched low, using the Hummer as cover.

"Hold your fire! Hold your fire!" the guy with the crewcut shouted.

McMurphy didn't stick around to see how peace-loving the new guy was. He ducked and ran, darting into the woods on the far side of the dirt road. He crashed through the darkness, zigzagging and getting slapped in the face with branches.

An expected barrage of bullets blasted into the woods, pinging off trees and snapping off branches and leaves around him. He ducked, covered his head, and ran. Over the gunfire, he heard a lot of shouting, but he didn't stick around to hear what they were saying.

Well, this is another fine mess you've gotten yourself into, McMurphy thought, baffled by what he'd stepped into and pissed he left his cell phone in the center console of the Hummer.

CHAPTER TWELVE

BANNON STOOD IN THE dark warehouse with his hands in the air. He told Barnes to do the same thing.

"Monroe Police Department," the officer said again. "Don't even think about moving."

As he stepped forward, Bannon could see the uniformed officer had his gun drawn and held in a two-handed grip. Bannon had no idea how well the small forty-man department was trained. He hoped well because he didn't want to get shot by a cop with a twitchy trigger finger.

He whispered as low as he could and yet be sure Barnes heard him.

"Follow my lead." He cleared his throat softly and stepped forward, keeping his hands in the air, very aware of the .45 he had strapped behind his back. "I'm ah… Who's there?"

"Monroe Police Department," the officer said for the third time. "Come out of the shadows so I can see you. Both of you."

To Barnes, Bannon said, "Come on, Bridget. It'll be all right. Officer, please don't shoot us. I know we shouldn't be in here, but—"

As he moved closer, the cop snapped on his Maglite and shined it in Bannon's face, freezing him in his tracks. "That's close enough. This is private property. Who are you? Why are you all in here?"

Bannon feigned nervousness. "I... my name's Cyrus Rosenthal."

Barnes knitted her eyebrows and mouthed the name Cyrus Rosenthal. *What?*

He shrugged, hoping she'd go along. To the cop, he said, "I'm an attorney with... well, it doesn't matter who we're with. Point is... oh, this is my associate, Bridget Doyle. She's the property manager with my, um... client's firm."

"Tell me why you're here, Cyrus—" the cop said.

Bannon held his arm up, shielding his eyes from the glare of the light. "Would you mind lowering that light? It's annoying."

The cop lowered the light. "But keep your hands where I can see 'em. Both of you. And no sudden movements."

"No," Bannon said. "Of course not."

He put his arms down but held them out away from his body. Barnes did the same.

"As I was saying, I represent a client who... they're interested in purchasing this abandoned building. They do a fair amount of import-export business, and this location here upriver from Lake Erie would be ideal. Ideal, isn't that right, Bridget?"

She smiled sweetly. "Ideal, Cyrus."

The cop frowned, keeping a wary eye on them as he holstered his weapon.

Bannon was a little shocked at that, but it played in his favor, so he wasn't going to complain.

"How'd you two get in here?" the cop asked.

"The door was open. Well, not open." He looked at Barnes, who nodded her head, concurring. "Not open but unlocked.

The chain around the door was loose. The padlock was open. That's what I meant to say."

Barnes agreed. "The padlock was open." She flashed the cop a sincere smile.

Bannon stepped closer to the cop. "Like I was saying, this location would be ideal, Officer…

"Fields. Officer Fields."

"Excellent, Officer Fields, it is. I—" Bannon looked at Barnes. She nodded. "We were wondering if you could tell me—us—a little bit about it. Anything special my clients should know?"

"You all need to leave." The cop took a step back and indicated the door.

"Right, of course." Bannon turned toward Barnes. "Bridget, the officer says we need to leave."

Barnes nodded. "Then we should leave."

"Absolutely." Bannon smiled at her, then at Fields. "We didn't mean to cause any trouble."

As they stepped through the door and went outside, Bannon kept talking while Fields pulled the doors shut and looped the chain around the gate, relocking it again.

"We've got a meeting with the bank in the morning," Bannon said, making things up as he went. "The property being foreclosed and all, but I thought… we thought." He indicated Barnes. "We'd get a jump on checking the property out tonight since we were in town already."

"Trying to be efficient," Barnes added.

"Right," Bannon agreed. "Efficient."

With the building secured, Fields rested his forearms on the butt of his holstered gun and his side-handle baton. "Efficient. You two are lucky I don't run you in for trespassing." He looked at the lock he'd just re-locked. "And breaking and entering."

"We didn't break anything. I swear."

"No breaking done by us," Bridget added. "No, sir."

Bannon exchanged a glance with her. "We did enter."

"Entering was involved, yes."

"You've got us there, Officer, for entering. We shouldn't have done that. For that, we're truly sorry. Now, about the building, what can you tell us?"

Relaxed, Fields said, "Not much really. It's been abandoned for two, three years now. Owned by some kind of logistics company before they went out of business. Like you said, it's in foreclosure. The bank's been trying to unload it for years." He paused as if giving it some thought. "All it was ever used for was warehousing, far as I know."

He started to walk, leading them toward the parking lot where their Camry was parked and his patrol car sat.

"Anything else?" Bannon asked. "No juicy insider information?"

Fields knitted his eyebrows. "That's illegal, ain't it?"

"Only if we're talking about stock tips," Barnes said. "The warehouse?"

Fields looked down at the ground, wrestling with a decision. Finally, he looked up. "There was one thing recently."

Bannon perked up. "Really."

"Yeah. I don't have all the details. I was off that night. We've got this old, homeless fella. Harmless guy goes by Desert Storm Bob. Hear him tell it, he was part of Task Force 1-41. You know what that was?"

Bannon and Barnes exchanged glances, shaking their heads, but Bannon knew. Task Force 1-41 Infantry was the first coalition force to engage in direct firefights with Saddam Hussein's army in the first Gulf War, Desert Storm.

Fields explained what it was.

"Did you serve, Officer Fields?"

"Naw, but I got a lot of friends who did. Admire the hell out of what those boys." He looked at Barnes, "and girls did and are still doing over there."

"Us, too," Bannon said, unable to resist giving it to Barnes.

"I feel bad for him. A vet, you know."

"You lost me," Bannon said.

"Well, being homeless, of course. On inclement nights, he'd camp out inside the warehouse you all are interested in. We let 'im, you know, because… "

"He was a vet," Bannon said.

"Sure. Anyway, it was never a problem until the other night. According to my sergeant, Bob found something in there."

"Found something," Bannon said, overly alarmed. "Nothing contagious, I hope."

"Naw, nothing like that," Fields said. "I can't tell you what it was 'cause I don't know. Only a handful of folks do, and they've been sworn to secrecy."

"Sworn to secrecy?" Bridget asked. "By whom?"

"By the U.S. government."

"The government?" Bannon asked.

"Yup. The Fed swooped in and cleared the place out. Lickety-split. Told everyone to forget about what Bob said he saw. Buttoned it up like one of them Roswell, New Mexico, things."

Bannon stared at the cop, wide-eyed. "You're not talking about alien autopsies going on in there?"

"That sure would drive the market value down," Barnes suggested.

"No. No. That was just an example. I just mean they made it all hush-hush. Very fast. Then they were gone. Since then, the place's been locked up tighter than a Navajo drum."

"But your boys back at the station," Bannon said. "I'm sure they're talking about it, no?"

"Nope. Not after what happened to Bob."

"What happened to him?" Barnes asked.

"Day after he reported seeing whatever it was he said he saw." Fields clapped his hands together loudly. "Splat."

"Splat?" Bannon asked. "What, splat?"

"Poor soul got himself a snoot full of Wild Turkey and stepped right in front of a moving car. Bam. Splattered all over the street. I was off that day, too. Thankfully. Didn't need to see that."

Bannon exchanged looks with Barnes. "That's terrible. The driver must feel awful."

Fields shrugged. "Wouldn't know. It was a hit-and-run. Driver came out of nowhere, hit old Desert Storm Bob, and then disappeared again like it never happened."

"That's a tragedy," Bannon said. "But why's it got your other officers spooked so they won't talk about Bob found?"

"They don't think it was an accident. Hit and run or otherwise," Fields said. "They believe Bob got eliminated to keep him quiet about what he found. But anyone else who knows anything they're staying quiet as church mice. Not taking any chances of being next, I guess."

CHAPTER **THIRTEEN**

TARA GLARED AT GHAAZI and shook her arm loose. Ambassador Pyotr Denikin, still speaking, his words droning on, like mosquitoes buzzing around her ears. All she could do was stare into the face of a man she thought was dead. Her brother. The lines at the corners of his eyes were etched deeper than she remembered. Gone was his scraggly dark beard. He stood clean-shaven and handsome as ever. If possible, maybe even more so with the touch of gray that streaked his temples. His chocolate brown eyes were as clear and sharp as ever.

Beside her, Chandra turned. He knitted his eyebrows and made a move toward Ghaazi. A large, dark-skinned man, who looked as if he did little else but shove weights around a workout room, took a menacing step forward. One of the many security personnel on board. He clamped a heavy hand on Chandra's shoulder, holding him in place.

"We should go somewhere private to talk, sister." Ghaazi tugged at the crisp white sleeves of the shirt under his tuxedo jacket. "We have much to discuss." He leveled Chandra with a stare. "So good to see you again, Kamal. We should get together sometime and catch up."

"No time like the present."

Ghaazi forced a smile. "I regret that will not be possible. Not tonight." The statement hung heavy in the night air, weighed down by innuendo.

"I'm afraid I must insist, Fares Terzi," Chandra said, taunting Ghaazi with his alias.

"And I'm afraid I must decline. In fact, I think it best you go with my men. They have a ridged-hull raft standing by for your immediate departure back to the harbor."

"I'm not going anywhere without Tara."

"Yes, you will." His tone discouraged argument. "I have it on good authority there is a pressing matter that has arisen that requires your immediate attention."

"What matter?"

"Be a good fellow and go with my men." Ghaazi waved his hand like a sheik would wave away the help. "All will be explained to you once you are back ashore."

Chandra risked giving Tara a look. She nodded. *Go. I'll be fine.*

Two others joined the security man who had his hand on Chandra's shoulder. The three of them escorted Chandra toward the stern without raising a commotion.

"You will not harm him," Tara said.

"Is that a question or a statement?" Ghaazi asked. When she didn't clarify, Ghaazi nodded. "Of course. He is an old friend. What do you think I've become, little sister?"

"That's the question of the day, isn't it, brother? No harm will come to Kamar. I have your word?"

Ghaazi placed a hand on his heart. "Hand to Allah. Now, please, accompany me below deck. I've a room. There is much for us to discuss."

Tara followed him through the crowd toward the ship's midsection. He never once looked back to see if she was following him. He didn't have to. She was flanked by three security people. And there would be others nearby, just waiting for her to get out of line.

They had little to worry about. She'd spent weeks getting to this place, to be in the same room with Ghaazi. She wasn't going anywhere until they talked. Until he gave her answers. Even if she had to beat them out of him.

He led her through the dining room, filled with dozens of round, linen-covered tables and gold and red appointed velvet chairs. The wait staff busied themselves with last-minute details while they waited for Denikin to finish his speech. Soon after, the guests—each having paid ten thousand dollars to attend—would gather in the room to eat, drink, and be seen.

Ghaazi brought her through the kitchen. The security detail following them had dwindled to two. Mistake number one, bro, Tara thought. Mistake number one.

They stepped into a two-sided elevator and descended two levels. The elevator doors on the opposite side of the lift opened. They came out in a short utility corridor that intersected between two carpeted passageways. They went to the left and then turned right. Two men guarded a door to the forward section marked private. Ghaazi indicated with a wave of his hand that they should proceed in the opposite direction. From the windows that lined the corridor, Tara could see the city lights of Manhattan. The tip of the island. It seemed a world away.

Ghaazi paused at a door and opened it, ushering her inside.

She stepped past him. He instructed his last two men to station themselves outside the door and await further instructions. He entered the room, closed the doors, and crossed over to a fully stocked bar. Over his shoulder, he asked, "Drink?"

"Answers," Tara replied.

Ghaazi poured himself a drink. He turned, took a sip, and smiled. "Straight to the point, as always. It is good to see you, sister. You've almost lost your accent. You sound very… American."

"Enough with the family reunion charade, Ghaazi. What insanity has gripped you?"

He stiffened, with his back still to her. "What have you heard?"

"It's what I know. You sent Aziza Faaid here and gave him a weapon capable of killing thousands of people. We barely stopped him in time. I know you have more weapons just like it. What is wrong with you?"

He took a sip from his drink. The ice clinked in the glass. His hand trembled slightly. He turned to face her for the first time since they entered the room. "Your information is coming from Miss Barnes, I presume."

"She's saving her own skin." Tara stepped closer. "Something you should be thinking about."

"How so, sister?"

"You were behind Faaid's attack. People died."

"And more people will die," he snapped. "But for a change, it will not be our people."

"Why are you doing this? What happened to you?"

"I am doing what you and I set out to do all those years ago, Tara. What we swore an oath to do together after Mother and Father were killed."

"We vowed to get revenge on the people who murdered them. We did that. The terrorists who built and detonated the bomb that killed them are dead. Those in the *Al-Jamā'ah al-Islāmīyah* who ordered the mission have been killed. Years ago."

"But the fight grew larger, didn't it?"

"It did. But it wasn't our fight, brother."

"It was. And you abandoned it. I did not."

"This isn't the same fight. This is your desire to kill. And obsession that has grown larger, insatiable. Killing those we tracked down in the *Al-Jamā'ah al-Islāmīyah* did not satisfy you. We moved on to Al Qaeda and the Taliban, but that did little to quench your thirst for death. After that, who became your target of choice, brother? ISIL. Al-Shabab. Boko Haram. And now the United States?"

She took a step toward him. She let her expression soften. "The Americans did not kill our parents, Yusuf." She used his given birth name. "Do not soil their memories to justify this course of action you've taken."

He returned to the bar, refilled his glass. Without looking at her, he said, "When I left you in Afghanistan, I fought alongside the coalition forces in Syria, fighting against ISIL until ally became enemy. I was captured by American special forces. They held me prisoner, tortured me. I was left to be humiliated, to die in a CIA black hole."

"That's what this is about?" Tara asked. "Revenge because you were mistreated?"

He pounded the bar with his fist. Glasses rattled. "It is so much more than that, dear sister. Left to rot in a dirt cell, in my own filth, I came to realize, it is the Americans who are to blame for it all. They did not activate the bomb that killed our parents, yet they might as well have. If not for their intrusion into the region, their interference, since—"

"What, Yusuf? There would be peace in the Middle East?" Tara shook her head. "Our people have been fighting this war for thousands of years. Sunni. Shia. Kurds. Israelis, Palestinians, the Iranians. They will be fighting it a thousand years after we are gone. It is all we know how to do. To blame America—"

"Is putting the blame squarely where it belongs," Ghaazi said. "We fought alongside them for years, only to have them turn against us. To side with rebels against their allies, to conduct cowardly airstrikes that indiscriminately kill... everyone."

"Oh, yes. *Munaqadh!*" Tara snapped. "The savior. You are the one among us who can do what dozens of governments have failed to do, accomplish what thousands of years of war and bloodshed could not. How egotistically narcissistic of you, brother. What you are doing is no different than the *Al-Jamā'ah al-Islāmīyah.* Worse."

Ghaazi clenched a fist. "You are wrong."

"No. I was there. You targeted six thousand people for death. Innocent people. How many more do you plan on killing with the remaining railguns in your possession? Ten thousand. A hundred thousand."

Ghaazi pounded his fist on the bar. "As many as it takes to get the world to wake up and the Americans to leave us alone!"

"And then what? America, the coalition leaves. What then? Sunni, Shia, and Kurds all come together and sing Kumbaya around bonfires in the desert? We celebrate our great *munaqadh* who vanquished the evil Americans from our lands?"

"Sure," Ghaazi said. "Something like that."

"It's a fantasy. You're delusional if—"

Ghaazi stormed toward her, raising his fist. His drink sloshed over the rim of his glass in his other hand. Tara stood her ground without flinching.

"That's right," she said. "Like the bully you've become. Trust me, Ghaazi." She went back to using his oldest alias. "Picking this fight is a fight you cannot win. America, Americans, will not back down. Hussein learned that. Bin Laden learned that. The only way this ends is with you dead."

"Not this time." Ghaazi reined in his anger and turned away. "You have no idea the devastation I plan to cause."

Tara grabbed him by the arm and spun him around. "Tell me. We can stop this. It's not too late."

"On that point, you are so, so wrong, dear sister. Nothing can stop what is coming next. Not even your little band of do-gooders."

Tara's expression clouded with concern. "What does that mean? What have you done?"

Ghaazi downed his drink in a single swallow. "Faaid's mistake was his hubris. Oh, and that he was an idiot, too. He overestimated his abilities while underestimating his enemy. I have not made the same mistake. Unlike him, and because of my time fighting side by side with them, I have a profound respect for your friends, Brice Bannon and the ever colorful Skyjack McMurphy."

"What have you done? If you've harmed them in any way... "

Ghaazi raised a hand. "I've simply set into motion... events to distract them. I've splintered your team, you from them, and them from each other." He used a linen napkin to dry his hands, then refreshed his drink. "Why do you think you were so easily able to find me after all these years?"

She didn't admit it had not been easy at all. She would not give him the satisfaction. "I've never looked for you before. I thought you were dead."

"Yes, until sweet, beautiful Bridget Barnes revealed to you my role in all this. How is Ms. Barnes? Cooperating nicely with Homeland Security?"

He sipped his drink. "You learned I wasn't dead because I wanted you to. You found me, dear sister, because I allowed it. I left the breadcrumbs that ultimately led you here. That brought you to me. Just as I have done with Bannon and McMurphy. Their manipulation was quite easy, actually."

"Brice and Skyjack? What of them? They were your friends, too. Once."

"No. They were simply people I met, two of many, along this long journey I have traveled. The one you started with me, but long ago abandoned." His eyes clouded with sadness. "As for your friends, they're alive. At least they were the last I was informed. They're being dealt with. That is all that concerns me."

"If you've harmed them, I swear, brother, you will have me to be concerned with."

"As menacing as that might be, normally your current situation makes that threat so empty as to be laughable."

"Then try laughing at this," she said, her hands clenched into trembling fists. "If just one more American life is lost because of you, or any harm comes to my friends, brother or no brother, I will kill you, and I will spit on your dead corpse when I am done."

CHAPTER FOURTEEN

BACK IN MONROE, AFTER getting escorted from the warehouse by Officer Fields, Bannon and Bridget found a seafood restaurant along the waterfront in Avalon Beach overlooking Lake Erie. Bannon enjoyed a large tiger shrimp boiled and served in a spicy bayou sauce, while Barnes ordered the fourteen-dollar appetizer sampler plate that included onion rings, fried mushrooms, mozzarella cheese sticks, mini tacos, and loaded potato skins, and still had room to consume the mussels entrée in a Cajun butter sauce.

Bannon limited himself to two beers with dinner and had coffee, while Barnes consumed an apple crisp, topped with ice cream and whipped cream, and three whiskeys.

"Must pay well, being Grayson's lapdog," she said between bites.

"Expense account," Bannon said. "Tell me about Ghaazi."

"What do you want to know?"

Bannon signaled for the check. "Your boyfriend knew him from over there. How'd you get involved with him here?"

"Josh never knew what happened to Ghaazi after he orchestrated his escape. Never knew if he was alive or dead, had been recaptured, or had given up the fight. Not until a few years ago. By then, Josh had become very vocal in his protest of the U.S. involvement in the war. He'd been a local organizer of such events and was becoming known as an important leader in the movement, doing interviews on local news stations and on podcasts that got picked up overseas, I guess.

"Not long after, Ghaazi reached out to him. He told Josh how much he appreciated the support he was giving the people of the Middle East, giving to their cause. They spoke a lot after that, over Skype and social media messaging boards, and what have you."

"Further recruiting him," Bannon said, signing for the dinner and pocketing his government-issued credit card. "Radicalizing him."

"Your perspective," Barnes said, walking with him outside.

The night had grown cool by the water. Bannon was glad he'd brought his jacket with him. "Don't give me that 'one person's terrorist is another person's freedom fighter,'" he said. "You, Ghaazi—you're targeting and killing innocent civilians."

"This is war, boy scout. There's collateral damage in war. Show me one that's been waged without that."

"You targeted a cruise ship with innocent men, women, and children on board. Your only goal was for a bigger body count than 9/11."

"That was Faaid's goal. But don't get all high and mighty with me. What about Hiroshima and Nagasaki?"

"9/11 and the Camp Speicher Massacre," Bannon countered. "We could go back and forth all night tallying the dead. What happened to Josh?"

They reached the Camry. Bannon keyed the fob and unlocked the car. They stood in the cool night air, not getting into the car yet.

"We helped organize and attended an anti-war march and protest in New York City. Josh and a bunch of his group led a march through the city, ending in Times Square. It was peaceful civil disobedience. We blocked traffic and prevented pedestrians from walking on the sidewalk or getting into stores. Just to get their attention. We had no intention of hurting anyone."

"But it got out of hand," Bannon guessed. "There were counter-protesters. People took exception to your presence, to your message."

"It turned violent, yes. The police rushed in. People were beaten up on both sides. Arrests were made. Josh was arrested, handcuffed, severely beaten by the police, and hauled off to jail. He was held and denied medical attention for over twenty-four hours. They found him dead in his cell the next morning. He'd sustained extensive internal injuries, very painful injuries. He bled to death, internally."

She blinked back tears at the memory. "The police did nothing to save him. They let him die."

"I'm sorry to hear that," Bannon said, breaking the silence that followed and meaning it.

They climbed into the Camry and pulled out of the parking lot.

Bannon was truly at a loss as to what to do next. Fields hadn't revealed the names of any of the officers who'd actually seen the railgun, not that they'd have any information Bannon himself didn't already know, but he needed a lead. A thread to pull that would lead him to who brought the weapon to Michigan, and why. With Desert Storm Bob dead, the trail was as cold as the Mount Washington summit in winter.

"Where are we going?" Barnes asked as he turned into traffic.

"Beats me," Bannon said honestly.

On the quiet streets lined with low industrial buildings, boat trailers, and small track houses, it didn't take Bannon long to pick up the tail they'd acquired. He drove, randomly turning onto roads called Lake Street, Miami Avenue, Shady Lane, and Beachway Drive, zigzagging through the lakefront community to confirm he wasn't being paranoid.

He wasn't.

It didn't take Barnes long to realize what was going on. "We're being followed?"

"Old gold Bronco with a white roof," he confirmed.

To her credit, Barnes didn't turn but instead glanced at the rearview, then at her side-view mirror. "Two front seat occupants, maybe one in the back. It's hard to tell."

Bannon continued to turn in and out of the roads, heading south.

"A second vehicle's joined them," Barnes announced.

His unfamiliarity with the neighborhood led Bannon to make a mistake. At the intersection with Biscayne, he chose to continue south along Lake Drive.

"This is a dead end," Barnes announced.

"Says who?"

"The sign you just passed that said, 'dead end.'"

"Crap." Bannon snapped off the headlights and quickly swung into the driveway of a tan brick beach house with wood trim. The garage door had been left open. There was a speedboat under a tarp on a trailer to one side of the driveway.

Bannon leaped from the Camry, keeping an eye on the pair of headlights speeding toward them. Three other vehicles had joined the chase. A souped-up red pickup truck with an oversized grill and roof fog lights, a white Jeep Wrangler, and a tricked-out throaty '68 Camaro.

He joined Barnes at the front of the car and grabbed her hand. "Come on."

They ran between the brick beach house and the small white clapboard cape next door.

Bannon flipped on his flashlight and waved it in front of them, narrowly avoiding tripping over a low, two-step deck. They could smell the burning wood of a nearby bonfire. Somewhere, a dog barked. Waves gently lapped on the sandy beach as they ran up the incline of grass that brought them to the shoreline of Lake Erie.

"Now what?" Barnes asked.

They heard several car doors open and close. A deep male voice said, "Spread out. Find 'em."

Bannon snapped the flashlight off, and they ran. He pulled Barnes along, cutting through the backyards of two smaller houses. Moonlight shimmered off the smooth water of the lake, sparkling like diamonds. The moon hung low and bright in the sky, making it easier for them to run and not risk twisting an ankle. The temperature had dipped with the absence of the sun.

At the third house they came to, Bannon veered toward the water.

"Where the hell are you going?" Barnes hissed. She brushed her hair out of her face, twisting around, keeping an eye on their pursuers.

He didn't answer but pulled her down the incline to a pair of docks and a covered boat slip. Under the pitched roof sat a speedboat tied to the dock. A rowboat bobbed against the dock in the other berth.

As they got closer, Bannon could see the speedboat was a nineteen-foot open-bow Chaparral.

"You're just going to sail away?" Barnes asked.

Bannon jumped into the boat. "You got a better idea?"

Her lack of reply was his answer.

The keys weren't in the ignition. Nope, it couldn't be that easy. They were in the glove box. Bannon snatched them out and twisted them in the ignition. The engine rumbled, sputtered, then died.

"Bannon," Barnes said.

He ignored her and tried again. The engine struggled again, longer this time, but again it banged and coughed and died. "Damn it."

"Bannon!"

"What?"

A shadowy figure stood at the top of the incline down to the docks. He pointed at them and shouted. "I got 'em! This way!"

"They're here," Barnes said to Bannon. "And you just rang the dinner bell."

The figure scrambled down the incline. He was armed with a small automatic. He stepped under the single pole light. Bannon could see he was Caucasian with a long, gaunt face. His cheeks were pockmarked, and he had greasy, stringy brown hair under a dark baseball cap.

Bannon leaped out of the boat, drawing his .45. Not that there was much more he could do than that. The man's buddies would be there in seconds. Already he could see the bobbing of flashlight beams and hear the stampede of the undisciplined group of men. Bannon could shoot the man before he got off a shot, but then what? The boat wouldn't start, and he couldn't get it started before the others descended on them. They were trapped.

All they could do was give up.

Bannon was about to do just that when baseball cap's expression changed from overly confident to confused. He knitted his eyebrows, his attention squarely on Barnes. "Hey. I know you. Bridget? Bridget Barnes. Is that you?"

In response, she snatched Bannon's gun from his hand, aimed it at the man, and fired. The bullet slammed into the man's forehead. His head snapped back, and his baseball cap went flying. He landed on the grass berm behind him.

The gunshot echoed in the air.

Bannon looked at Bridget, puzzled. "What the hell?"

A chorus of gasps and surprised expletives came from the approaching group. Collectively, they put on the brakes, stumbling to an indecisive stop.

Before Bannon could react, Barnes smacked the butt of the .45 down on the back of his skull. He dropped to his knees. Starbursts filled his vision. He reached for the back of his neck, confused and spitting mad.

Barnes slammed the butt of the weapon—his weapon— across his jaw. He spat blood and collapsed to the side. Barnes kicked him, and he keeled over. He tumbled over the speedboat's gunwale, bounced off the seats, and crashed to the deck of the boat that wouldn't start.

A second later, everything went black.

CHAPTER **FIFTEEN**

AT ABOUT THE TIME Brice Bannon was getting his brains bashed in by Bridget Barnes on a dock in Avalon Beach, Michigan, Skyjack McMurphy was darting through the forest, doing his best to evade a group of military vets with a burning desire to kill him.

When the bullets started flying, McMurphy made a beeline into the woods, putting as much distance between him, the cabin on the lake, and the trigger-happy welcoming committee as he could. Crouched and moving low, he moved from tree to tree. The ground was soft and moist from a recent rain, making it easier for him to move quietly through the woods.

His new pals hadn't paid the same amount of attention when their drill instructors taught that module in training. The initial pursuit had been noisy and chaotic, involving a lot of rustled leaves and snapping twigs. Without discipline. He could easily follow their progress by watching the beams of the bobbing flashlights and listening to loud whispers shouted back and forth.

To his surprise, the sounds of the search had quickly faded and then stopped.

Either the group had suddenly developed mad ninja tracking skills, or the search for him had been called off. The group seemed willing to return to the campground empty-handed. McMurphy voted for the latter, but he wondered why. He didn't rule out a ruse that left one or more highly skilled trackers still on his tail, hoping he'd overconfidently give himself away. Maybe they were laying a trap for him, for when he returned to the cabin to attempt a rescue of Mary.

Anyone who knew him would know that would be his play. McMurphy wouldn't leave Mary to the mercy of these men, and he still needed to find Andy. The mission hadn't changed, he reminded himself. It had just gone sideways and gotten more complicated. What else was new with his life?

He gave it ten minutes, then began his careful return to the house.

Moving slowly and with the stealth of a Navajo tracker, McMurphy crept to within striking distance of the cabin. Crouched in the wood line, concealed by trees and darkness, he waited and watched.

The night had turned muggy and thick with patchy overhead clouds drifting past the moon. He could use the irregular periods of cloud-covered darkness when it came time to advance on the cabin. If only he could do something about the buzzing mosquitoes making a meal of his sweaty neck and arms.

There was the main house, the single-story log cabin McMurphy had spotted earlier. He estimated it to be about two thousand square feet, not including the open deck that faced the water. The lawn graded softly to the crescent-shaped beach where a plethora of Adirondack chairs, log stubs, and cheap lawn chairs circled a fire pit. The fire had been left to smolder and die out. There was a flagpole in the middle of the yard. A spotlight embedded in the ground illuminated the stars and stripes hanging limply in the damp night air.

Army surplus tents littered the grounds. People, mostly men, crawled into them after taking leaks in the woods, belching, and stripping down to T-shirts and shorts. McMurphy counted thirty people preparing to bed down for the night during the hour he stoically watched the compound.

He also determined there were five men and two women inside the cabin. The men were mostly hanging out on the deck, smoking and drinking, and entertaining each other with war stories from back in the day. The women joined them for a while but eventually went back inside. As time wore on, one by one, the men went inside, too. Not too much later, the lights in the cabin, except for one over the kitchen sink, went out.

Tucked in behind the main cabin, near the woods to the right of the property, was a second cabin of similar design but far smaller, about half the size. It was there he focused his attention.

A man remained by the back door of that cabin. He sat in a plastic chair under a yellow porch lamp designed to repel bugs. It wasn't doing the job, by the way the guy kept slapping his neck and arms, and face. In between bouts of self-abuse, he tilted his chair back, leaning it against the side of the cabin. He held a shotgun across his lap, chewed tobacco, and spat.

From his position in the dark, McMurphy spotted a second individual leaning against the back of the cabin. He faced the lake. There was a sliding glass door beside him, a concrete pad that served as a patio under his feet. There were two lounge chairs on the patio, but the man didn't sit. A rifle leaned against the wall next to him.

Through a window, McMurphy caught glimpses of a woman. She moved past the window a couple of times. It wasn't Mary. But with two guards assigned to the building, dollars to doughnuts, the woman was there to keep an eye on Mary.

McMurphy frowned. "Good thing the element of surprise is on my side."

He retreated into the woods, fading back into the shadows as if he melted into the darkness behind him. It took another twenty minutes for him to silently make his way around the far side of the cabin house. This put him on the tobacco-chewing, Skoal-spitting guard's left.

It was darker on that side of the property. If the overhead cloud cover cooperated, McMurphy figured he could sneak up and practically be in the guard's lap before the guy noticed him coming.

As he'd guessed, the guard remained unaware until McMurphy snaked his arm around the man's neck and pressed his head forward, applying a chokehold that is generally forbidden to use by most law enforcement and military circles.

McMurphy didn't care. He'd use every tool available to him to get Mary and Andy back. "Don't fight it," he whispered in the guard's ear. "Just go nighty-night."

The guard struggled for a while. He then grew weak and finally went limp.

McMurphy pulled him off the chair and away from the back door. Careful not to bang the chair against the cabin or drop the shotgun the man held. He dragged the man back into the shadowy woods, out of sight.

With the shotgun in hand, a Remington pump-action—nice gun—McMurphy circled to the far side of the cabin. There, he quickly emerged with the shotgun set to his shoulder, aiming it at the man leaning beside the sliding glass door.

Startled, the guard straightened up and reached for a holstered sidearm. McMurphy shook his head, his eye aiming down the shotgun's sights. "I wouldn't."

The guard surrendered, spreading his arms wide.

"One peep and I blow your head off." McMurphy turned him around and pressed the shotgun barrel in the small of the man's back. He relieved the guard of his sidearm, a Smith & Wesson 9mm, and held it in his left hand while keeping the shotgun jammed in the man's back with his right.

"How many inside?"

"Three."

"Who?"

"The woman we caught snooping around, Sally, and her man Teddy."

"Listen to me very carefully. You're going to open the slider and go inside, tell 'em you need to take a leak or something while I stick to you like glue. You do anything other than that, I'll blast a hole through you so big a tractor-trailer could drive through it." He jabbed the man's back with the gun. "Got it?"

The guard nodded.

"Say it like you understand."

"I understand."

McMurphy pushed him. "Well, get on with it."

The man reached out with a trembling hand and slid the glass door open. He stepped inside with McMurphy close behind him. McMurphy blinked in the sudden brightness of the lights inside. He kept the shotgun to the guard's back and aimed the Smith & Wesson over the man's shoulder.

"Pom-Pom, what the hell you doing?" the unidentified woman said. She stood by a counter in the kitchen space.

"Nobody move!" McMurphy shouted, turning quickly, trying to locate all the players in the room.

"Funny, John," Mary Pawlowski said. "We were about to say the same thing to you."

It took McMurphy a moment to grasp the situation he'd walked into.

Andy Pawlowski sat in a straight-back kitchen chair in the middle of the living space. His arms were tied behind his back. His ankles were duct-taped to the front legs of the chair. He looked a little roughed up. Had a black eye, but otherwise not seriously hurt.

Mary—his wife, McMurphy reminded himself—stood with a gun pressed against Andy's temple.

Behind the kitchen counter, a woman stood—the one he'd seen walk past the window a few times—holding a shiny stainless steel revolver in two hands, aimed squarely at McMurphy. To Mary and Andy's right were three more men in a hallway that probably led to a couple of bedrooms in the rear. They were armed with shotguns and AR-15s. Every weapon was aimed directly at McMurphy.

He lowered the Smith & Wesson, pulled the shotgun from the guard's back, aimed it in the air, and surrendered. The man they called Pom-Pom spun around and angrily snatched his weapon back from McMurphy. Then he grabbed the shotgun and patted McMurphy down, finding his Sig, too.

"Three, huh?" McMurphy said.

Pom-Pom, in an over-the-top, dim-witted, redneck accent, said, "I ain't never been too good at the counting. The schooling up in these parts ain't what it should be."

McMurphy ignored him, focusing his attention on Andy instead. "You okay?"

He glared at McMurphy. The flesh around his eye was the color of an eggplant. His eyes were watery and bloodshot. And he looked as if he hadn't bathed in days. "Do I look okay to you?"

He was alive and otherwise unharmed. For McMurphy, that would do for now. He shifted his attention to Mary, ready to demand an explanation. "Oh, Mary, this had better be good."

CHAPTER **SIXTEEN**

THREE HUNDRED MILES AWAY from where Skyjack McMurphy was facing down the barrel of Andy's ex-wife's gun, in a stateroom on the *Morskoy Skat,* Tara watched with trembling fury as Ghaazi Alvi filled his empty tumbler with more bourbon from a crystal decanter.

Over his shoulder, he asked, "Sure you don't want a drink? You look like you could use one."

"I'm particular about with whom I drink these days."

"Oh yes, Brice and Skyjack. I do miss our late nights around the campfire in beautiful Kabul. Those were the days."

"Go to hell."

"*Jahannam.* Or have you forgotten Mother's teachings?"

"Don't bring her into this," she snapped. "You bring shame to our parents' names."

They were interrupted by a knock on the door.

"Yes?" Ghaazi called out.

One of his burly bodyguards poked his head in. "It is time. You're needed on deck."

"Time for what? Tara asked.

108

Ghaazi threw down the last of his drink and sighed. He placed the empty glass on the credenza, buttoned his tuxedo jacket, and squared his shoulders. "Pyotr is nearing the end of his speech. I'm needed to make nice with the generous, if unsuspecting, donors. Revolutions do not come cheap."

He checked his watch—a gold Rolex. "I wonder how all these pretty people would react if they knew the truth about how their donation dollars were really being used? Do they not care," he wondered out loud, "or would they simply prefer to remain ignorant? Warm in their self-indulgent comfort. Pleased with themselves over how they've helped all the poor little refugees. Even if it's all a lie?"

"What are you planning to do?" She took a step toward him. "The railguns? Where are they? What are your targets?"

He smiled. In that moment, she didn't recognize him at all. "Faaid showed you what a standard ballistic missile fired from one railgun could do. The destruction it could cause. Imagine if it were fired into a building, maybe two or three of them at the same time. Or several rounds from the same weapon."

"It would bring a building to the ground," she reasoned. "Like the World Trade Towers."

"Now, imagine if that ballistic missile were replaced with something more… epic. Can you imagine the death toll then?"

"Epic?" Tara's blood ran cold. "What the hell does that mean?"

"Imagine a warhead, or three, filled with a deadly toxin, such as VX gas."

"You can't be serious." Tara knew VX gas was an odorless, tasteless nerve agent. Exposure to it caused muscle spasms, asphyxiation, and heart failure. The smallest amounts could be fatal.

"Now imagine those same warheads exploding over a large concentration of people. A place where—oh, I don't know—forty thousand people might congregate. Imagine the panic as clouds of VX vapor drift down over that crowd. Those who aren't killed by the gas or by the collateral damage of the bombs' blasts will be trampled to death in the stampede. Forty thousand people trying, and failing, to escape."

Tara felt her mouth fall open. "You're a monster, Ghaazi. Insane."

He snapped. "Call me by my given name, sister!"

She looked at him with disgust. "I will not. Never again. Yusuf is dead." With even greater disgust in her voice, she added, "You are not him."

He swung his arm so fast, so unexpectedly, Tara didn't have time to dodge the backhanded slap across her face. She cried out in surprise and cupped her hand on her hot cheek. She did not cry. All the tears she had for her brother had been shed many years before. There were no more. As she'd said, Yusuf was no more. Her brother was gone from her forever.

Ghaazi tugged at the cuffs of his shirt. He glanced at his gold Rolex. "Fear not, sister. You will have little time to contemplate what will happen because the time is close. The world will soon be changed, and it will be glorious."

She stepped in front of him, blocking his path to the door. "I will stop you."

The bodyguard who had remained in the room stepped forward.

Ghaazi waved him off.

"I'm begging you, Ghaazi. Is that what you want? Then I beg. Stop this madness. There's still time. We can set it right."

He clasped her by the shoulders. "That is precisely what I am doing, Tara. Setting things right." He moved toward the door.

"No. All you are doing is making it worse. The people have suffered too much already. Theirs. Ours. Put a stop to this, Ghaazi. Stop this!"

The bodyguard opened the door and stepped to one side, giving Ghaazi room to pass. In the passageway, he stopped and turned to her one final time. Tara saw two more bodyguards filling the doorway behind him.

"Don't do this, brother," she pleaded a final time.

Ghaazi addressed the largest of the three guards. "Adnan, she can kill you seven times in seven different ways in a split second. Do not underestimate her and do not let her out of your sight."

He left.

The door closed.

Adnan and one other guard remained in the room, standing, watching her, with their backs to the door. They were both large. Adnan was larger, but both looked to make formidable opponents. Their jackets remained unbuttoned, giving them unobstructed access to their holstered sidearms.

These were dark-skinned men, Middle Eastern. If Chandra was correct, they were likely current or former Syrian National Defence Force. If so, they were highly trained. That made them extremely dangerous.

Tara crossed to the credenza. Her cheek stung, and it fueled the fire in her belly. "Drink, anyone?"

Neither man responded. She had no illusions they would. Tara lifted the decanter from a silver serving tray and poured herself a generous amount of bourbon as she continued talking, the one-sided conversation that had a single purpose—to distract. She put the decanter down on the glass-top credenza next to the decorative silver serving tray it had been on.

"I so hate drinking alone, boys," she pouted. "Sure you won't join me? One drink. I won't tell Ghaazi on you. I promise."

Neither man reacted.

Tara sipped her drink—it was excellent bourbon—then she put the glass down beside the decanter, next to the serving tray. The tray was empty now.

On the credenza was a stack of brightly colored, slick brochures, the kind found in the lobby of hotels to advertise the area's biggest tourist attractions. She thumbed through them. The Jacob Javits Center. The Plaza at Thirty Rock. The Empire State Building. Yankee Stadium and Citi Field, where the other New York baseball team played. Madison Square Garden. Her blood ran cold in her veins. The World Trade Center Memorial and Museum.

Potential targets. All of them.

She took a sip of bourbon, regretting that she'd not be able to finish her drink. In a flash, she grabbed the tray and flung it across the room, Frisbee style, aiming for the guard to the left.

He ducked and drew his weapon. The tray banged noisily against the door.

Tara grabbed the decanter and hurled it end over end at Adnan as he twisted and stepped away, also drawing his gun. She rushed them, kicking a club chair across the room.

It crashed into the guard on the left.

She leaped onto the low coffee table and jumped at Adnan.

He was the first to squeeze off a shot. The bullet whizzed under Tara's leap and chewed a deep gouge into the teak-paneled wall behind her. She dropped from the air, driving her tightly wound fist down across Adnan's jaw. He lost a tooth and spat blood.

His partner fired a shot that skimmed over Tara's head. His bad aim had been aided by the third guard stationed outside, who, upon hearing the commotion, threw open the door at that moment, knocking the guard forward as he fired.

Tara grabbed Adnan's wrist and twisted him around. With his arm cradled against her side, she aimed his gun at the entering guard. She wrapped her hand around his, inserted her finger inside the trigger guard, and squeezed his finger. The gun fired. The third guard slammed against the open door, grabbing at the bloody wound in his shoulder.

He twisted away and stumbled out into the passageway.

Tara elbowed Adnan across his already damaged jaw. With a savage yank, she tore the gun from his grasp and double-tapped the guard still by the door in the chest. Two bloody spots formed on the white shirt of his tuxedo as he went down, firing a third shot into the ceiling before he fell back dead.

Tara fired a bullet into Adnan's head and pushed his dead body away from her. She went over to the guard sitting against the door and put a bullet into his temple, making sure he was dead.

She relieved him of his weapon, a Soviet-made Makarov .380. Just like Adnan's gun. The standard-issue service weapon of the Syrian Army, thus confirming Chandra's theory: they were National Defence Force. Did that mean this whole operation was sanctioned by either or both the Russian and Syrian governments?

Armed with both weapons, she cautiously stepped out into the passageway. There she found the third guard bleeding out on the floor. With a final shot, she ended his life, too. She kicked off the four-inch-heeled sandals she wore and raced barefoot down the corridor.

She fired several shots at the guards down the hall, keeping a watchful eye over the door marked 'Private.' They ducked and returned fire, one calling into the mike sewn into his cuff. She hit the elevator call button. The doors sprang open.

A waiter stood in the middle of the lift behind a linen-covered wheelie cart. Behind him were two more dark-suited security people. Before they could react, Tara shot one in the forehead. He crumpled to the floor after a sharp cry of surprise and pain.

The second guard, reaching for his gun, stopped.

"Smart move."

The waiter cowered behind his cart. She entered the elevator, keeping her gun trained on the security person. She grabbed the waiter by the shoulder and pulled him to his feet. She pushed him out of the elevator. She hit the button for the top floor. Before the doors closed, she tossed one of her guns out into the corridor and relieved the remaining guard of his weapon. Another Soviet Makarov PM .380.

The elevator would open up in the kitchen. It would be filled with innocent workers just trying to put a fundraising dinner together. She'd do her best to minimize the collateral damage, but she needed to get off this yacht. She needed to get word to Bannon, to Grayson, and Homeland Security. Tell them Ghaazi was here in the States. Let them know whatever it was he planned to do, he planned to do it soon. That whatever it was, tens of thousands of lives were at stake.

She pushed the guard face-first against the closed elevator doors. A trail of sweat rolled down the side of his face. He knew what was coming.

The elevator came to a stop, and the doors opened.

She stood behind the security person. She winced as he screamed. His body jerked and shuddered, riddled with sudden automatic gunfire.

She shoved his body forward and grabbed the cart, still in the elevator. She wheeled it out, crouched low and firing over it as she raced into the kitchen, then ran past the stainless steel stoves and commercial-size refrigerators, gunfire chewing into the walls, shattering tiles, and pinging off metal hoods, pots, and pans. Lights exploded over her head.

She reached a set of double doors, not even sure of how many people were shooting at her.

She crashed through the doors.

Beyond them, the dining room was a mess. Tables were overturned. Linen tablecloths covered the floor, and broken stemware, shattered plates, smashed flower centerpieces, and scattered silverware littered the carpeted floor. The result of a panicked stampede when the gunfire started.

Tara ran through the room, leaping over tables and zigzagging around overturned chairs. She burst through the far doors and out onto the stern deck, which was also the yacht's helipad. The deck was crowded with partygoers, milling around, crying and screaming, and not sure what to do. Among them were several armed, tuxedo-clad guards. The guards and guests spun around at her sudden appearance. The guards moved to chase after her. She ran to the breezeway between the yacht's accommodation section and gunwale. More guards were racing toward her from the front of the yacht.

Boxed in, Tara had only one choice.

She ran for the railing, leaped, and with guns in both hands, she twisted in the air and fired at the converging guards to keep them pinned down. To keep them from shooting at her until she hit the dark water below.

The impact loosened her grip on the guns. She dropped them and dove.

Around her, bullets pierced the bracing water, creating stinging contrails of air bubbles in their wake. Tara twisted around, ignoring them, and kicked her feet hard, diving deeper, deeper, deeper into the black, chilly water until she was swallowed by the depths of Manhattan's Upper Bay.

CHAPTER **SEVENTEEN**

WHILE TARA SARDANA DODGED bullets by swimming through the cold waters of New York's Upper Bay, Brice Bannon woke up with a groan and a splitting headache. Still, on the deck of the Chaparral speedboat in Avalon Beach, the deck was slick with water and blood. His blood. He rolled over and sat up, resting his back against the captain's seat.

Tenderly, he touched the back of his head. His hand came away bloody.

His senses scattered. His head pounded like a five-alarm fire bell. It took him a minute to even realize he was clutching his .45 in his hand. Slowly, that realization became surprise, then blind panic when he heard the sounds of sirens and police radios.

Careful not to leave a bloody palm print on the floor—not that it mattered; his fingerprints were already all over the boat—Bannon climbed to his feet. He holstered the .45. Unsteady on his feet, he climbed out of the swaying boat, fighting the urge to vomit. There wasn't time for that.

Electric blue emergency lights were flashing on the sides of the houses along the bank. The lights inside most of the houses were on. Dogs barked at the commotion.

Bannon went to the body lying dead on the grassy berm. The bullet hole in the center of his forehead leaked surprisingly little blood. Dead instantly. He silently gave credit where credit was due. Barnes was a hell of a shot. Also, something to keep in the back of his mind for the next time they met up.

He patted the body down but found no wallet, nothing at all to identify the dead man. Bannon snapped a picture of the dead man's face with his cell phone. He forwarded the picture to Kayla, then put in a call to her as he climbed up the berm, glancing south to see a group of cops already making their way along the waterfront, searching.

Bannon blinked, trying to focus his eyes as he moved through the backyards, moving away from the police. A resident must have called the cops, either to report the dangerous-looking posse moving through their backyards or the gunshot that was fired.

Kayla Clarke answered the ringing phone. "Charming pic, Brice. Who is he?"

"That's for you to tell me."

"That's all you've got? A picture of a dead guy." Kayla sounded exasperated. "Fine. I'll run it through face recognition, see what we get. Anything else you can tell me?"

"He tried to kill me."

"I meant that could help me identify him. And why do you sound like you've got a mouthful of marbles?"

Because his jaw ached from the pistol-whipping he took. He ignored that question. "He was with a group of others, about half a dozen of them. They came at us in an old gold Bronco, a red pickup truck. A Jeep Wrangler, white, I think, and a '68 gray Camaro." He reached a house and leaned against it to catch his breath, staying deep in the shadowy overhang of a big red maple. His nausea churned again, threatening to have him relive his dinner again. "And he knows Barnes."

Kayla hesitated before she spoke. "Not to state the obvious, why don't you ask *her* who he is?"

116

He closed his eyes and held a hand against his clammy forehead. "I did, right after she killed him and just before she bashed my brains in with my own gun. Now she's gone."

"Oh. Okay," Kayla said. "That sounds complicated."

"You have no idea. I need to speak to Grayson.

"I can patch her in. Hold on."

Bannon pushed off from the side of the house. He couldn't go back to the Camry. If Barnes hadn't already taken it, it would be surrounded by cops. He needed to put as much distance between himself and the cops. Unless he got out of there, and fast, there was no other way for the evening to end than him in custody, his gun confiscated and tested for ballistics, and a lot of questions about why he killed the dead man on the berm.

He drew a deep cleansing breath of fresh night air. His teeth hurt. His jaw was sore. And his body ached like he'd been hit by a UPS truck.

At the corner of the house, he peered through the pine needles of a blue spruce. Seven patrol cars filled the dead-end road. Many of their doors were open. Lights flashed. Cops rushed back and forth, talking on the radio and calling out, relaying instructions from headquarters as a search was initiated.

A single dark sedan sat among the patrol cars. Detectives had already arrived on the scene. Soon, ambulances and whatever served as a coroner's unit in a small town like Avalon Beach would arrive as well.

And as he suspected, the Camry was gone.

Grayson came on the phone. "Brice, is everything okay? What is going on up there?"

"Depends on your definition of okay, but I'll live. Here's the Cliff Notes version. Barnes killed a man and knocked me out. She's on the run." He heard the sound of more sirens approaching. "And set me up as the fall guy for the dead body she left behind."

"Slow down. You're not making any sense."

"Probably due to the concussion she gave me." He was being snappy. He knew it, and he didn't care. "I don't have time for a detailed debrief at the moment. I'm too busy evading an entire police department determined to arrest me for a murder I didn't commit." He took a deep breath. "And yeah, you can bet there will be an I told you so coming, but for now, Barnes is in the wind. I sent Kayla a picture of the recently deceased. He knew Barnes. Called to her by name. Call me when you know who he is. In the meantime, I need to go dark."

Bannon disconnected the call and pocketed the phone before Grayson could reply.

He ducked low into the shadowy bushes that ran along the front lawn of the house he was using to hide behind. None of the lights were on inside, meaning no one was home. He considered hiding inside but rejected the idea. They would eventually conduct a house-to-house search. He'd only be delaying the inevitable.

He remained concealed in the shadows, watching the arrival of yet more police and the slow, methodical process of securing and processing the murder scene. The newly arriving cops were from different jurisdictions, called in from surrounding areas to aid in the canvassing of the neighborhood, a canvass that would eventually turn into a manhunt.

Bannon stayed one step ahead of the cops as they literally beat the bushes looking for him.

As the night wore on, the number of cops on the scene fluctuated. An ambulance arrived. Soon after, the body was lifted inside, presumably to be transported to the county or state morgue. Some patrol officers were released back to their sectors. The rest of the city still needed protecting. As lead detectives were assigned, others were dispatched to run down leads, make notifications, or, if not needed, return to their other cases while the forensics and coroner teams conducted their work, some of it a bit gruesome.

Bannon's cell phone vibrated in his pocket. He checked it. An incoming text from Kayla.

Body Identified. Call Me.

Bannon retreated from the scene, backing two more houses away. There, he made the call to Kayla. He covered his mouth and the glow of the cell phone screen with his hand. Whispering, he said, "Talk to me."

"His name is Travis Millar," she said without preamble. "He's twenty-nine and a mechanic at one of those drive-through oil change places. He's lived in Michigan his entire life except for two tours in Afghanistan. An infantryman with the local National Guard unit. They deployed about two years ago."

"I need to know his known associates, local friends, family. That sort of thing. Track down the vehicles I gave you, too."

"I'm already working on it."

He noted a bite in her tone. "I know you are. Sorry."

"No worries. The Camaro came back belonging to someone named Steven Van Sistine. It's the only '68 registered within a hundred miles of Monroe. He's a sergeant on the Monroe, Michigan police department. Coincidence?"

"I'm going to say no."

"Especially when you consider he served in the same National Guard unit as Millar. They deployed together. Looks like they grew up together."

Bannon wasn't surprised. Monroe wasn't very big. But still, the news disturbed him. It meant Millar's death would take on personal meaning for Van Sistine and the police in general. Van Sistine and his buddies would leave no stone unturned to find the man's killer and deal with him. Bannon was pretty sure that wouldn't involve an arrest, trial, and due process.

"That still doesn't explain how Millar knew Barnes." Just mentioning her name boiled his blood.

Grayson's voice came on the line. "We're working on that. I made some inquiries with the local FBI office up there. They tell me Millar is also a member of a small militia group. Call themselves the Michigan Minutemen. Law enforcement has been keeping an eye on them for quite some time."

"I know I was just hit on the head, but how's that connect to Barnes?"

"Hear me out," Grayson said. "Barnes was part of a group called the White Mountain Militia. They operated out of the Lakes Region in Northern New Hampshire. The group was founded by her boyfriend, an ex-Army MP named Josh Starling."

"Her boyfriend. She told me about him. Tell me about the group."

Kayla answered. "They call themselves a patriot movement. Starling formed the group about five years ago by recruiting disgruntled ex-military types. Their stated purpose was to protest governmental overreach and intrusion on the citizenry and their lack of proper support for returning vets, especially those wounded physically and emotionally."

"Don't tread on me," Bannon said. "That sort of rhetoric?"

"Several of these groups are trying to expand, grow their base beyond geographical restrictions," Grayson chimed in. "By unifying, they believe it gives them a louder, stronger voice in which to get their message heard. We believe this was something Starling and Barnes were trying to do before Starling died. It's possible that's how Barnes and Millar knew each other."

"Extremist unification, great. But why kill him, and where has she gone off to?" Bannon thought about it for a moment, but he couldn't make sense of it. He was missing something. "Let me guess, this Van Sistine's a card-carrying member of this Michigan Minutemen group."

"He has been on the FBI's radar," Grayson confirmed. "Yes."

Bannon tried to think things through, but his splitting headache and aching jaw made the job difficult. "Could it be it was these knuckleheads and not some Islamic extremist group that had possession of the railgun?"

"It's starting to look that way," Grayson said.

"Which means Barnes knew that and kept it from us. She used us to put herself right back into the thick of it." Bannon wanted to kick something, but he figured his body had taken enough abuse as it was. He didn't need to add a broken big toe. "Looks like I need to have a chat with this Steven Van Sistine."

It was Grayson who spoke up. "Sit tight, Brice. Don't do anything rash."

"Like kidnap a police officer, take him to an undisclosed location, and do whatever it takes to get answers out of him."

"Yes," Grayson said with a sigh. "Like that."

"I can't do that. I have too many questions," Bannon said, watching as more police cars pulled into the dead-end street and others left. They were widening their search grid. "Like, how'd they know we were at that restaurant at that time? We weren't followed there. I would've spotted them. I did as soon as we left. Now with Barnes out there, we're running out of time."

"I can tell you how they found you," Kayla said. "But you're gonna be mad."

"Just say it."

"Barnes called them. She placed a call to the Monroe police department at seven thirty-seven this evening."

"That's impossible. She was with me. We were eating." Thinking back, it dawned on him. "Wait. She went to the ladies' room. I checked it out before. There were no windows, no exits. No payphones. I didn't think... how the hell did she get a phone? Wait. How do you know she made a call?"

"The phone," Grayson said. "I gave it to her."

"Wait, what? Why?"

"Here's the good news," Kayla said, circumventing an argument they didn't have time for. "The phone's got a GPS tracker embedded in it."

"Let me tell you the bad news," Bannon said. "It's been deactivated."

"Yes," Kayla admitted.

"Then it's back to Plan A. I grab Van Sistine and get him to talk."

Not interested in debating it with Grayson, he disconnected the call, cutting off her protest. "Brice, don't. Think about—"

He pocketed the phone as fortune smiled down on him for a change. Bannon recognized a figure walking down the row of late-arriving patrol cars. He smiled grimly. Here was his way to get Sergeant Steven Van Sistine, and it came in the form of Officer Freddie Fields.

Fields reached the last patrol car in line. He pulled open the driver's side door.

Bannon rushed across the open yard, risking exposure. But he was quiet enough and quick enough no one noticed, not even Fields. Not until Bannon slipped a hand over his mouth and jammed the barrel of his .45 into the cop's ribs.

"I won't hurt you," Bannon whispered in the cop's ear. "Unless you call attention to us. Then I'll kill you. Nod if you understand."

Wide-eyed, Fields nodded.

"Keys."

Fields held them out.

Bannon walked him to the secure back of the car, stripped him of his duty weapon, and shoved him into the back seat as he snatched the keys from his hand. He shut the door and climbed quickly into the driver's seat. He started up the patrol car, swung a quick U-turn, and drove away from the crime scene.

Bannon looked at the cop in the rearview mirror as he drove. Behind the security screen, Fields looked pale, sweaty, and frightened. Good.

"You. You're that guy from the warehouse. Cyrus Rosenthal."

"I am, but that's not my real name."

"Where are you taking me?"

"For a ride."

CHAPTER EIGHTEEN

WHILE BRICE BANNON WAS evading police custody and kidnapping police officers in Michigan, McMurphy was being roughly tossed into a hardback chair in the back room of the small cabin in New Hampshire. It had been a bedroom at one time, but the windows were boarded over with plywood, and the hardwood floor was scuffed and stained, and in desperate need of attention. There were two old cots with thin green Army blankets on them, and that was about it.

Overhead, a single lightbulb burned.

Mary watched from the door at gunpoint as Pom-Pom tied McMurphy's legs and arms to the chair. He was efficient with knots, McMurphy noticed, much to his irritation. When he was done and stood up, McMurphy said, "Why do they call you Pom-Pom? You the cheerleader for this band of misfits?"

Pom-Pom slugged McMurphy with a right cross.

McMurphy worked his lower jaw and spat blood. "That all you got?"

"You're a tough guy, huh?"

Pom-Pom pulled back to take a second shot at him, but Mary told him to quit it. He spit on the floor at McMurphy's feet instead.

"His name's Pompey," Mary said. "He hates being called Pom-Pom. That's why everybody does it. He's got a nasty temper, John. I wouldn't antagonize him if I were you."

"I'm feeling pretty antagonistic myself right about now."

Still tied to his chair, two men tilted Andy backward and dragged him into the room. They set him down—roughly—a few feet from McMurphy, facing him. Done, they left the room. Mary backed out and closed the door. McMurphy heard the dull thud of a deadbolt being locked.

"Okay, Andy. Time to start filling me in on what the hell's going on?"

"Skyjack, man. What are you even doing here?"

"I'm here because your wife… " He tossed his head toward the closed door. "Played me for a fool with her 'I'm oh so worried' act. Going on and on about the trouble you might be in. In other words, she conned my dumbass to come looking for your dumbass."

"I am in trouble. She didn't lie about that."

"You're in trouble because of her, dumbass. Start talking," McMurphy demanded. "What's going on?"

"Yeah, yeah. Okay. Right." From the stubble on his face, Andy hadn't shaved in two days. Always skinny as a rail, he now looked like an emaciated meth addict. "Why'd she even bring you into this?"

"You're asking me?" Murphy angered easily. He knew that about himself. At that moment, his temper was creeping into loose nuke territory. And to make matters worse, his nose itched.

"Okay. Okay. I've been hanging around with these guys… well, this one guy, Peter Lynch. I met him at a VA support group. He introduced me to the others. They seemed like okay, good ole boys, ya know. Vets, most of 'em, like me. A lot of 'em having trouble adjusting back into civilian life. All of us with a lot in common, you know."

"What are you doing up here?"

"I've never been up here before. Lynch came to me a few days ago, said he needed a favor. Had a job he needed doing."

"As a driver. Mary told me that."

"That was part of it."

McMurphy closed his eyes, not sure he wanted to know the rest. "What's the other part?"

"You know I'm still with the National Guard. Do drills one weekend a month."

"Get to the point," McMurphy shouted.

"I am," Andy shouted back. "Listen. Lynch told me he needed an M925. A five-ton he knew we had in the motor pool."

"Don't tell me you stole a cargo truck from the National Guard."

"I didn't steal it. We borrowed it. Just for the weekend," he justified.

"Oh, Andy."

"He said he needed it for a parade. A rally they were part of. This militia of his."

"Where's this rally gonna be?"

"He didn't tell me. Just said it was south of here."

"South, where?"

"I don't know. We didn't get that far. All I know is I took the five-ton a couple of days ago—the guard won't be looking to use it until next month—and I drove it up here. Since then, we've just been hanging out, you know, just partying, swimming, doing some fishing out on the lake. We've been tooling around on some old four-wheelers on the trails around here. They've even got a couple of surplus LSVs."

Light Strike Vehicles. They were high-speed, lightweight, sand-rail vehicles that looked like dune buggies. The military had them designed specifically for desert combat. In the sandbox, they were armed with a heavy .50 caliber Browning machine gun and two mounted single-shot anti-tank weapons. The vehicles were introduced in the first Gulf War and used extensively during Desert Storm, though they were called Fast Attack Vehicles at the time.

McMurphy closed his eyes, trying to rein in his impatience. "Get to the point, Andy. Please."

"Yeah, sorry. Like I said, we played around during the day. At night, we were doing BBQ and burgers, drinking beer and tequila around the fire pit, telling war stories. It was cool, you know, sitting on the lake and all."

"Can you fast forward to the part where you ended up hogtied with a gun to your head?"

"That was yesterday morning. I got up, feeling more than a little hungover. I know I shouldn't be drinking—"

"Focus, Andy."

"Yeah, yeah. We had breakfast—eggs and bacon and toast and—"

"The point."

"Lynch came to a bunch of us and said they needed to load up the five-ton for the parade. I had no idea what they were loading up, I swear. Lynch took us to the barn on the other side of the property. That was where he had me park the truck when we got up here. He told me to back the five-ton up to the barn. Them other boys opened it up, and that's when I saw it for the first time.

"Skyjack, man… it was a gun. Not like any kind of gun I've ever seen before. I'm talking big, really, really big."

McMurphy groaned. "Oh, you have got to be kidding me."

"What?"

"This gun. The barrel. It has two parallel metal rails, about thirty feet long, a big generator with it, all of it on a base so the gun can swivel."

"Yeah. Yeah," Andy said, excited. "How'd you know?"

"I've seen it before. Not that one. One like it. What happened next?"

"I kinda freaked out, you know. I should have kept my cool and acted like it was no big deal, but I freaked the hell out. I started asking about the gun. What kind was it? What was it for? How come they had it? What'd they plan to do with it? I guess I made Lynch nervous thinking I was gonna go running to the cops. Because I was gonna. First opportunity. But they figured that out, I guess, and well, here I am."

McMurphy couldn't believe his luck—dumb, stupid, bad luck that it was. Here every law enforcement agency in the country's out looking for this stupid gun, and it fell right into his lap.

"A gun like that," Andy said, breaking the silence. "They've gotta be up to something not good, right?"

McMurphy didn't answer directly, his mind reeling. "Did they say anything else? Think, Andy. Anything about what they plan on doing with it? Where? When?"

"No, man. Only thing Lynch said—a couple of days ago, he got a little liquored up, more than usual, and was going on about how Washington was gonna finally hear their voices."

"That was it?"

"Well, I'm not exactly part of the inner circle, now am I?" Andy twisted his bound hands as if to demonstrate. "But it's gonna be soon."

"Why do you say that?"

"First off, Lynch was yelling about how they had a schedule to keep. That they had to have the gun properly mounted by the morning."

"The morning? You mean tomorrow morning?"

"That's my guess since he told me I'd have the five-ton back so I could return it to the motor pool early next week. That would make this rally of theirs scheduled for this weekend. Tomorrow's Saturday."

"But we still don't know where?"

"South of here. That's all he said. If we can even believe that."

He had a point, McMurphy thought. "Andy, we need to get to that gun. We need to stop this."

"Yeah, I got that sense, too. But with our situation here, you got any bright ideas on how we're gonna do that?"

McMurphy frowned, giving it some thought. "Not yet, but something will come to me. It always does."

CHAPTER NINETEEN

TARA DOVE AS DEEP as she could, kicking powerful strokes to put as much distance between her and the bullets being fired blindly at her into the river. Her heart pounded in her chest. Her lungs felt like they were about to burst. She needed to stay underwater as long as possible. She'd trained for this in the Algerian Navy, of course, but that had been many years ago. It wasn't a technique she practiced regularly behind the bar at the Keel Haul.

When she couldn't hold her breath any longer, she arched upward and swam for the surface. A twinge of panic set in. Had she dived too deep? Was the surface too far away? Would she end up inhaling a lungful of water before...

She burst through the surface, taking in a great gasp of air.

Her lungs burned. Her hair shrouded her face like so much seaweed. She brushed it away, breathing hard, and looked around, mindful to remain as low and splashing as little as possible. The water was chilly. She shivered. Then she giggled with relief, seeing how much distance she'd put between herself and the *Morskoy Skat*. Way more than she'd have guessed.

The shooting had stopped.

A crowd still gathered along the starboard rail of the yacht, but it was too dark, and she was too far away to be seen, only her head with her dark skin and black hair bobbing in the water for the guards or the privileged rich, with their exciting story to tell, to see her.

She swam toward land, staying low in the water and doing a butterfly stroke so only her head remained above the surface. She made her way toward the Hudson River side of Battery Park.

Once she put the yacht well behind her, she watched as dozens of small boats raced to the *Morskoy Skat*. The ones with flashing lights were the police responding to the gunfire. After, she was sure, a slew of 9-1-1 calls. Others were probably dispatched en masse to begin evacuating the guests from the yacht, the fundraiser dramatically cut short.

Tara reached Slip 12 at the south end of Battery Park, west of the Staten Island ferry terminal.

She dragged herself up on the wharf where the Clipper City, a one-hundred-fifty-eight-foot, two-mast, topsail schooner, was moored. Available for charter and touring during regular business hours, it sat dark and foreboding at the moment. She sat on the dock, catching her breath. Like a drowned rat, exhausted and chilly, she stared into the dark water below her dangling bare feet. The water and air temperatures were a chilly seventy-two degrees at night, when you were soaking wet.

Tara gathered up the hem of her ruined designer dress and twisted it, squeezing the water from the soiled, ivory material. With her strength returning, she climbed to her feet, careful to avoid splinters. The dress dripped, forming a large puddle on the rough wooden wharf under her. She shook out her long, wet hair, squeezed the water from the wet ends, and flung it off her face, finger-combing away the strands pasted to her cheeks.

When she reached the end of the wharf, two uniformed NYPD officers were standing there, watching. They blocked her path.

"There's better places you could have picked for a midnight swim, hon," the female cop said. Her nameplate said Torres.

Tara's shoulders sagged. Inwardly, she groaned.

Her male partner, Bradley, chimed in. "Legal places."

"Oh, no, it's not...I didn't jump in intentionally." She looked down at herself. "Not in a Carolina Herrera dress."

"No. Of course not," Bradley said. "What were we thinking, Torres?"

"Seriously," Tara said. "I fell in."

"How much did you have to drink?" Bradley asked.

Tara mentally took down his badge number: 4183.

"We're going to need to see some ID," Torres said.

Tara held her hands out. Palms open. She pointed back at the water she'd just climbed out of. "You're kidding, right?"

"Your shoes down there, too, Cinderella?" Bradley asked.

"Look, it'll take too long to explain. If you could give me a phone, I can make a call. Clear this up."

"Have you been drinking, ma'am?" Torres' badge number was 3422.

"No." Tara remembered the bourbon she had aboard the yacht. "One drink. What does that matter?"

"You're sure?" Bradley asked. "Sober women don't normally take a swan dive into the Hudson River in the middle of the night. Unintentionally."

"I wasn't out... Can you just give me a phone, please?" Tara held her hand out.

From the way Bradley's eyebrow arched under the brim of his uniform hat, Tara assumed he didn't like her tone.

"How'd you end up in the water, miss... "

"Tara. Tara Sardana."

"That's some necklace you're wearing, Tara," Torres said. "Where'd you get it?"

Tara fingered the diamond-encrusted necklace Chandra had loaned her. Thinking of him caused a pang of concern to form in her gut. She rubbed at her bare wrist where the matching bracelet had been. It must have slipped off in the water. She hoped it wasn't as expensive as it looked.

"Looks pretty expensive," Torres added.

"What are you suggesting? I stole it?"

"Your words," Bradley said.

Torres snapped her flashlight on and shined it on Tara's arm. "And how'd you hurt your arm?"

Her upper arm and forearm were streaked with blood. A cut creased her skin just above her elbow. It was still bleeding. She hadn't realized she'd been cut. "I, um, I don't know. I must've cut it on something falling in."

Tara glanced at the *Morskoy Skat* visible in the distance. Several boats surrounded it, yet the police lights had ceased to flash. From where they stood in the shadow of the Clipper City, nothing appeared out of the ordinary out there.

Did she tell these cops who she was, what had happened? Or would that slow her ability to get word to Bannon and Grayson? Why were these cops giving her such a hard time?

"What were you doing out here?" Torres asked. She kept her voice low and soothing. "All alone? At night?"

"I wasn't alone." Tara wiped her hand over her wet face in frustration. "Look, I work for the government. I need to speak with Elizabeth Grayson. It's a matter of national security."

"I want to speak to the President of the United States," Bradley said. "He's not taking my calls."

"I can arrange that for you," Tara said.

"Ha. Ha. Very funny." He rested his forearms on his holstered weapon and the handle of his baton. To Torres, he said, "We need to run this one in."

"I am serious," Tara said.

"So am I, Ariel."

"Who's Ariel?"

He looked at her like he couldn't believe she said that. "The Little Mermaid. You came crawling out of the river. Never mind. Torres, let's take her in."

"You mean to arrest me?" Tara asked. "On what charge?"

"Swimming in the river," Bradley said.

"Is that a crime?"

He hesitated. "I think it is."

Torres said, "We need to verify who you are and the ownership of that very expensive necklace."

"It's mine. Given to me as a gift." She couldn't get Chandra involved.

"So, you say," Torres said. "We can't just take everyone's word for what they tell us. You understand. We'll check the hot sheets. Then we'll know."

"I know I've done nothing wrong." Tara shivered as a breeze blew across the wharf.

"Let me make a deal with you," Torres said. "You want to make a phone call. You should get out of those wet clothes, out of the night air, before you catch a death of cold. Come on down to the precinct with us. We'll get you something dry to change into. Get that cut of yours checked out. You can make that call to someone who can verify who you are. Win. Win."

"You won't try to arrest me?"

"Like you said." Torres smiled. "You've done nothing wrong."

If they wouldn't give her a phone to use here, maybe the quickest way to resolve this would be to go to the precinct. She'd call Grayson, get her on the phone, and she could straighten all this out.

"Let's go then," Tara said. "We don't have time to waste."

The back of the patrol car smelled like vomit. Luckily, the drive to the precinct, the Oh-One as Bradley called it, didn't take long. The precinct was an old three-story building. Several patrol cars were parked on the street, angled nose in toward the building. The entrance doors were painted bright blue with an oversized NYPD emblem across them.

Bradley and Torres opened the back door of the cruiser and walked with her into the building's lobby. They approached an elevated front desk where a desk sergeant sat like a lord looking over his court. A disheveled man sat handcuffed to a bench in the corner. He held a bloody rag to his forehead. The sergeant had a small TV on his desk, tuned to the Yankees-Red Sox game in the Bronx. The Red Sox were winning three to two in the bottom of the seventh.

"What've ya got, Bradley?" the sergeant asked, keeping his attention on whatever he was writing.

"Woman we fished out of the Hudson, Sarge."

The sergeant looked up. He gave Tara's ruined party dress and diamond-encrusted necklace a once over. Tara knew immediately what was going through his mind. A high-priced prostitute got rolled or roughed up by her pimp. Dumped in the water. "What's your name, toots?"

"Not toots."

He frowned and waved his hand impatiently. Come on.

"Tara Sardana, I work for—"

The sergeant's expression turned angry. "What the hell, Bradley? Bringing a prisoner in here without cuffs? What are the two of you thinking?"

Tara said, "Wait. I'm not a prisoner."

The desk sergeant hit a button under his desk. A door to the right buzzed. Torres went over and pulled it open, holding it open. "This way, Tara."

"Secure your prisoner and get her processed," the desk sergeant shouted. "I'll deal with you two later."

"Hold it," Tara demanded. "I am not a prisoner." She looked from Torres to Bradley. "You said I'd be able to make a phone call." To the desk sergeant, she said, "I demand to see your commanding officer."

"Demand? Get her out of here. Now!"

"You can, miss," Torres said. "We've got to go through the process first."

"You are lying."

Bradley grabbed her by the arm. "Don't give us—"

Tara spun and cut him off with a punch to the throat. Bradley gagged, grabbed his neck, and staggered back, a wide-eyed, surprised look on his face. Torres rushed over as the sergeant jumped to his feet.

"Son of a—" He called out, "We need some help in here!"

Uniformed officers rushed through the door Torres had held open. She reached a hand out to grab Tara, but Tara seized the cop's arm, pulled her forward, off-balance, then twisted her arm around her back. She spun Torres around until she was facing the open door into the precinct as a rush of cops came running out.

Tara shoved Torres forward.

The woman stumbled into the cops, knocking them down like bowling pins.

Tara spun and ran for the door out to the street, but more officers were running down a flight of stairs to her left. They cut off her means of escape. Surrounding her, they piled on. Even a couple of plainclothes cops joined in. A fist struck her cheek. She kicked someone in the groin. Her arm was yanked to one side. She jabbed an elbow into a nose. Someone drove a fist into her stomach, driving her breath from her lungs. She scratched the face of one cop holding her arm. Having freed it, she swung a punch. Her fist crunched a cop's jaw. He spat blood.

She didn't intend to hurt anyone, but if she could get her hands on a gun... Fire it into the ceiling. Use it to hold them off. It might buy her some time, give her a chance to escape.

But there were too many of them.

The sheer weight of bodies forced Tara to the ground. Fisted pounded into her. She kicked out, but it was a wasted effort. Just prolonged the inevitable. Hands grabbed her arms, wrenched them behind her back. Her cheek was pressed hard against the tile floor. She heard the ratcheting of metal handcuffs, the bite of metal around her wrists.

With a few parting punches and kicks, the mob withdrew. Three burly police officers yanked her to her feet and propped her up in front of the desk sergeant.

He stared down at her, a frown on his weathered face. "Take her in the back. Book her."

"On what charge?" Tara asked. She spat more blood on the floor.

"Assaulting a police officer, several of 'em, and resisting arrest."

"You're making a mistake," she yelled. The two big cops pulled her toward the open door. "I work for Homeland Security, for Elizabeth Grayson."

"Sure, you do," the desk sergeant said, sitting back down. "And I'm an altar boy for the Pope."

Torres and Bradley followed Tara and the two cops inside. Behind her, Torres said, "You all right, Bradley?"

He cleared his throat, still rubbing his neck. His voice, barely a whisper. "Yeah. But she'll get hers for that. Trust me."

The two cops, with Torres trailing behind, led her through a door and down into a large, cold room with gray cinderblock walls. There were two cells along one side, both empty. A narrow space about five feet wide in front of the two cells. Torres opened a cell. The metal gate squeaked as she pulled it open. She indicated to Tara she should step inside.

She did. And then she tried to get through to Torres again. "Please, just call Secretary Grayson's office. Tell her you have me in custody. Tell her you have Tara Sardana in jail."

Torres handed her a folded gray sweatshirt and dark blue sweatpants through the bars. Each had the NYPD logo stitched on them. "Your dress is a mess. This is all we've got in the way of spare clothes. I'll make sure you've got a few minutes of privacy to change. Oh, and I'll need to check that necklace into evidence."

She held her hand out.

Tara removed the necklace and dropped it into her outstretched palm.

Torres locked the cell door. She returned to the door leading into the room where the other cops were waiting to make sure Tara behaved. Torres nodded at them. "Thanks, guys."

Before Torres left, Tara called out again. "Just make the call. Lives depend on it. If you don't, the blood that's spilled will be on your hands, Officer Torres. Make the call!"

The outer door slammed shut, and in the echo that followed, Tara was left alone with nothing but her thoughts and a change of clothes.

CHAPTER **TWENTY**

BANNON DROVE THE STOLEN police car west on Route Fifty. He turned south for no particular reason when he reached Lewis Avenue. He drove slowly down the rural road. Bannon leaned forward as they cruised through a middle-class residential neighborhood full of one-story ranch houses, searching for a place he could park the cruiser that wouldn't raise suspicions.

He found it when the headlights reflected off the sign for a local high school. Go Blue Streaks, whatever the hell a blue streak was.

He drove the cruiser toward the back of the large brick building, only to discover the high school was actually a campus of three different buildings. Straight ahead was the middle school, and to the left, a road that led to the elementary school. He pulled around into the shadows of the gymnasium building. There, he pulled up onto the paved basketball courts next to a practice football field.

Surrounded by dark woods, the area was secluded enough for what he needed. There were security lights on the corner of the building and two pole lights providing enough light. A Friday night in late August, so long as no one came around to walk their dogs or play a late game of pickup basketball, he and Fields could chat with little chance of being interrupted.

Bannon climbed out of the cruiser and pulled open the back door of the patrol car. He stepped back as the cop climbed out of the backseat. Bannon covered him with his .45.

"Do you have any idea how much trouble you're in, whatever your real name is?"

"Do you know how dead you'll be if you don't do exactly what I say?"

"As dead as Travis Millar, I suppose."

He'd pieced it together, Bannon thought. Maybe he wasn't the Barney Fife Bannon first assumed him to be. "You won't believe me, and that's fine, but for the record, Bridget Barnes killed Millar, not me."

"The redhead with you?" When Bannon nodded, Fields shrugged. "Doesn't matter who pulled the trigger. You're both good for it."

Not concerned with convincing Fields of his innocence, Bannon said, "Tell me about Millar. I know he's a member of the Michigan Minutemen."

"Why should I help you?"

"Because I've got a loaded .45 aimed at your gut."

"A compelling point," Fields said. "But since you'll never let me go anyway, I might as well die with my dignity intact."

"Tell me about Steven Van Sistine."

"What's the Sarge got to do with any of this?"

"He's a member of the minutemen, with Millar, isn't he?"

"What's that pack of whack-a-dos got to do with anything?"

"You're not associated with them?"

Fields screwed his face up, giving Bannon a sour expression. "Don't be ridiculous. I've got better things to do with my time than hang around the VFW telling old war stories and complaining about the government. I'm married with a couple of kids to raise. My spare time's spent coaching football and mowing grass."

Bannon sized up the cop, decided on a different tactic. Taking a chance he was on the level, Bannon holstered his weapon.

"My real name is Brice Bannon. I'm a Commander with the U.S. Coast Guard. I'm on assignment here, working directly for Elizabeth Grayson, the Secretary of—"

"Homeland Security. I know who she is. Can I say that's an even less convincing story than you being a real estate attorney searching out waterfront properties."

Bannon tossed his badge case to Fields, who caught it against his chest. The cop opened it. Inside were Bannon's military ID and his Coast Guard Special Agent badge. Though he wasn't technically a part of the Coast Guard Investigative Service, Grayson had made arrangements for him to carry a badge and ID identifying him as such. Any check would verify it.

Fields scrutinized the card and badge. Bannon read uncertainty in his expression. "Assuming they're legit." He tossed the badge case back to Bannon. "Why didn't you start with that from the beginning?"

Bannon started from the beginning now, at least Officer Fields' beginning. "What Desert Storm Bob found inside that warehouse was a weapon. A powerful weapon called a railgun. It's fallen into the hands of terrorists."

"Terrorists? Here in Monroe, Michigan?" Fields asked. "What were they going to attack, the Red Lobster?"

"We believe the site was simply a staging area."

"What kind of terrorist group operates out of Monroe, Michigan?"

"That's what we came here to find out."

"You and that woman? The one you said killed Millar. Does the Coast Guard typically go around shooting innocent civilians?"

"She's not Coast Guard. It's complicated, but I get your skepticism," Bannon said. "The weapon. It's one of four. The first one was used recently to attack a cruise ship off the East Coast a few weeks ago."

"The *Oceanic Princess*. It was all over the news. They said a generator overheated. That's what caused the explosion."

"A story planted to prevent a panic."

"You don't think the public deserves to know the truth? Maybe Millar and Van Sistine are right about—"

"A debate for another time, Officer Fields. Here's the bottom line. Four of these weapons have been smuggled into the United States. We dealt with one of them. A second one was discovered and confiscated from that warehouse."

"You think Van Sistine and Millar brought that weapon... here?"

"It's starting to look that way. I also think they're responsible for Desert Bob's death. Killed to make sure he couldn't tie the railgun back to them. What can you tell me about these minutemen?"

"They're harmless loudmouths." He shoved his hands in his pants pockets and leaned against the rear fender of the patrol car. "They gather at the VFW. Day drink and mouth off about how bad the government treats them. How none of them can catch a break. How they sacrificed so much and got nothing in return. When they've had enough, they sleep it off at home or in the drunk tank."

Fields looked at the ground and kicked at a pebble. "I'm not saying there's not a legitimate beef they're grousing about. A lot of vets do get the shaft from the system, from the V.A., but personal responsibility plays a part, too. Am I right?"

Bannon ignored the question. "After you let us go at the warehouse, who'd you talk to?"

He shrugged. "No one. I mean, I logged the call in with dispatch. Spoke to my sergeant about it."

"Steven Van Sistine?"

"Yeah. Sure."

"I don't have time to get into all the details, but Bridget Barnes, the woman with me, has ties to a similar organization operating out of New Hampshire. She knew Millar."

"And she shot him anyway?"

"She's a piece of work. Let's leave it at that. Any idea how there's a connection? My boss thinks some of these like-minded organizations might be banding together."

Fields frowned, thinking about it. He crossed his arms over his chest. "I don't know. Them ole boys are pretty much homebodies. Some of 'em—outside of their military service—never even left the state, far as I know. I can't believe… Wait. Did you say New Hampshire?"

"Yes. That mean something to you?"

Fields stood straight up. "Like I said, they're all local boys. I grew up with most of 'em since grade school. I stay friendly, but I can't say I'm friends with 'em, you know what I'm saying."

Bannon nodded.

"I'll share a drink and a barstool with 'em on a Friday night. Shoot a game of pool or two with 'em. Happy to take their money," he said with a smile.

Bannon waited, his patience ebbing, for a point to the story.

"Anyway, they've been going on about joining a larger movement, kind of like you're saying. Van Sistine's always complaining that a bunch of locals in a small place like Monroe, can't get heard. Nobody's listening to 'em. He said they have to go national. I never knew what he meant by that. I dismissed it. Drunken rambling, but now with what you're saying… "

"What?"

"Millar, he pulled Van Sistine off to the side a few weeks back when we were playing pool. He's a loud drunk, so most of the bar heard 'em. I don't remember the exact words he used, but he told Van Sistine something like, remember those people they met last year—them like-minded folks he called them. Said they were planning on doing something. Something big."

"Like what?"

"No idea, and he didn't say. But he did mention New Hampshire. Said the group's name, too. Militia something. No, wait. White Militia." He snapped his fingers as it suddenly came to him. "The White Mountain Militia. That's it."

"Anything more about what they were planning?"

"No. Van Sistine realized how loud Millar was getting, shut him up after that, but I did hear one more thing."

"What's that?"

"Millar and a bunch of his guys were putting plans together to go join them. I figured it was gonna be one of their drunken camping trip debacles. They do them a few times a year. Usually, someone ends up getting hurt, shot, or in a DWI car crash or something. But now hearing what you're saying…"

"Anything else? Anything at all."

Fields shook his head. "A lot of drunken rambling about piling a bunch of them into their pickups and their RVs and setting out to 'exercise their free speech rights' and give 'em hell at this rally, he called it."

"This rally. Did he say where it was being held?"

"No. Just that they were heading east. That would mean New Hampshire makes as much sense as anywhere."

"Listen, I need to talk to Van Sistine. Where can I find him?"

"Don't know. He's taken a bunch of personal days."

"When? Now?"

"Had it scheduled for a while. Left today."

Bannon pulled out his cell phone. The phone connected. Kayla answered. "Brice?"

"I need a way out of here," Bannon said. "Now."

"Okay. Out of where? Where are you?"

Bannon turned to Fields. "Where are we, exactly?"

"The town of Ida," the cop said. "Ida High School, specifically."

To Kayla, Bannon said, "You get that?"

"Got it. How fast do you need to go?"

"Yesterday."

"No sweat. I'll get you out. Where do you want to go?"

"New Hampshire. The Lakes Region."

Less than an hour after hanging up with Kayla Clarke, Bannon looked up, searching the night sky, hearing the first faint thrumming of an approaching helicopter. A bright searchlight flickered across the trees, then over the practice football field behind the gymnasium. The chopper's rotors grew louder. The updraft created a mini-whirlwind of dust and grit as a large white, red, and blue Coast Guard HH-65 Dolphin helicopter touched down on the high school football field fifty yards away.

Fields shielded his eyes from the sudden bright light and stirred-up dust and dirt. "If the badge and ID didn't convince me, that sure does."

Bannon and Fields stood near the trunk of the patrol car. They'd spent the last hour talking. Bannon believed the cop to be a good man, not involved with Millar and his group of crazies. He didn't let that stop him from doing what he had to do next.

"I hate to do this," Bannon said as he pulled Fields' handcuffs from his equipment belt and walked the cop over to the basketball hoop. Fields didn't resist as Bannon handcuffed his arms behind his back around the metal pole.

"You don't need to do this. I'm not involved with Van Sistine and Millar."

"I believe that. I truly do. But I need to keep this contained, just until I can get to New Hampshire and put a stop to it."

With Fields' gun already in the patrol car, Bannon pulled the cop's radio and cell phone from his belt—after letting him text his wife to say he'd be stuck at work but not to worry, he was safe—and locked them inside the patrol car along with the car key.

"It'll be dawn in a few hours," Bannon said, looking skyward. "Not long before someone finds you."

He headed for the waiting chopper.

Fields called out, "Still not necessary."

Bannon called back. "No hard feelings."

"Yeah," Fields shouted back. "Some."

Bannon leaped into the co-pilot's seat of the waiting chopper. The pilot handed him a set of headphones. "Buckle up, Commander."

He placed the headphones on his head, and they lifted off.

The chopper had been dispatched from Air Station Detroit, located at Selfridge Air National Guard. The station was responsible for the southern portions of Lake Huron, Lake St.

Clair, Erie, and Lake Ontario. The chopper crewed with four personnel.

"New Hampshire's a bit far afield for us, Commander," the pilot said over the roar of the Dolphin's twin engines. "Our orders are to drop you at Erie Station." As in Erie, Pennsylvania. "I'm told arrangements are being made to take you from there."

"Appreciate the lift, lieutenant," Bannon shouted back. "Sorry to get you out of the rack this late at night. National emergency."

"That's what the orders said. No sweat, Commander. We're always up for a little unscheduled sightseeing. At least we're not getting wet this time."

Bannon put another call into McMurphy. Again, it went immediately into voicemail. He was starting to worry. It wasn't that Skyjack couldn't take care of himself. It was just this wasn't like him.

Unable to do anything about it at the moment, Bannon leaned his head back. Inside of five minutes, he was fast asleep.

SATURDAY

CHAPTER **TWENTY-ONE**

McMURPHY WOKE UP WITH a start. Their captors had left the overhead bulb on all night, probably just to torture them. He'd slept with his head slumped forward. Now he had a crick in his neck and a splitting headache. He blinked the sleep from his eyes and rolled his head from side to side, trying to relieve the pain in his neck.

"How the hell can you sleep tied to a chair?" Andy asked. He remained bound in the chair, facing McMurphy. His eyes were puffy and dark from lack of sleep.

McMurphy had an uncanny ability to fall asleep instantly and sleep anywhere, in almost any position. People would attribute it to his time in the military, and while it had been a handy talent during his years of service, the truth was he'd been like that since he was a little kid. It was something Bannon and Blades loved to rib him about.

"Is it morning yet?"

"Can't tell." Andy glanced at the window, but it was boarded up tight. If it was daylight outside, it didn't leak through any gaps between the window and the boards. "Feels like we've been here forever. I did hear voices in the other room. A little while ago."

McMurphy wondered if that might've been what woke him up.

Just then, the door opened. The guard he'd prodded with a shotgun the night before stood in the open door. Pom-Pom glared at McMurphy. His ego was still bruised over how easily McMurphy got the drop on him.

Fine by me, McMurphy thought. His sore jaw reminded him of the man's cheap shot the night before. That wouldn't go unanswered.

"Oh, good," McMurphy said. "Room service. I was afraid I'd have to give this dump a poor Yelp review."

"Wiseass."

A second man pushed into the room behind Pom-Pom. McMurphy recognized him as the guard he'd put in the sleeper hold the night before. McMurphy smiled at him. "Sleep well, honey."

He scowled at McMurphy, then snapped open a switchblade knife. He crossed the room. "Nothing smart to say now, huh?"

"Smart would be over your head."

He circled behind McMurphy. Pom-Pom said, "Lynch wants to meet you."

"That the guy in charge?" McMurphy asked. "The one pulling your strings."

"Quit your jawing," the guy with the knife said.

The ropes around McMurphy's wrists fell away. He rubbed his wrists where the ropes had chafed his skin. "Give me the knife. I'll be happy to cut myself the rest of the way free."

"Thanks. I've got it." The man knelt and cut away the ropes around McMurphy's legs.

McMurphy calculated his odds of overpowering him and getting the knife from him. They were high, except for the Browning .380 Pom-Pom had pointed at him. A gun that could easily be turned on Andy as well.

"You wouldn't want to be that guy," Pom-Pom said, clearly reading McMurphy's mind.

"What guy is that?" McMurphy asked, standing up while Andy was cut loose.

"The guy brings a knife to a gunfight." Pom-Pom smirked at his own joke.

Once they were both freed, Pom-Pom took them to the front room of the cabin.

A fire crackled in the fireplace. Several people were crowded in the small living space. They were all in their twenties and maybe early thirties, dressed in a mishmash of military and hunting clothes. All of them were armed with either a sidearm or had a long gun slung over their shoulders. Mary was among them, but it was the rail-thin man with long, stringy brown hair talking to her that caught McMurphy's attention.

In scuffed work boots that had seen better days and baggy, straight-leg blue jeans, he wore an olive green T-shirt under an open camouflaged shirt. His right sleeve was flat and pinned to his shoulder. The man had lost an arm. The name tag stitched over his left pocket read Lynch.

"This must be the infamous Skyjack McMurphy, the source of so much trouble." Lynch kept his hand in his pocket while he sized McMurphy up. From Lynch's expression, he didn't seem impressed.

"I do what I can," McMurphy said. "How'd you lose your arm?"

"Didn't lose it. Got it blown the hell off when an IED took out the Humvee I was in."

"Afghanistan?" McMurphy thought the man too young for the fighting in Iraq.

Lynch nodded. "Kunduz. Three years ago."

"Tell me how you got your hands on a railgun?"

Lynch rubbed his hand over his mouth and scruffy beard. His fingernails were bitten down to the quick and lined with dirt. "It was a friend of a friend kind of thing."

"What do you plan on doing with it?"

"You'll find out soon enough," Lynch said. He shrugged. "Unless we kill you first."

"We're not killing him," Mary said, taking a step toward Lynch. She'd changed into a military uniform, though she'd never served. Her hair was pinned up under a camouflage patrol cap. She wore a camouflage holster with a Beretta 9mm in it. "Or anyone."

"Mary, it's time for you to do some 'splaning," McMurphy said.

She faced McMurphy. "I'm sorry you're involved in all this, John. It wasn't my idea."

"Whose idea was it?"

"We're going to make a statement," Lynch said, interrupting. McMurphy guessed he didn't like not being the center of attention. "For once, our message will finally be heard by the world."

McMurphy ignored him, hoping it would piss him off. "Mary, you can't be part of whatever this is."

"It's not like that, John. We don't want to hurt anyone, but we need to get them to listen. We need to be heard."

"A gun like that's not just for making a loud noise. I've seen what it can do." McMurphy didn't want to give away too much of what he knew, but if he could convince these crazies to stand down... "It's made to kill a lot of people. What's the target?"

"The Capitol building," Lynch said.

Which one, McMurphy wondered, but before he could ask, Mary slapped Lynch's shoulder. "Shut up, Peter."

"It's not like they're going to live to tell."

"I told you. We're not killing anyone." She was more forceful this time. "That's not part of the deal. And besides, Andy's still my husband."

Andy had taken a seat on the couch and put his feet up on a coffee table. His eyes were closed. McMurphy didn't think he was asleep, but after the sleepless night he'd put in, it probably wouldn't be long.

"If he's not with us..." Lynch let the implication hang. "We can't just let them go. They need to be dealt with. Permanently."

"That's not your call."

"Whose call is it, Mary?" McMurphy asked. She'd said bringing him there wasn't her idea. He wanted to know whose it was. "Who told you to bring me here?"

She looked genuinely upset. "I was only following orders, John. I'm sorry."

"Whose orders?" he demanded.

"That's not something you need to concern yourself with, Skyjack." A woman's voice.

The voice came from behind him. He turned; his blood had run cold. He wouldn't say it was the last person he expected to see standing there, but she was probably in his top five percent. "Bridget Barnes," he said. "This day just keeps getting better and better."

The striking redhead who'd tried to kill him on multiple occasions and blow up a ship with six thousand people on it, stood at the back door with a police officer standing behind her. From his expression, McMurphy didn't mistake him for a means of rescue.

"You know this woman?" Andy asked.

"As much as I hate to admit it," McMurphy said. "She's tried to kill me a few times."

"A task that's harder than one would imagine." She smiled. "I must say, I've seen you looking better, Skyjack."

He bristled at her casualness. "You try sleeping tied to a straight-back chair all night."

"Yes. I can see where that would be uncomfortable." She looked past him to Lynch. "Is everything ready?"

"We finally got the gun loaded this morning. Both generators are installed and ready to go. My specialist is working on the final connections and doing a diagnostic as we speak."

"Good." She nodded toward the door. "Go supervise him. Make sure it's done correctly."

Lynch took her orders in stride. He pushed through the circle of people and left. Most of the group left with him. They knew Barnes well and accepted her as the alpha dog.

Alone in the cabin with just Andy, Mary, Barnes, and the uniformed cop, McMurphy was intrigued by the new dynamic and full of even more questions.

"In case you get any stupid ideas about trying to escape," Barnes said. "I've posted two armed guards at each door. Naturally, they have orders to shoot to kill."

"Naturally." McMurphy leaned against the kitchen counter and crossed his arms over his chest. "Do I have you to thank for this party invitation?" He crossed his legs at the ankle and glanced at the coffee machine with a full pot of brewed coffee on the hot plate. "If so, a good host would offer me a cup of coffee. Why yes, I would like a cup, thank you very much."

Mary glanced at Barnes, who nodded. Mary poured a cup of black coffee and handed it to McMurphy, and also handed one to Barnes.

"Actually, no. I'm not responsible for you being here," she said, sipping her coffee. "I was still enjoying the hospitality of Homeland Security and the Federal Marshall's Service when this part of the plan was hatched."

McMurphy sipped his coffee. It was hot and good. "How many people did you kill to get away?" He kept his tone conversational.

"No one you need to worry about."

A curious answer, McMurphy thought.

Barnes' cup was a chipped mug with the 82nd Airborne Rangers logo on it. She began to pace the living room. Sleepless shiners rimmed her bloodshot eyes. She'd pulled her red hair, frizzy from the humidity, into a sloppy ponytail with a simple rubber band. Her clothes were wrinkled. McMurphy suspected from a long drive. Much longer than the two hours north from Boston, where she was being held. The last he'd heard.

He glanced over at the cop. Which begged the question, what was a police sergeant from Monroe, Michigan—a town McMurphy had never even heard of—doing with her? The cop's name tag read Van Sistine. At McMurphy's scrutiny, he placed his hand on his holstered sidearm and kept a wary eye on McMurphy. The leather crinkled.

McMurphy turned his back on the cop, dismissing him to address Barnes. "Bring me up to speed. What'll it hurt if you're going to kill me anyway?"

"Who said anything about killing you?"

"Lynch."

Barnes looked out of the glass sliders and sipped her coffee. Beyond the concrete patio and sloping lawn, an early morning mist drifted over the surface of the lake. The sun was still low in the sky, just beginning to crest the tall pines.

Between sips of coffee, she said, "Bannon sends his regards. Well, he would have if he'd known I'd be seeing you. He tried calling you yesterday."

McMurphy concealed his surprise. How would she know that? "I was too busy helping a friend to pick up." He glanced at Mary. "That was a mistake."

Barnes looked away. "He's fine, by the way. We took a little road trip together. After several weeks inside, being held against my will, it was nice to get out. To get some fresh air."

McMurphy glanced back at the cop. "How is Michigan this time of year?" he asked Barnes.

"Bannon's still there. Probably trying to convince the local police he didn't kill someone."

"I'm assuming you did." When she didn't answer, McMurphy pressed. "What do you plan to do with the railgun?"

She turned from the glass door. "The FBI and Homeland Security discovered another one in Michigan." She glared at Van Sistine and shook her head. "Hidden by children. Easily found." The cop bristled but didn't say anything. "They have it now."

"Is that why Brice was called to Boston yesterday?"

"Yes."

Van Sistine stepped forward. "I don't think this is—"

"Shut up, Steven. No one cares what you think. You want to be useful? Go help them with the gun. Make sure we're not late getting started."

"I'll stay here and keep an eye on this lot if it's all the same to you," Van Sistine said. "And you."

McMurphy had almost forgotten Andy and Mary were still there. They were sitting on the sofa. Andy was struggling to keep his eyes open. Oddly, Mary stood beside him. They looked like the loving couple he thought they were. Not a woman who'd hog-tied him to a chair all night.

"Counting the railgun here, that's three," McMurphy said. "Where's the last one?"

Barnes shrugged. "Beats me." She turned to Mary. "Why did you bring him here?"

By him, she meant McMurphy.

"We received orders," Mary said. "From Ghaazi Alvi."

Barnes seemed surprised by that. "Ghaazi told you to bring him here?"

"Yes."

"And what brought you here, Barnes?" McMurphy asked.

"What doesn't matter," she replied. "It's the why that's important." She finished her coffee and put it on the kitchen counter. "There's an anti-war rally going on this afternoon at the state capitol building in Concord."

"Mass. Or New Hampshire?"

"New Hampshire," Barnes confirmed. "Because it's an election year, politicians representing both parties will be there, also the governor, his opponent. All the candidates for the open Senate seats."

She didn't need to finish. McMurphy got it. "You're bringing the railgun to the demonstration."

"When the Governor stands up on the steps of the Capitol building, we're going to blow it and him to the moon. We'll take as many political cronies and civilians with him as we can." She smiled grimly. "It won't be the death toll we hoped for from the *Oceanic Princess*. We're going for quality over quantity this time. A bunch of high-level political warmongers has to be worth something, don't you think?"

CHAPTER **TWENTY-TWO**

IN HER JAIL CELL, Tara curled up on the hard shelf bolted to the wall, laughingly called a bed, and slept. At least she tried to. She didn't have McMurphy's ability to fall asleep anywhere at any time. She always teased him, saying he suffered from narcolepsy. In response, he'd give her that big grin of his and say, it's not suffering, it's a gift.

As she tossed and turned, struggling to grab a few hours of sleep, she had to agree. It would've been a gift. Thinking about the big, redheaded Irishman, she realized how much she missed him and Brice.

She did sleep, if fitfully. They cleaned and bandaged the cut on her arm. She had a foggy memory of a couple of people coming in and tending to it while she tried to sleep. Now her arm ached. The next time anyone came back, maybe they could spring for an aspirin.

The two cells in the cinderblock room had no windows, so Tara had no sense of how long she'd been left there. After what felt like days, the steel door to the outer room opened. Tara swung her feet to the floor and sat up. Her stomach growled, so maybe it was time for breakfast. She finger-combed her hair, not for vanity's sake but because the tangled mess hung like a rat's nest in her face. A shower would not have been unwelcome.

From the commotion coming from the other side of the door, Tara quickly realized this wasn't room service.

Loud, unruly voices echoed off the cinderblock walls as a parade of young people was escorted into the room by a handful of cops. The group consisted of men and women whose ages ranged from late teenagers to mid-thirties. The vast majority of them were Middle Eastern. The men were shoved into the empty cell while the women, three of them, were put in with Tara.

At the cell bars, Tara called out over the shouting and grumbling young people, "What is this? What's going on?"

Officer Torres, among the cops bringing the prisoners in, gave her an arched eyebrow. "What? We answer to you all of a sudden?"

"Did you call Grayson?"

Torres paused at the open steel door. With both cells closed and locked, the other cops had filed out. "It look like I've got time for that? What with dealing with these snowflakes and their silly ass sit-in, protesting who gives a crap. Here's what I did do. I talked to my watch commander about your situation. And you know what he told me?"

Tara shook her head.

"He told me about an incident out on some fancy celebrity booze cruise or whatever. He said there were a bunch of diplomats and big shots wining and dining and having a good old time until some Middle Eastern woman in an ivory dress started shooting up the place. Then he told me how witnesses said that a woman jumped overboard and dove into the water. That she was last seen swimming toward Battery Park. Sound familiar?"

"Okay." Tara gripped the iron bars hard. "If that was me, would that get you to call Secretary Grayson?"

"Are you confessing?"

"Would it get me out of here faster?"

Torres let the door close behind her and crossed the space to stand face to face with Tara. "According to my watch commander, according to all the morning news shows, you're a radical right-wing nut job who snuck onto that boat to kill people in protest of whatever crazy cause you're protesting. Far as I know, you're protesting the same damn thing these jokers are protesting."

"Hey," the men grumbled in protest.

"Settle down," Torres warned them.

She looked at Tara and narrowed her eyes. "There are three dead bodies on that boat, several more wounded."

"You've got to believe me, Tara said. "There are people on that yacht. They're planning to do something terrible. An attack. I need to speak to Elizabeth Grayson. Please. Thousands of lives are at risk."

Torres returned to the closed door. "Everything we've got, we turned over to the District Attorney's Office. They're handling it, along with our counterterrorism and intelligence unit. Your dress and the blood sample we got from dressing your wound have been turned over for forensic analysis. If you truly are who you say you are, the right people will get wind of it, eventually."

"By then it'll be too late!" Tara called out as Torres left. "A simple phone call! That's all I'm asking. How hard can that be to do?"

Her answer was a slammed metal door.

Tara pounded her hand against the bar. "Idiots."

She set about pacing the cell.

Her three new cellmates huddled together, sitting on the shelf bed. They were barely twenty years old. They had on blue jeans and wore colorful blouses and hijabs. They clasped their hands together, holding each other tightly, and looked worried. Mumbling among themselves in Arabic.

The men in the adjoining cell were equally quiet. They were all dressed in Western clothes. Only two were Caucasian.

"What are you in for?" Tara asked the women, almost laughing at the line she'd heard in every cop show ever.

Before any of them could answer, a young man in the other cell, leaning casually against the bars, spoke up. "We were demonstrating the President's overabundant use of airstrikes in Afghanistan by staging a sit-in. Peaceful civil disobedience. Turns out you need a permit for that sort of thing." He gave Tara an awkward smile and shrugged. "Who knew?"

"Everyone," she said.

"Yes. You are probably right, Miss Tara Sardana."

She crossed the cell in a flash and grabbed his arm through the bars. "How do you know my name? Who are you?"

He did not pull away. As the others in the cell stared at them with greater interest, he shouted, "Mind your own business. All of you."

They looked away. The women mumbled about what a rude young man he was.

Tara tightened her grip and shook his arm. "Tell me who you are before I rip your arm from your body."

"Call me Max."

"You don't look like a Max."

"I'm not, not really, but you can call me that." He looked down at her hand. "You may let go of me." He indicated the nine-by-nine cells they each occupied. "Where can I go?"

She released him. "Start talking."

He lowered his voice. "We have a mutual friend. Kamal Chandra."

"Kamal! Is he okay?"

"Yes. He apologizes for not being available to assist you in your time of need. He has sent me with a message instead."

"What's going on?" she asked. "If he's okay, do you know, has he contacted my... superiors? Do they—"

"He is unharmed, but... "

"Spit it out, Max."

"Your mutual acquaintance has made it impossible for him to provide any aid to you or information to your... superiors."

"Impossible? Why?"

"Mr. Chandra's family, back home. He has received clear warning that his family is in danger. If he takes any action to aid you or your adopted country, his wife and daughter will pay the price."

Tara could hardly believe what she was hearing. "Ghaazi's done this?"

"So it would seem. I am sorry."

"Max, I need to get word to my people."

"Mr. Chandra understands this. He has instructed me to tell you he is dealing with his family's situation as rapidly as he can. Once resolved, he'll be able to contact your people. Let them know where you are. But you must be patient. It may take him some time to resolve his issues."

"That's not good enough, Max. Kamal doesn't know this, but my brother... " She glanced at the young women and the others in Max's cell. They were paying them no undue attention now. Tara lowered her voice anyway. "He has a very powerful weapon."

"The railguns, Mr. Chandra informed me."

"It's worse, Max. He has VX-loaded warheads. Missiles he intends to fire with the railgun."

"VX? That is nerve gas, is it not?"

"Yes. He has two, maybe three of them."

"Fired over the city." Max's expression darkened. "The effect would be devastating."

"You don't know the half of it," Tara said. "Ghaazi boasted that his intended target would be greater than six thousand people, maybe as many as forty thousand. Since he told me, I've had a lot of time to think about it. I think I know what he intends to do."

"An aerially dispersed nerve agent. The target could be anything. The affected area would be quite large."

"You seem to know a lot about this sort of thing," Tara said.

"I am older than I appear. I have served covertly overseas with the coalition forces for many years."

"The railgun has an effective range of fifty miles. I think he plans to target a sports stadium."

Max's jaw dropped. "The only major sports arena is...no."

Tara nodded. "I believe Ghaazi plans to attack Yankee Stadium during a game. They're playing the Red Sox this weekend."

"That would mean a sellout crowd," Max said. "Then he must strike tonight or tomorrow night."

"You see why I can't wait for Chandra to save his family," Tara said. "If I'm to stop Ghaazi, I need to get out of here now."

Max nodded as if thinking about it. "Yes. There may be a way."

CHAPTER **TWENTY-THREE**

THE REST OF THE evening and early morning were a blur for Brice Bannon. From Coast Guard Erie Station, which shared real estate with the state park on Presque Isle on Lake Erie, he was whisked by car to the Erie International Airport ten minutes away. There, a chartered jet sat on the runway, prepped, fueled, and ready to go.

Three hours later, they landed at Laconia Airport in Gilford, New Hampshire. A mid-morning sun seared in the sky overhead. Bannon deplaned and slipped on his Ray-Bans. Wearing the same clothes since yesterday, he wished he had time for a shower.

A green government sedan sat at the edge of the tarmac. The driver tapped the horn.

Bannon crossed the tarmac and climbed into the passenger seat, taken aback to see Kayla Clarke behind the wheel. She dropped the car into gear, and they roared from the airport.

"Have to say, this is a pleasant surprise," he said.

She smiled from behind a fashionable pair of sunglasses of her own. With her thick auburn hair tied in a ponytail, she wore a casual—civilian—light green jumpsuit with the pant legs rolled up to mid-calf and the sleeves rolled up to her forearms, with white canvas shoes.

"Grayson sent me to keep you out of trouble."

"A day late for that, I'd say." He leaned his head back against the soft leather headrest. "You're driving like you have a specific destination in mind."

"I do. And it won't be long enough for a catnap. Unless you're Skyjack."

Bannon forced himself to sit up straight. He took off his sunglasses and rubbed his grainy eyes. "I'm good. Bring me up to speed."

"Let's see. There's a region-wide manhunt out for you. Congratulations on that one, by the way. You're officially a person of interest in the murder of Travis Millar."

"Thanks to Bridget Barnes."

"Grayson's working on smoothing that over. The White Mountain Militia operates out of an old summer camp on Lake Kanasatka near the northern tip of Winnipesaukee."

"That's where we're heading now?"

"Yes. We think Barnes is trying to hook up with some of her old posse there."

"The drive east from Monroe would take over nine hours," Bannon said. "Should put us a few hours ahead of her."

"We're not. They're already there."

Bannon looked at Kayla.

"We've re-tasked GPS satellites to follow their procession. A motley crew of campers, RVs, off-road trucks, and Van Sistine's stolen police cruiser."

"Lights and sirens the whole way would sure cut down the travel time." Bannon stared out the front window as they drove. A break would be nice, he thought. Just one. "Tell me about this militia."

"Started up by Barnes and her boyfriend Josh Starling."

"She told me."

Kayla shot him a look. "She was pretty tight-lipped about him during the debriefs she had with the FBI and Homeland Security."

"They should have pushed harder. It was through Starling she came to be involved with Ghaazi Alvi. He was a prisoner in a CIA black site in Afghanistan. During a prisoner transport, they came under attack. Starling helped Ghaazi and about two dozen other prisoners escape."

Kayla took the information in. "I'll follow up on that as soon as I can. What else did she tell you?"

"He's dead, for one thing. Happened during an antiwar rally in New York City. I'm guessing he put it together with this militia of his. The cops broke it up. Violently. During the arrest, Starling sustained injuries that were left untreated while in custody. He died as a result. Barnes blames the government for that."

"Making this, what? Revenge?"

"I suppose," Bannon said. "And to carry on Starling's misguided mission."

"Which is what?"

"Help Ghaazi win the jihad against the West."

"You knew Ghaazi," she said. "Why's he doing this?"

Bannon sat silently for a minute. Ever since they'd learned Ghaazi was the driving force behind the attack on the *Oceanic Princess*, he'd been asking himself the same thing. It didn't track. But then he hadn't seen the man in years. Thought he was dead for most of them.

"The Ghaazi Alvi I knew wouldn't do this. He was driven, determined, sure. A man with a singular focus, but his goals were always clear: get revenge on the people responsible for his parents' deaths. He and Tara accomplished that long before I even met them." Bannon shook his head. "Of course, by then, they'd expanded the fight, teaming with the allied coalition to combat Al Qaeda, the Taliban. ISIL. What changed for Ghaazi that he now sees us as the enemy? I don't know. The guy I knew wouldn't be doing this. But things change. People change. Especially over there."

"There's something else I need to bring you up on," Kayla said. "There was an incident in New York City last night. The details are sketchy. Grayson's been up all night trying to get to the bottom of it."

Bannon waited for her to go on, steeling himself for the bad news.

"There's a yacht in the Upper Bay, off the southern tip of Manhattan. They were having some kind of fundraiser dinner cruise with a lot of dignitaries aboard. Celebrities, diplomats, Fortune 100 captains of business types."

"What happened?"

"A shooting. At least three people are dead. Pyotr Denikin, the former Russian ambassador to the United States, was hosting the event."

"What's that got to do with… anything?"

"The lone gunman… was a woman. She shot up the yacht, killed a few people, and dove overboard. She escaped."

"You think it was Tara."

Kayla shrugged. "You tell me. They described her as a beautiful, dark-skinned woman with raven black hair. Witnesses said she fought like a tiger. Like out of an action-adventure spy movie."

"That sounds like Tara."

"There's something else. One of the passengers aboard the yacht was the Deputy Director General of the India Defence Intelligence Agency."

She glanced over at Bannon to gauge his reaction. He frowned.

"Kamal Chandra. Tara and Chandra were close back in the day," Bannon said. "Have we heard from her?"

Kayla shook her head. "We know Chandra's okay. There's been no word on Tara. Radio silence."

"That's odd," Bannon thought.

Tara was back in the United States, but she hadn't contacted them. Him. Why not?

If she'd found Ghaazi, she'd have reported that to Grayson, to somebody. That she hadn't meant that she couldn't. Add to that, he still hadn't managed to reach McMurphy. Two of his closest friends were MIA at the same time. That couldn't be a coincidence.

"Has Grayson spoken with Chandra? He's a good man."

"She's reached out, but he's not returning her calls. His advisors tell her he's dealing with a family emergency and is unavailable for the time being."

"They got to him. Shut him down somehow."

"They?"

"Ghaazi. It has to be him."

They drove on in silence until Kayla said, "We're five minutes out."

"Have you heard from McMurphy?" Bannon asked. "I've been trying to reach him, but he's not picking up or returning messages."

"Us, too. No word from him in at least the last twenty-four hours." She forced a smile. "That's why you've got the B team."

He returned the smile. "Kayla, you're not the B team. Not by any stretch of the imagination."

"Thanks." Her smile brightened. "It does seem like old times, doesn't it?"

"It does," he said. "Let's go get 'em, tiger."

She turned at a break in the trees and drove along a dirt road after passing a wooden sign. In carved yellow letters, it read *Camp Cove* across the top board and *Kanasatka Lake Reservation* along the second weathered board. She slowed.

"In the glove compartment is an aerial photo of the camp," she said.

He pulled it out. The quality was very good. "Re-tasked satellite surveillance?"

"Google Earth."

"Ah." Bannon nodded.

The compound was surrounded by thick, dark woods. The photo revealed about half an acre of property had been cleared to the water's edge. He saw the roofs of two structures, one larger than the other, at the end of the dirt road. There was also a dock and a sandy beach area with a fire pit.

Kayla pulled to the side of the road. "The clearing's a half mile up the road. There's a main cabin and a smaller one tucked in the back."

"I see that. What else?"

She shrugged, shutting off the car. She pointed to a series of little gray rectangles dotting the cleared property. "Near as we can tell, those are tents."

"Any idea how large a group they are?"

"The White Mountain Militia boasts over a hundred members. According to the FBI, there are maybe twenty or thirty of them, at most. We can only guess at how big a contingency Barnes and Van Sistine brought in from Michigan."

"There's one way to find out." He got out of the car and gently eased the door closed.

Kayla did the same. She went to the back of the car and popped the trunk. Inside, she had enough arms and ammunition to supply a battalion three times over.

"We doing recon or starting a war?" Bannon asked as she handed him a camouflaged ballistic vest.

"Semper Paratus. Always ready," she said, quoting the Coast Guard motto.

She tried to hand him an Army-issued Colt .45 1911. Vintage. It was a lot like his.

"I have mine." He lifted the tail of his shirt.

Kayla yanked it from his holster. "Which has been used in a homicide out of state."

"Not by me."

"Doesn't matter. God forbid you need to shoot someone here and ballistics tie it to the Travis Millar murder. Can you imagine the tap-dancing Grayson would have to do to smooth that over?"

"Yes, mother." He accepted her .45, dropped the magazine to check it, and snapped a round into the chamber. Locked and loaded.

She put on her vest, seated her Coast Guard-issued Beretta 9mm in her holster, and handed him an M16 before taking a second one out for her and closing the trunk.

"Ready?" Bannon asked.

Kayla nodded. "Ready."

Like McMurphy the night before, they crept through the woods, staying low and going slow because of the daylight hour. They reached the wood line and settled behind a thick oak that gave them cover and a panoramic view of the clearing.

The tents shown on the satellite photo were still in place around the property. The stars and stripes hung limply in the humid August air from a flagpole in the center of the clearing. Under it was a picnic table with attached benches, two large, propane-fueled outdoor grills, and lying overturned on the embankment near the beach area were several rowboats and kayaks.

In the clearing where the dirt road ended were several vehicles, mostly trucks, SUVs, and a Jeep, most of them old, all of them muddy. Conspicuous by its absence was Van Sistine's Monroe Police Interceptor. Also missing were all the people.

"Looks like we missed the party," Bannon said.

"Or the party's moved elsewhere and could be getting started any minute now."

"If that's the case, we better figure out where and fast. I'll take the main house. You check out the cabin in the back."

"What are we looking for?"

"Clues to where they've gone off to. Anything that might tell us what their next move is."

She started to move out.

"Kayla. Be careful. They might have left people behind."

She nodded. "You, too."

He watched her slip into the woods and disappear, confident she could take care of herself.

Bannon gave it another minute to make sure no one unexpectedly appeared. When no one did, he made his way toward the big log cabin. Five minutes later, he came out again. The cabin was empty but probably hadn't been for very long. He noticed matted tracks in the grass that led into the woods at the far side of the property, in the opposite direction of the smaller cabin.

He followed them and found a ramshackle shack built deep under the cover of a particularly dense thicket of towering pine trees. Big blue spruces, perfect for hiding the existence of the shack from satellite tracking and even Google Earth.

The doors were open. Several planks had been laid out end to end, forming two tracks over the soft ground. The boards were muddy. Some of them had split in two. The mud and grass around where the boards ended were deeply tracked with big tire marks.

The shack was empty.

Kayla joined him. "The camp's deserted, but not that long ago. The coffee pot in the small cabin was still on."

"The embers in the fire pit on the beach were still warm, too." Bannon stood staring into the empty shack. "Something big and heavy was stored in here." He pointed at the deep tire tracks leading away from the shack. "Something with a wide tread left those tracks, and not that long ago. The mud on the boards hasn't dried yet."

"You're not suggesting?"

He nodded. "One of the railguns was stored here. I'd bet my pension on it."

"So, where is it now?"

"That's the million-dollar question."

Kayla retrieved her cell phone from her pocket. She looked at the screen and frowned. "That's odd?"

"What is it?"

"Remember I told you we installed a GPS tracker in Bridget Barnes' phone?"

"Yeah." Bannon ground his back teeth, still annoyed over the fact they gave the woman a phone in the first place. Something he was going to get to the bottom of with Elizabeth Grayson just as soon as possible.

"It just activated," Kayla said.

"Where?"

She looked at the phone again. "On a back road about two miles south of here."

Kayla started to walk back toward the clearing.

"Where are you going?" Bannon asked.

She turned, looking confused. "To the car. We can catch her."

"I've got a better idea. I found something else."

CHAPTER TWENTY-FOUR

McMURPHY DROVE THE M939 five-ton military heavy cargo truck loaded with the railgun in the back. Because of the weight, their top speed was a little more than forty miles an hour. He had no incentive to push it. Before climbing in, at gunpoint—the only way they could make him drive the truck—he made note of the bumper markings. They told him the truck belonged to a local National Guard unit. It was the one Andy had stolen. Excuse me, borrowed.

The olive drab cab was stripped down to its most bare-bones basics. Green metal doors. Green metal floor, no floor mats. A green metal dashboard with only an instrumental panel embedded in it. Not even a radio. But worst of all, the seat was so thinly padded he felt every bump, dip, and pothole in the road, jarring his spine without mercy.

He glanced over at Bridget Barnes, who sat in the passenger seat, a Smith & Wesson .40 pointed at him. He knew she also had a holstered Lady Smith revolver on her hip. Even if he managed to wrestle the big automatic away from her, he'd still have the little .38 to contend with.

From his prior dealings with Bridget Barnes, he knew that would mean a bullet in his brain and a very messy truck cab afterward.

"I'm bored," McMurphy said.

"Suck it up, big boy."

"I need stimulating conversation," he said. "Otherwise, I might fall asleep and overturn this lumbering beast in a ditch."

"Try it and you'll nap permanently," Barnes warned.

"How'd you break out of federal custody?"

"I didn't break out. They let me go."

McMurphy barked a laugh. "Yeah, right."

"Listen, believe me, or don't. It doesn't matter. All you need to know is I'm on your side."

His expression said she'd lost her mind. "If that's your idea of a joke, remember, I'm slow. You're gonna have to break it down for me."

"I was in Michigan with Brice—"

"You're on a first name basis with him now, are you?"

"Shut up and listen." She glanced ahead at the stripped-down military Humvee they were following. Ahead of it, Van Sistine drove his police car, leading the convoy. There were seven vehicles in a line behind them. Back at the summer camp when they mounted up, McMurphy had taken a headcount. Thirty-seven nitwits and knuckleheads, including Mary and Andy. They were riding in the back of the five-ton, Andy in handcuffs, his wife holding a gun on him.

McMurphy could imagine the marriage counseling sessions that lay ahead for those two.

"When I heard a railgun was found in Monroe," Barnes said. "I suspected it was the Minutemen who had it. Bannon and I were sent to investigate."

McMurphy didn't know anything about a recovered railgun and wasn't sure he believed her. *Why send her with Bannon to Michigan to investigate? Why didn't he call me?* McMurphy thought, then recalling the calls Mary had asked him to ignore.

Idiot, he told himself.

He let Barnes go on without interrupting her, keeping a watchful eye on the gun she had trained on him. "A condition of my cooperation," she said, "was to go to Michigan and help Bannon. Grayson made it very clear what would happen if I didn't. She wanted me to reconnect with the Minutemen. She hoped they would know where the other railguns were. That's why she sent me."

"Was shooting someone and pinning it on Brice part of that cooperation?" he asked.

"I didn't know how it was going to go down. I had to improvise."

"Some improv. Who are the Minutemen?"

"The Michigan Minutemen, an anti-government, alt-right survivalist group, Josh and I had had some dealings with in the past."

"That cop? Van Sistine?"

"Part of the group. Same with the others that came along with us. More of them are back in Michigan, the ones that couldn't make the trip." She fell silent and looked away.

McMurphy wondered what was going through her mind. He figured it had to be a very scary place.

When she spoke up again, her voice was emotionless, like ice. But McMurphy noticed a vein pulse under her jaw. "I had to kill him. His name was Travis Millar." Despite her cold demeanor, this seemed to bother her. "I knew him from…before."

"Had to?"

"I needed to get them to trust me. Quickly. If I killed Millar and blamed it on Bannon, told them I escaped from his custody…It was the only way I could convince them I hadn't sold out. For Grayson's plan to work, Van Sistine needed to take the bait. He did."

"You and Grayson hatched this plan?"

"She gave me a cell phone. I used it to contact the Minutemen when we got into town." She pulled the phone out of her pocket. "When Bannon and I were at dinner, I called Van Sistine. I told him I'd," she made air quotes, "borrowed his phone to contact him."

"Then what?"

"Van Sistine told me about this. Said my old group, the White Mountain Militia, had one of the guns. Before my capture, Ghaazi had promised one of the railguns to them. I didn't know it had been delivered. Nor did I know where they were or what they planned to do with it. But Grayson had called it."

"How do you mean?"

"She'd learned from FBI sources several of these groups were starting to work together, coordinating efforts, sharing intel, resources. It was something Josh and I had started before he was killed."

McMurphy wished he'd had a pair of sunglasses. The sun was high in a cloudless sky and glared off the truck's windshield. He squinted, keeping the Humvee in sight a few car lengths ahead.

"Van Sistine filled me in on the details," Barnes continued. "Told me the Minutemen were joining up with the White Mountain Militia to help carry out today's attack on the New Hampshire State Capitol building."

"Where's the last gun?"

"I don't know. I swear. Van Sistine says he doesn't know either."

"You believe him?"

"I think I do, yeah."

As they bounced along toward Concord, McMurphy thought about what she'd told him. "Say I believe you, and I'm not saying I do. Why are you telling me all this now?"

"I want to stop them. Stop this. Just like you."

McMurphy arched a bushy red eyebrow, waiting. "What? You've suddenly grown a conscience? Did the humanitarian fairy come down and sprinkle you with morality dust or something?"

"Hardly," she said. "I would still love to watch the government crash and burn. Make every last politician pay for the casual disregard they have for the men and women they sent to war, sacrificed without a second thought. Destroy them all for the survivors they mistreat and ignore."

"So then, what is it?"

"Simple self-preservation." She lowered the gun she held to her lap. "Grayson made it very clear. I had two options. Cooperate or wait on death row until they got around to jabbing a needle in my arm. That hasn't changed."

McMurphy could buy that for now. "What do Mary and Andy Pawlowski have to do with any of this? And why the hell was I dragged up here?"

"Mary's been a part of the group for a while now. That's a woman with some serious hate for what happened to her husband. She's one seriously pissed off military spouse, and she's all in." Barnes shook her head. "Andy? I don't know him. From what I've seen, he's a groupie. Hangs out, drinks booze, tells his BS war stories like the rest of them. As you've seen, the rubber hit the road, and he bailed. Not like Mary."

"And me?"

"Lynch got a message from Ghaazi instructing him to lure you up here. Hold you captive, kill you if necessary. Sounded like Ghaazi didn't much care either way."

"Never did like that guy," McMurphy said as they hit a pothole big enough to jar his molars. "Damn. Still don't understand why."

"I hope your delicate ego can handle this, Skyjack, but it's not you, per se. It's you, Bannon, and Sardana, the whole more than the parts. Ever since you three interrupted Faaid's efforts to smuggle those Russian missile launchers into the country, he's kept an eye on you. I don't know, because I was captured, but when you dismantled Faaid's attempt to destroy the *Oceanic Princess*, I imagine Ghaazi decided he needed to deal with you three. Didn't want to risk you ruining his master plan."

"Separate us. Divided we fall."

"Something like that." She stared out the windshield. "I'm speculating, but once Tara found out he was alive, he had to know she'd come after him. And that she'd do it alone."

"Protecting Brice and me from any blowback caused by her going off-book."

"Exactly. Luring you up here was simple enough."

"Thanks," McMurphy said, already feeling enough like an idiot for being so easily duped.

"It's not a knock on you," she said. "You've got a big heart, McMurphy. Mary would know you'd do anything to keep Andy out of trouble."

He leveled her with a stare. "How'd Ghaazi manipulate Brice?"

"Knowing Ghaazi the way I do, I suspect he orchestrated the discovery of the Michigan railgun. A big price to give up, but worth it, knowing it'd be too juicy a find for Grayson to not send Bannon to investigate."

"Sacrifice the railgun just to keep us apart?" McMurphy asked, not sure he bought that.

"Pawns on a chessboard. Ghaazi doesn't care about the Minutemen or the White Mountain Militia, or anyone or anything else. Just the mission. That's what makes him such a good strategist."

"Say all that's true. What's your play now?"

Barnes pulled out her cell phone. As they rumbled down the road, she inserted the SIM card and a battery into the device. Done, she powered the phone up.

"We bring in the Cavalry."

CHAPTER TWENTY-FIVE

TARA'S STOMACH GRUMBLED. SHE hadn't eaten since she'd indulged in the platter of crackers and cheeses and very expensive malt scotch whiskey at Chandra's hotel terrace balcony the night before. She tried to forget the revolting rice and bean entrée and really bad coffee on the plane before that.

Her three cellmates remained huddled on the shelf bed. Max sat on the floor of his cell with his back against the adjoining bars. The others in his cell alternately sat, stood, and paced. Tara remained at the bars, gripping them until her knuckles blanched, counting the seconds, then the minutes, worrying as time passed and disaster grew closer.

"How much longer are they going to keep us in here?" she asked. It had felt like an entire day had passed. "I need to get out of here."

Max didn't get up but said, "I may have a way."

The outer steel door opened.

Like dogs in a kennel, the prisoners all turned expectantly toward the sound.

Torres came through the door with a group of police officers. "Listen up."

Everyone gave her their full attention.

"It's time to take you all for arraignment. We'll be transporting you to the courthouse via a prison bus. You will be handcuffed behind your backs. You will be shackled to one of your new best friends. I hope you've been getting along with your fellow cellmates."

"My phone call," Tara demanded. "Did you call Grayson?"

Torres ignored her. "If you haven't made prior arrangements for representation, public defenders will be available to you at the courthouse. Otherwise, your attorneys have been notified. They should be there to meet you."

Max flashed Tara a smile.

She frowned. What was that for?

"Once there, you can discuss such things as pleas, bail arrangements, and," she looked at Tara, "making phone calls."

"How long will that take?" Tara asked.

"Depends," Torres said.

"On what?"

"On how long it takes."

Tara slammed her hand into the bar. "That's helpful."

Torres glared at her, making sure Tara took note. "If any of you get out of line, trust me, it will be the worst mistake of your day, if not your whole life. Do we understand one another?"

After a murmur of replies, Torres nodded to the other officers with her.

Officer Bradley was among them. He gave Tara a sneering grin as he rattled the chains he carried. Torres opened the women's cell first. The women filed out. They placed their hands behind their backs and were cuffed, then shackled one behind the other.

The officers led them out to the squad room.

A few minutes passed, then Max came out. The line of male prisoners behind him. He stood next to Tara. "Stick as close to me as you can," he said under his breath. "I have a way to get you out."

Led by Torres and Bradley, three more armed cops walked with them out of the building. Bradley marched next to Tara. He held a Mossberg 590 pump-action shotgun. He asked, "Miss me?"

The prisoners were taken out to Ericsson Place, where a Department of Corrections short bus sat idling. White, it had Corrections – New York City painted across its side in blue. Security screens covered the windows.

At the bus's open door, she gazed at Max. He shook his head no. She boarded the bus as directed. The other women followed behind. They didn't have a choice, being chained to her and all.

The bus drove south on Broadway, then east on Chambers Street, before looping north to go up Centre Street, which brought them to the Manhattan Criminal Courts building in no time at all. The bus pulled to the curb. Torres and two of the cops got out. Bradley and the other cop remained on the bus with the prisoners until they were given the all-clear.

Once all the prisoners were off the bus and lined up on the sidewalk, Tara squinted against the bright sunlight, surprised at where in the sky the sun was. "What time is it?"

Torres glanced at her watch. "Nearly four."

A sense of panic surged up in Tara. Locked in the cell with no windows, just cinderblock walls and iron bars, she'd lost all track of time. What time did the game start? Seven? Eight?

"Why has this taken so long?" she demanded.

"What? We owe you an explanation?" Bradley asked. "We're working for you now?"

"How's your throat?" Tara asked. "Your voice is still a little scratchy."

Bradley instinctively reached for his neck. He stopped and frowned. He muttered something under his breath.

Pedestrians walked around them. Most talked into cell phones and barely looked up. It was probably not a very unusual sight. Then again, it might just be a case of New Yorkers being New Yorkers.

The courthouse loomed large with its block-long, wide gray steps and classical Roman-style design. There were even Corinthian columns covering most of the building's frontage and a triangular granite pediment. At the street corner, Tara noticed a black town car parked and idling. Its black tinted windows rolled up. Her first thought was that it looked like Kamal Chandra's car from the night before. But that was crazy.

She glanced at Max.

He smiled grimly and nodded. This was it.

Suddenly, Max screamed and charged at Bradley, slamming his shoulder into the cop's chest. Shocked by the sudden attack, Bradley stumbled back and fell into Torres behind him. Both cops tripped over each other and crashed to the pavement with Max on top of them.

Tara wasted no time. She dropped to the ground and tucked her knees up to her chest. She swung her handcuffed hands under her bent legs. She hit the pavement hard. Pain jolted up her backside as she rolled onto her back and brought her hands forward.

The sudden drop and roll yanked the next woman chained to her to the ground. She cried out.

With her hands in front of her now, Tara pulled the girl back to her feet. She clasped her fists together and slugged the cop beside her across the jaw, stopping him from bringing the pump shotgun up and aiming it at Max. The cop staggered back and fell against the side of the bus. He held the side of his face where Tara had punched him. Tara stomped on the back of his leg, driving him painfully to his knees.

With Max on top of Bradley and Torres, the others chained to him, piled onto the downed cops, too. They swung fists and knees, punching and kicking, their chains rattling with each blow.

Tara yanked her chain, pulling the women well along with her as she swung her arms over the head of the last cop standing. She wrapped the chain around his throat and pulled back, hard. He gasped and dropped his shotgun, grabbed for the chain biting into his neck. He wore a keyring on his belt, attached to an elastic pull-string.

Tara shouted to the woman chained next in line to her. "Get his keys."

The women didn't move.

The cop gurgled.

"Get them!"

The woman jumped as if she'd been zapped with a stun gun. She grabbed for the keys. Her hands shook so badly she yanked the whole pull-string keyring off his belt.

"Here." She held them up proudly.

While still contending with the struggling cop she was choking, Tara told the woman which was the handcuff key and instructed her on how to unlock the cuffs and release Tara's wrists.

Once freed, Tara pulled the cop's gun from his holster and aimed it at the other one she'd kicked in the leg. He still had his shotgun. "Drop it! Now!"

He bent down and put the shotgun on the pavement.

"Get over here," she ordered. At gunpoint, she directed them to the back of the bus. There, she relieved the second cop of his sidearm and handcuffed them to the emergency door.

When she came back around, the women were freeing themselves from their chains.

Max and the others were still roughing up Torres and Bradley, preventing them from getting up. The two shotguns remained lying on the sidewalk. The bus driver stood at the door of his bus. He looked old, frail, and shaken. "I… I called for help. The cops will be here soon."

As he said it, Tara glanced at the courthouse where uniformed cops and security guards were already charging down the steps, drawing their guns. She glanced at Max, who had mostly removed himself from the pile, standing over it while the others kept kicking and punching.

Panting, he wore a big grin on his face. He caught her gaze and nodded toward the idling town car. "Go!" he shouted.

When she looked down the street, she saw Varma, in his chauffeur's uniform, standing at the open back door. He looked worried.

"Go!" Max shouted again.

"Thank you," she shouted and ran toward the car.

A couple of the cops racing down the courthouse steps veered off to chase after her. She had a pretty good head start but redoubled her effort to reach the car. When she got there, she dove into the backseat.

Varma slammed the door shut and raced around to the driver's side. He jumped in, slammed the vehicle into drive, and peeled away from the curb on screeching, smoking tires.

Tara sat up, breathing hard. She looked over to see Chandra sitting beside her. He held out a glass half-filled with his insanely expensive single malt scotch. "Drink?"

She rolled her eyes and dropped her head back against the soft, luxurious leather seats. "You need to ask?"

CHAPTER **TWENTY-SIX**

THE CONVOY CONTINUED DRIVING south on Keyser Road, a secondary back road that more or less ran parallel with Route 3, the main artery through the Lakes Region. The road cut through a mostly flat landscape of green grass and middle-class homes set back from the road. A warm overhead sun baked the pavement and the cab of the truck. McMurphy opened the window. The hot breeze did little to cool him off.

There was a thick stand of tall maples and oaks on the left side of the road. Their leaves, full and green, remained motionless in the heavy air. To their right was a grassy berm. He'd noticed a matted trail that ran along the side of the road. Probably used by kids four-wheeling in the summer and snowmobilers in the winter.

Bridget Barnes had activated the GPS on her phone ten minutes earlier, but so far, nothing had happened. McMurphy glanced expectantly through the windshield, looking first left, then right, then even upward. A pale blue sky with a single cloud formation that looked like a crab was all he saw. He sat back. "As far as cavalries go, I'm calling this one a dud."

Barnes looked concerned, first at the phone, then at McMurphy. "Does this mean you don't believe me?"

"Have to say, the sudden arrival of the 82nd Airborne or Seal Team Six would've gone a long way toward establishing some credibility." He looked at her. "Any chance you've got a plan B?"

"Hate to say it," she admitted. "I don't."

Assuming he could trust her, which was a big ask, two— three if he could cut Andy loose—against thirty-seven heavily armed vets, cops, and good ole boys weren't odds McMurphy was particularly anxious to take on. Especially since said odds were only slightly less than totally suicidal.

Thinking about it, McMurphy was trying to come up with a workable plan B when he heard the high-pitched whine of an engine. At first, he thought it was a plane or a drone. No, it's more like the sound a motorcycle makes on a jump when it blasts over a hill and catches air.

That's crazy, he thought, until he glanced in his side-view mirror and caught a glimpse of something shooting past, cutting across the space between the back of the five-ton truck and the battered RV camper following behind them.

"What the hell... " he twisted around to look out the open window as he slammed on the brakes.

"What is it?" Barnes called out.

The big truck's brakes locked up, smoking the tires as they squealed to a stop.

Two seconds later came an explosion.

BANNON'S BETTER IDEA INVOLVED something else he'd found while searching the militia's base camp—several military light strike vehicles. Camouflaged off-road Army dune buggies. The LSV was a fast strike, low-ride, open tubular framed vehicle with an integrated roll cage, high flotation smooth front tires, and special rear paddle tires that gave it the ability to skim over the sand without getting bogged down. A two-hundred-horsepower air-cooled diesel engine powered the lightweight machine to speeds of sixty miles an hour.

Bannon had used such vehicles extensively during his time with the Coast Guard in Afghanistan. It would be more than enough to catch up with a slow-moving convoy transporting a piece of heavy equipment like the railgun.

But the real reason Bannon opted for the strike vehicle over Kayla's tired, government-issued green sedan, besides that they were cool as hell, was the fact—and to his dismay— these were equipped with mounted 84-mm portable, single shot, recoilless anti-tank weapons, and rear-facing .50 caliber M2 Browning machine guns, along with all the appropriate ammo to go with them.

"The tank's full." He climbed into the driver's seat of one. Kayla took the gunner position in the elevated rear seat, testing its swivel as Bannon goosed the engine. He smiled as the machine roared down the dirt road in pursuit of Bridget Barnes' suddenly activated GPS locator.

Kayla shouted directions to Bannon and then called Grayson to update her. Next, she called the New Hampshire State Police, requesting whatever backup they could provide. Already put on high alert by Homeland Security earlier, they promised to set up a roadblock on Keyser before it intersected with Route Twenty-five, thus trapping the convoy on the back road. They'd also request all available units from as many local departments as could respond.

In grim silence, Bannon and she drove on. Unprotected from the wind whipping in their faces and with the roar of the rear-mounted 200-horsepower engine in their ears, normal conversation was difficult at best. Not that it mattered. It wasn't long before they caught up with the convoy, spotting the tail vehicle ahead of them.

Kayla spun her seat forward. "How do you want to play it?"

"The railgun'll be near the front," Bannon called out over the engine noise and wind. "We cut off the head—"

"The snake will die."

"Precisely." He knew how to do it, too. "Can you call up a satellite image of that trail next to us?" He nodded to the right. There, a serpentine dirt track ran roughly alongside the road.

"Can I call up a satellite… " She repeated in a tone suggesting how ridiculous his inquiry was. In less than a minute, she shouted, "It looks like an old snowmobile trail. It runs uninterrupted until it reaches Route Twenty-five, then loops left through the fields behind a mobile home park."

"Twenty-five. That's where the State Police are staging their roadblock, isn't it?"

"It is."

"Perfect." Bannon twisted the vibrating steering wheel hard to the right. He shouted, "Hold on."

The Army dune buggy hit the low grassy berm. The special tires and suspension did an admirable job of absorbing the impact. The incline launched the vehicle over the deep rain gully beside the road. When the vehicle touched down on the steeper grassy incline on the other side, the tires slipped and spun, emitting a high-pitched whine. Bannon floored the engine and zigzagged the wheel back and forth. The tires caught a ripple in the ground, then a large rock, giving it enough traction to surge onward. The LSV leaped forward and was again airborne before it bounced to the matted grassy path at the top of the ridge.

The impact was jarring. The padded seats helped. Bannon spun the back end into a fishtail, then righted the vehicle and roared south, quickly catching up to the slow-moving convoy ahead.

The trail switched back and forth, and at times Bannon lost sight of the road to his left. He trusted Kayla's assessment that the trail followed along the side of the road far enough for his purposes, so it was full speed ahead. When the trail veered close to the road, Bannon caught a fleeting glimpse of the ragtag convoy between the trunks of trees flashing past them. They had not only caught up with the string of vehicles, a hodgepodge of pickup trucks—some expensive and well taken care of, others rotting, rattling deathtraps—SUVs, and civilian Jeeps, and two RVs. They were on the verge of overtaking it.

Interspersed with them were half a dozen military vehicles—Humvees, pickup trucks, and one big tanker, commonly referred to as a water buffalo—and what caught Bannon's attention the most: an M-939 five-ton truck. Painted Desert Camouflage. It had a canvas cover stretched over rickety ribs covering the truck bed. It moved slowly. And rode low on its upgraded tires. The railgun had to be inside it.

Directly behind it was an old white Chevrolet camper truck with blue trim. Rust stained the side of the camper. The window in the overhang section was cracked. Ahead of the five-ton truck was a stripped-down Humvee. Leading the pack was Van Sistine's Monroe police cruiser. Its lights were flashing, but they ran quietly. No sirens.

"You ready?" he shouted.

"For what?" Kayla shouted back.

"This."

He floored the gas pedal, and the strike vehicle surged forward. Ahead of them, the trail veered toward the road. When they were neck and neck with the five-ton, Bannon whipped the wheel to the left and up the embankment. They hit the grass. The tires slipped underneath them, but momentum sent the powerful dune buggy into the air.

The engine whined.

Kayla shouted, "Are you crazy!"

The strike vehicle arched high in the air, hit its apex, and began its descent.

At first, Bannon feared he'd misjudged the jump as the front of the strike vehicle aimed for the backend of the five-ton. He had images of them crashing through the canvas sides of the truck. The five-ton sped along, maintaining its sluggish speed. The strike vehicle crossed over the convoy between the back end of the five-ton and the camper behind it.

As they passed, Bannon shouted, "Now!"

Kayla knew what he wanted. She turned the antitank weapon, tracking the camper as it sailed past it. She fired. There was a rush of air and a puff of fire and smoke from the weapon. The high-explosive projectile slammed into the grill of the camper truck. The munitions exploded on impact. The hood blew upward. The engine block exploded into a black and yellow fireball that roiled skyward. The camper's back wheels came off the ground as the front end locked up. It looked like the camper had run into an invisible wall and stopped dead. The back end bounced back to the pavement, and the camper skidded to an angled stop, partially blocking the road.

By that time, the strike vehicle had hit the ground on the other side of the road. It bounced and rambled across the grass behind another thicket of trees. Bannon fisted the wheel, his knuckles blanched as he struggled to keep the dune buggy from spinning out of control. Kayla grunted as they hit but held on tight and somehow managed to remain within the confines of the vehicle's roll bars.

The strike vehicle sped around the sparse grouping of trees, driving south as it spun over grass and dirt, and pebbles, kicking up a cloud of dust in its wake.

McMURPHY CAUGHT A FLASH of the strike vehicle disappearing behind the trees to their left. He didn't know how—he never knew how—but he had no doubt the crazy driver of that buggy was Brice Bannon. McMurphy slammed on the brakes, bringing the five-ton to a screeching halt.

Seconds later, the Chevy camper behind him blew up. The front end was engulfed in a fireball of bright flames and oily smoke.

McMurphy shoved the five-ton into park and pocketed the keys. The truck wasn't going anywhere. Not unless someone pried the keys from his cold, dead fingers.

"What the hell was that?" Barnes demanded.

"The Cavalry." He grabbed the Beretta from her hand before she could react.

He pushed open the door and leaped to the ground. He ran to the back of the five-ton.

The driver of the camper and his passenger had jumped out of the truck cab. The driver ran a couple of steps from the camper, his arm covering his head, protecting him from any flying shrapnel and the heat from the burning engine compartment. He carried a handgun. He saw McMurphy and raised it. That was as far as he got. McMurphy put a bullet in his forehead.

On the other side, the passenger fumbled trying to get his gun out. When he did, he aimed it at McMurphy through the roaring fire consuming the camper's engine.

McMurphy swung the Beretta in his direction, but before he could squeeze the trigger, the guy's head snapped to the left. Blood and brain matter flew from his temple. He fell against the camper's open door, slamming it shut, then slid down it to the ground, leaving a thick trail of blood down the smooth metal door.

Barnes stepped around the back end of the five-ton, the Lady Smith in her hand. "You can thank me later."

BANNON SPUN THE BACK end of the strike vehicle through the field, sending a fan of grass and dirt into the air. He floored the gas, racing to the front of the convoy where the lead Humvee and the police cruiser had skidded to a stop. Kayla had switched to the .50 caliber M2 Browning machine gun.

The M2 had a selectable rate of firing—single shot, slow, rapid, and fully automatic. In slow-firing mode, which Kayla had chosen, the machine gun fired forty rounds per minute in five to seven-round bursts with different pause lengths between bursts.

Van Sistine rolled out of his cruiser low, with a shotgun in hand. Several men dressed in desert fatigues piled out of the Humvee. They were all armed with an array of shotguns, rifles, and handguns.

Kayla opened fire, spraying the police car with rapid-fire bullets. The side windows burst into white, gummy glass. Bullets pinged and dented the doors and fenders. She fired high, trying to avoid hitting anyone.

Van Sistine dove to the ground and fired the shotgun.

Bannon gunned the strike vehicle. The front end rose up as the vehicle shot forward.

The shotgun blast missed.

"Don't be nice!" Bannon shouted. "This is a war!"

Kayla fired another short burst at the men hunkered down behind the Humvee. Bullets chewed through the metal, sparked, and starred the windshield. One man popped up at the wrong moment. A round pierced his neck, nicking his jugular. Blood spurted from the wound like a water fountain.

Bannon aimed the strike vehicle at the road. It climbed the berm. He swung onto the pavement. The tires smoked as they slid across the smooth paved surface. With the strike vehicle aimed at the convoy straight away, Bannon stomped the gas pedal.

Kayla swung the machine gun, facing forward again.

Van Sistine sat up on the pavement next to his cruiser.

He racked a round into the shotgun's breach and set the stock to his shoulder.

Bannon drove straight at the cop. He pulled the .45 Kayla gave him. He rested his wrist on the roll bar ahead of him to steady his aim. He shouted, "I've got this."

He and Van Sistine fired at almost the same time.

Bannon's bullet slammed into Van Sistine's cheek, shattered his jaw, and knocked him backward. The shotgun fired harmlessly into the air.

The men huddled behind the Humvee gave up the fight as the strike vehicle raced closer. They ran toward the back of the convoy, probably intending to get to the last few vehicles to escape. Turned out, it wasn't just Bannon and Kayla they were running away from.

Behind the speeding strike vehicle had appeared a formation of police cars from various agencies speeding toward the convoy, too, lights flashing and sirens screaming.

McMURPHY DIDN'T HAVE TO wait long for the chance to thank Barnes for saving his life. Nor did he do it with words. From the stopped vehicles behind them, several members of the militia charged at them, all armed to the teeth, including one-armed Peter Lynch. He had a handgun extended, pointed at Barnes as he ran.

"I should've known you'd betray us," he shouted. "I knew the government turned you! Knew it!"

McMurphy stepped in front of her, pointed the Beretta, and squeezed the trigger. Two rounds, double-tapped. They hit Lynch in the chest, center mass. He fell forward, stumbled, tripped over his feet, and hit the pavement. Dead.

With their leader dead, the others stopped short, deciding the fight wasn't worth it. They turned tail and ran.

"Guess we're even now," Barnes said.

McMurphy turned around. "Don't mention it. I mean that. Don't tell anyone I saved your life. Bannon and Blades would never forgive me."

Together, they turned at the sound of the approaching police vehicles. In a V formation, the cars and SUVs barreled down the road and even extended off-road on either side, kicking up clouds of dust behind them. Some slid to a stop near the forward vehicles. Others sped past, pursuing the militiamen who'd decided to run. A futile attempt at escape.

McMurphy and Barnes ignored them and turned their attention to the rear of the truck carrying the railgun. The back canvas cover was down, hiding the devastating weapon concealed inside from the curious—casual, and otherwise.

McMurphy climbed up the tailgate and reached for the canvas cover to pull it back.

Pom-Pom leaped out of the back of the truck. His face twisted into a deranged grimace.

He body-slammed McMurphy, who lost his grip on the handle he was holding onto. The two of them went flying to the pavement below. McMurphy took the brunt of the impact, landing on his back and smacking his head on the pavement so hard he saw stars. The Beretta he held bounced from his hand.

McMurphy blinked. "Son of a—"

Pom-Pom held a Ka-Bar knife in his hand. He raised it over his head. The blade gleamed in the sunlight as he plunged it toward McMurphy's chest.

McMurphy fisted his left hand and swung a punch at his attacker's jaw.

It knocked Pom-Pom to the side, but not swiftly enough to keep the blade of the knife from slicing across McMurphy's shoulder. He rolled over, knocked Pom-Pom to the ground, and stood up. Pom-Pom took a swipe at McMurphy's leg with the knife. McMurphy sidestepped the attack and slapped the knife from his attacker's hands.

With him weaponless, McMurphy fisted the front of Pom-Pom's shirt and pulled him up from the ground. He delivered a punch to his jaw. "That's for the cheap shot last night."

He punched him again. This time, a straight shot into the man's mouth. Blood spurted from Pom-Pom's lip. "And that's because you're a dick."

The third punch knocked Pom-Pom out cold. "That one's for... " he told the unconscious man. "Oh, forget it."

From the back of the five-ton, Mary poked her head out and held two empty hands up for McMurphy to see. "I surrender."

Behind her, Andy popped his head up over her shoulder. "Can someone take these cuffs off me now?"

Rather than respond, McMurphy stepped toward the strike vehicle as it skidded to a stop beside the five-ton. McMurphy grinned.

Bannon leaped from the dune buggy with a puzzled expression and a wide grin. "What the hell are you doing here?" He pulled McMurphy into a deep embrace. "You old walrus."

McMurphy returned the hug. He winked at Kayla over his old friend's shoulder as she climbed down from the strike vehicle's gunner position. "I can't tell you how good it is to lay eyes on you two."

"Same," Bannon said. He stepped back, still clasping the big man's shoulders. "But what are you doing here?"

"It's a long story."

Kayla slipped in between the two men and gave McMurphy a tight hug, too. "I'm so glad you're okay." She pulled back and surveyed his bruised jaw and bloody lip, the knife wound in his shoulder. "You are okay?"

He shrugged. "A little worse for wear, but I'm in one piece. More or less." He gave Bannon's bruised jaw and fat lip a sideways glance. "Looks like you've been through the wringer, too."

Bannon glared at Barnes standing behind McMurphy. "Can't say I approve of the company you're keeping these days."

McMurphy turned, following his gaze. "Wish I could say she was the worst of my questionable companions lately."

Barnes stepped up to Bannon and handed him the Lady Smith she held. "I guess you're looking for an explanation."

Bannon scowled, taking the gun from her. "And it had better be a good one."

CHAPTER TWENTY-SEVEN

VARMA DID HIS BEST impersonation of a New York City cabdriver, zipping in and out of slower-moving cars, his hand pressed permanently to the town car's horn. Tara and Chandra were tossed back and forth across the backseat. Only her tight grip on the handle strap kept her from getting dumped into Chandra's lap.

She gulped down the offered scotch quickly before it could slosh out of the glass. She had to admit, if bodyguarding and chauffeuring didn't work out for Varma, there was a New York City taxi medallion with his name on it for sure.

He drove them west on Chambers Street. After putting a good bit of distance between them and the courthouse, leaving dozens of angry motorists and pedestrians in their wake, Varma's driving settled down to something close to normal.

"What the hell is going on, Kamal?" Tara asked. "What happened to you after Ghaazi took you off the *Morskoy Skat?* Did they hurt you?"

"No, no. Nothing like that."

It being a Saturday, he wore a gray sports coat, a blue Oxford shirt with the collar open, dark blue slacks, and canvas sneakers with the brightest white laces Tara had ever seen. His black hair remained slicked in place, but his eyes were puffy from lack of sleep. "When we reached shore, Ghaazi's man there informed me they had taken my wife and child. That if I interfered no further, they would not be harmed."

He fisted his hand and visibly trembled at the memory.

Tara shifted in her seat and put a hand on his knee. "This was my fault. Did he take them? Are they okay?"

"He did. But they are fine now. It will take more than a *dusht* such as him to get the better of the Deputy Director General of the DIA. But it took me valuable time. For that, I apologize, *mushkil ek*. My delay in aiding you is unforgivable."

"Shush. You have nothing to apologize for." Tara glanced through the back window. She saw no sign of pursuit. "Max. He will be okay?"

"Yes. I already have personnel working on getting him and the others released. They shall all be fine."

"The police. They can be—"

He cut her off. "It is handled."

"How did he, how did you, pull this off?"

He simply smiled. "Max—and not to sound overly conceited, I—can be most resourceful when we need to be."

Chandra didn't want to give away his secrets. She respected that. She was tired. Her sleep in the jail cell overnight had been uncomfortable and fitful, at best. Her body was sore and bruised, and she smelled of briny water and fish. Exhausted, with her head back, she covered her eyes with her hand.

"I need to know where he is," she said, opening her eyes again.

"That isn't a problem. I know exactly where he is."

She sat up, surprised. "You do? Where? How?"

He gave her a tight smile. "He might have removed me from the playing field temporarily, but he did not immobilize my army of resources. I have eyes and ears all over this city."

"And the world," Tara said. "Now's not the time to be humble."

His smile warmed. "Very true. Ghaazi remains on the *Morskoy Skat*. Denikin refused the police request to return to port. He convinced authorities the incident was an internal matter, one that didn't involve the U.S. He insisted NYPD's assistance in the matter was neither required nor wanted.

"It took the rest of the night and a good portion of the day today, but Denikin succeeded in keeping law enforcement and all government officials off the *Morskoy Skat*, demanding permission to leave."

"Wait. They let him go?"

"Diplomatically, it is a sticky matter. But since none of the casualties were U.S. citizens… " Chandra shrugged.

"Only Ghaazi's henchmen," she said with disgust.

"To avoid an international situation, the State Department opted to allow the *Morskoy Skat* to depart without further harassment."

"Damn it." Tara pounded a fist into the side of the door.

"What is it, my dear?"

"I know what Ghaazi plans to do. And now I know how he plans to do it."

"Tell me."

"Better yet," she said. "Give me your phone."

He dug a cell phone from his jacket pocket. "It's secure," he said, handing it over.

Which meant his people would have access to the conversation, but no one else. The situation was now desperate and time sensitive. Such concerns were no longer worries. She dialed Grayson's private number.

"Grayson," the former Army General said, answering cautiously. Few people had the number Tara had called, but Chandra's phone number would come up as restricted or blocked, Tara was sure.

"Madam Secretary, this is Tara Sardana." She rattled off her ID code, proving she was who she said she was. Voiceprint recognition software would do the rest.

"Tara, are you okay? We've been so worried."

She heard the concern in the older woman's voice. It brought a lump to her throat. "I'm okay, thank you, Madam Secretary. But I need to talk to you about Ghaazi Alvi."

"I have a lot to talk to you about, too."

"I'm with Kamal Chandra," Tara said. "I'm going to put this on speakerphone, if that's okay?"

"Certainly."

"Varma, you know where to go?" Chandra said to his driver.

"Yes, sir."

"Good." Chandra activated the partition between the front seat and back, securing the compartment. "A pleasure to speak with you, Madam Secretary."

"And to you, Deputy Director General."

"Please, call me Kamal. We can speak freely without concern of being overheard."

Grayson didn't return the offer of informality. "Very good. I trust your family is in good hands, sir."

He exchanged a glance with Tara. She shrugged. The woman's plugged in. Don't underestimate her. "They are. Thank you for inquiring."

Grayson got right down to business. "What's going on, Tara? Where are you?"

Tara drew a deep breath. Where to start? "Time is short, ma'am. My brother Ghaazi Alvi is here in the United States, in New York City."

"On a Russian yacht with Pyotr Denikin. We've been monitoring the situation closely since... Can I assume you were involved in last night's disruption?"

"Yes, ma'am, I was."

"Bring me up to speed."

Chandra settled back and listened as Tara told Grayson about her narrow escape from the *Morskoy Skat* and her frustrating night spent in an NYPD holding cell. "With Kamal's assistance, I escaped police custody. There may be some fallout from that."

"Understood."

"What you need to know, ma'am, is that Ghaazi is in possession of at least one of the railguns."

"I am not surprised," Grayson said. "You don't know this since you've been AWOL." Her tone made it clear she wasn't pleased with Tara over it either. "We recovered one of the weapons a few weeks ago in Michigan. Brice and John are neutralizing another one as we speak. Those weapons are no longer a concern."

"How?"

"I'll explain later. Tell me about your brother."

"Madam Secretary," Chandra said, speaking up. "I have assets keeping an eye on the *Morskoy Skat*. Ghaazi is still on board, while my intel suggests they have permission to leave New York Harbor but have not yet done so."

"Our information tells us the same thing," Grayson said.

"Trust me," Tara said. "They won't be going far."

"Why do you say that?"

"I believe the fourth weapon, the last railgun, is on that yacht. Madam Secretary, I believe I've figured out Ghaazi's intended target."

"I'm almost afraid to ask. What is it?"

"Yankee Stadium."

There was a sharp intake of breath over the phone. "You can't be serious. That stadium holds forty thousand people, more when you include employees, players, and coaches. Is he insane?"

"He plans on unleashing an attack tonight or tomorrow night, during the game."

"Against the Red Sox. The attendance will be at maximum capacity."

"And it gets worse, ma'am. He claims to have three VX gas warheads."

The other end of the phone remained quiet. Tara feared they'd lost the connection. "Ma'am?"

"I'm here. How?"

"I don't know. What I do know is I've inadvertently forced his hand. Exposed, with the world watching them, they can't afford to wait another twenty-four hours. I believe he will attack tonight."

"If he manages to explode even one warhead... the dispersal... "

"I know," Tara said. What else could she say?

"That game starts in less than three hours."

"We're on it, ma'am," Chandra said, sitting up to rejoin the conversation.

Tara looked at him with a surprised expression. "We are?"

He smiled that handsome, winning smile of his at her. The one she'd fallen in love with all those years earlier. "I have a plan."

"Don't even waste time telling me about it," Grayson said. "Just do it, whatever it takes. Meanwhile, I'll see what I can do about getting you some backup."

CHAPTER TWENTY-EIGHT

WHILE BANNON, KAYLA, AND McMurphy wrapped up their reunion, the formation of police cars had swarmed to a stop around the convoy. The overwhelming show of force—more cops than Bannon could count leaped out of patrol cars and racked shotguns and aimed handguns at anything that moved—took out what little fight the militia and the Minutemen might have had left.

Arms were laid down, and the cops moved among the ragtag vets, ordering them to the ground and to put their hands on their heads. Cuffed, the men and the few women along with them were led to the backseats of patrol cars and a prisoner transport van the troopers had had the foresight to bring along.

A state police lieutenant named Leslie came up to Bannon and the others. He wore mirrored Ray-Bans under his Smokey the Bear hat and had a serious demeanor. At six feet tall, he was eye to eye with Bannon and McMurphy. He ignored them both and tipped his hat to Kayla Clarke. "You're Lieutenant Clarke, ma'am?"

"I am."

"Orders from my commander tell me you're in charge here," he said. "We'll handle hauling away those into custody. Beyond that, you let me know what else you might need."

"Thank you, Lieutenant." She gave him an endearing smile. Bannon had seen her use it to melt away her fiercest opposition. "We'll need a few men to secure the scene until the proper federal agencies can get here."

"Sure. What is it we're securing?" Leslie asked.

McMurphy pulled the five-ton's canvas flap back to reveal the railgun inside.

The cop whistled. "That's some peashooter."

"You can't even begin to imagine," McMurphy said.

"They planned to use it at a rally being held in Concord," Bannon said. "The target was the State Capitol building."

The cop stared at the railgun. "The whole building?"

"Pretty much." Bannon extended his hand. "Commander Brice Bannon."

They shook hands. "Where'd you learn to handle a strike vehicle like that?"

"You're familiar with them?"

"Did two tours in Afghanistan. MP naturally. Saw a few in operation, never got my hands on one to give them a go."

"We did a few turns in the sandbox ourselves."

Leslie cocked his head. "Thought you all were Coasties?"

"We are," Bannon said.

"Long story," McMurphy added. "A lot of 'em."

"Wouldn't mind hearing them, maybe over a few beers sometime," the state cop said. "But business first. Start with this one?" Leslie jutted his chin at Pom-Pom, who remained unconscious on the ground.

"Oh, yeah. He goes for sure." McMurphy indicated his wounded shoulder. His work shirt and the black T-shirt underneath were wet with blood. "Happy to press assault charges. Just let me know what I need to do."

McMurphy reached into the back of the five-ton and pulled out a plastic Army canteen. He tipped it over, splashing water on Pom-Pom's bloody face. When that didn't completely rouse him, McMurphy gave him a sharp kick in the side.

Pom-Pom jumped up and sputtered.

Leslie held out a hand. "I think we'll take it from here."

He waved two troopers over and ordered Pom-Pom removed. They hauled the man to his feet, cuffed him, and half-dragged him to the transport van.

When they were gone, Leslie asked, "And these three?"

Mary, Andy, and Bridget stood in a small group near the drop-down gate of the truck.

"I need a moment with these two," McMurphy said, indicating Andy and Mary. "Then they're all yours."

"And I need to speak to this one," Bannon said, grabbing Bridget Barnes by the arm.

McMurphy walked Mary around to the side of the five-ton. Andy followed meekly behind. When they were out of earshot of the others, McMurphy pushed her up against the side of the truck. She gave him a sharp look but said nothing.

"What were you two thinking?" he asked.

"I told you," Mary said. "We had orders to bring you up here. They wanted to kill you."

"So, what?" he asked. "I should thank you?"

"No." She looked at the ground.

"And that's not even what I'm talking about. What are you doing with these knuckleheads?" He waved an arm at the convoy, at the men and women being put into police cars. "They... you were going to blow up a building. How many people do you think that would've killed? What were you thinking?"

Andy kicked at a pebble. "I just borrowed a—"

"Shut up," McMurphy said, staring at Mary.

She stared back. "You think it's easy. This government took the man I loved and destroyed him. He came back broken. Scared. Paranoid. Angry. Violent." Her green eyes burned holes in McMurphy. "We're supposed to just let that go? Accept it? 'Thank you for your service' is supposed to be good enough while everybody else goes on about their lives, unaffected."

"Mary," Andy started.

"I know it's been hard," McMurphy said.

Mary wagged an angry finger in his face. "You don't know anything. You come around once in a while, make a phone call or two, coach a little league game here and there, and think that's enough. Makes it okay to tell yourself you've done your part."

McMurphy opened his mouth to say something, but snapped it shut again as Mary kept going.

"I'm the one left to deal. Deal with Andy's crap. Deal with Tommy. Deal with the mess our lives have become because of them."

She slammed her finger into her chest.

"It's me, trying to get help and being told I can't. Me trying to buy medicine that we can't afford, being told our benefits don't cover it. Or the therapy, the treatment, the doctors order for him. He needs because of what they put him through. I'm the one, me. And Tommy, who have to deal with the violent outbursts, the terrible depression—his and mine—the mood swings, being afraid… All. The. Time."

She wiped tears from her face.

"All while putting on a brave face for your occasional pity-motivated appearances. Yeah, I wanted to do something drastic. I wanted my voice to be heard. I wanted this country, our leaders, and the world to know the pain I'm suffering." She pointed at Andy. "The pain they caused by what they put him through. If people got hurt. If that's what it takes, so what?"

"And what about Tommy?" McMurphy asked simply. "What happens to him after his parents commit mass murder. Kill hundreds or thousands of people?" He shook his head. "So your voices could be heard?"

Mary covered her face with her hands and sobbed.

Andy glanced at her, then at the ground, unable to look at McMurphy.

"I don't know what more I could have done," McMurphy said. "What you wanted, expected from me, but I would have done it. All you had to do was ask. I reached out. How many times? I told you, told you both, whatever you need, just ask. You chose not to grab the lifeline, but it was there. You wanna put it on me? Fine. Tell me there was more I could've done. Whatever. But own your part of it, damn it."

He waved at two troopers waiting a discreet distance away. "Get 'em out of here."

The cop turned Mary and Andy around and cuffed them. As the cops led them away, McMurphy realized neither one of them had asked what would happen to Tommy now.

He returned to the rear of the five-ton, feeling lower than he could ever remember feeling.

Bannon and Kayla were there. Their arms across their chests, squaring Bridget Barnes with their hard, dagger stares. She stood pinned against the rear gate by their gazes.

"She tells us she activated the GPS on her own," Bannon said. "She's the one who alerted us, getting us here. That true?"

"As much as I hate to admit it, yeah," McMurphy said. "And you're not gonna like this, Brice, but that had been the plan from the beginning."

"Plan?"

"She and Grayson figured the best chance of finding out where the other railguns were was to put her in play. Give her an opportunity to rejoin her old group. The plan was once they revealed where the railguns were, she would use the phone to call in the Cavalry. It halfway worked."

"Halfway how?" Bannon asked, clearly not happy.

"We've got one." He patted the back of the five-ton. "But Ghaazi's playing things close to his chest. He never let on to anyone else where the remaining railgun is."

With his attention back on Barnes, Bannon said, "That true? You and Grayson cooked this scheme up?"

"Yes."

Bannon looked at Kayla. "Were you part of this?"

She raised her hand in surrender. "No."

Bannon took a deep breath. "So, all this and we've still got Ghaazi and one more gun to track down. A weapon he could use at any time now."

"Brice," Kayla said. "We stopped this." She pointed at the railgun. "That's not nothing."

"And we ain't done yet," McMurphy said. "They lured me up here to keep us apart. They revealed the railgun in Michigan so you'd go there to investigate. All of it was Ghaazi's plan to divide us. Well, it didn't work. We're back together, and as soon as we find Tara, we'll hunt that son of a camel turd down."

"Actually, we think we know where she is," Bannon said.

"We do?" McMurphy brightened. "That's great. Where?"

"New York City."

McMurphy beamed. "See? Ghaazi's plans are falling apart even as we speak." He clasped Bannon on the shoulder. He winced at the stinging pain the movement caused from the knife wound. "We've got this, brother."

Bannon again turned toward Barnes. "Give me something that convinces me not to put a bullet in your brain."

"This," she said. "This was all a distraction."

"How do you mean?"

"Skyjack said it. This was meant to keep you separated, busy. An attack on the State Capitol building? In New Hampshire? I mean, no offense but…

"What's that?" she said. "Symbolic, sure, during an anti-war rally and all, great, but what would the impact be… the death toll? A few hundred. Maybe a thousand?"

"Does seem like a waste of a railgun's potential," McMurphy said.

"Nothing compared to the six thousand lives that would've been lost on the *Oceanic Princess*," Kayla said.

"That was the beta test," Barnes said. "A trial run. If that was just practice, whatever he's planning, Ghaazi's endgame will be worse than that. Much worse."

"Go big," McMurphy said. "Or go home."

"What's he planning?" Bannon asked. "Where?"

Barnes shrugged. "I don't know, but if Tara Sardana's in New York City, I'd start there."

CHAPTER **TWENTY-NINE**

THE BLACK TOWN CAR carrying Kamal Chandra and Tara Sardana in the backseat pulled to the side of the Battery Park City Esplanade at the North Cove Yacht Harbor, a small docking facility along the Hudson River and a stone's throw south of the Holland Tunnel and Brookfield Ferry Terminal.

Tara glanced out the window. The boat club was full of large yachts and smaller sailboats, and she saw a single, sleek speedboat tied to a dock. It bobbed in the water.

"Your idea is to steal a boat?" Tara asked.

"No," Chandra said.

"Good thing. They'd blow us out of the water before we got within fifty feet of them."

Chandra powered the town car's divider down. "Arrangements have been made?"

Varma twisted around in his seat. "Yes. But I must advise against this course of action."

"Your objections are noted, old friend." Chandra reached out and placed a hand on the big bodyguard's shoulder.

"Thank you for your years of service. It has been an honor having you by my side."

Chandra pushed his door open and got out on the sidewalk side of the car. Tara slid across the backseat. Before she got out, Varma said, "Good luck."

Tara nodded. They climbed out of the car. Chandra closed the back door. Varma drove off.

"If I didn't know better," she said. "I'd swear that was a 'goodbye, I'm never going to see you again' send-off."

He gave her a grim smile. "One must be prepared for such unfortunate outcomes in our business, don't you think?" He grabbed her by the hand and led her across the street. "Come on."

They dashed across the street and along the concrete walkway to the far end of the wharf.

The Hudson River wasn't a river in the truest sense. It was a tidal estuary where the saltwater from the ocean mixed with fresh water from the northern tributaries, giving the water a brackish quality. The humid evening air held a strong mix of scents: oil, salt, and fish.

Chandra led her into a gray building with a sign overhead that read *Upper Bay Jet Ski Tours. Experience the city from a brand new perspective.* Before she could question what he had in mind, Chandra pushed through the front door. Overhead, a bell rang. A young man in a tank top T-shirt looked up from behind the counter. He had a mop of greasy blonde hair and a lopsided grin on his sun-tanned face. "Hey, man."

"My associate was in earlier," Chandra said. "He made arrangements for a special tour package."

"Oh, right." The kid shot Chandra with his finger-gun and a wink. "Yeah. Follow me. My name's Kyle."

Of course, it was, Tara thought.

Kyle came out from around the counter, locked the front door, and hung a sign on it that said *Be Back in Ten Minutes.* That done, he led them to a back room.

Tara grabbed Chandra by the arm and leaned into him. "PWCs, Kamal? They'll hear us coming before we clear the harbor."

He smiled at her. "Have a little more faith in me than that, *mushkil ek*."

They were led through a workshop where several wave runners and other personal watercraft—commonly called by the brand name jet skis—lay in varying degrees of disrepair. A strong odor of motor oil and gasoline stung the air.

Kyle pushed through a back door, and they were outside again. This time, on a wharf designed to be a patio for the workers and customers of the touring company. There were two redwood picnic tables complete with umbrellas and a rolling stainless steel serving cart, and ice machine. A billboard overhead listed the foods, snacks, and drinks available, including beer and wine. The latter required approved ID, of course.

The young man trotted down a flight of wooden steps to a lower dock below. There, several brightly colored watercraft were pulled out of the water. Their cowls were open, as they patiently waited for someone to perform maintenance on them.

What caught Tara's attention was not the run-of-the-mill wave runners and other personal watercraft. It was the two other vehicles tied to the dock. They bobbed in the gently lapping water of the Hudson.

"Are those hydrofoils?" she asked.

Chandra smiled, and Kyle beamed.

The vehicles were space-age-looking sleds with sleek, molded, white glass-reinforced plastic. They had aquamarine blue racing stripes, black padded seats for two, front and aft hydrofoils, and they were even equipped with cup holders.

Like a salesman at a boat show, Kyle gave them the rundown of the vehicles' specs. "A thing of beauty, aren't they? With a hull length under ten feet and just eight feet in width, they have four C-shaped foils, they're lightweight at two hundred twenty pounds, have an integrated electrical system for raising and lowering the foils, multi-functional steering, an interactive color touch screen display, GPS positioning, and navigation lights. And," he said excitedly. "They're powered by a lithium-ion battery pack and a 5.5 kW electric outboard motor with a max speed of twenty-five miles per hour while being virtually soundless."

Now we're talking, Tara thought. When in motion, the hydrofoils resembled a four-legged crab as the fore and aft foils raised the hull out of the water, decreasing drag and increasing speed capability as it practically skimmed over the water's surface. She'd read about them but had never driven one before. She was anxious to do so now.

"We'll need to wait until it gets dark," Chandra said.

Tara glanced at the sun, burning low but bright in the eastern sky. "That'll be cutting it close. The baseball game starts at seven."

"We'll have to risk it," Chandra said. "Without the cover of darkness, we'll be sitting ducks."

She didn't like it, but she knew he was right. All she could do was hope Ghaazi would wait for the game to start. "Any chance we have time to get to a gun shop?"

"When did you start to underestimate me so?" Chandra smiled. "Follow me."

He led her to a bench next to a couple of port-a-johns, where a dark, rigid plastic case sat. He snapped open the latches. As he opened the lid, Kylie crowded in behind them to see what was inside, too.

She had to admit, Chandra was full of surprises lately.

Inside the case were two Beretta pistols. Each had two spare seventeen-round magazines, a detachable silencer, and there were four military green fragmentation hand grenades inside as well, all packed in molded green foam.

She turned to him. "Where did you—no. I don't want to know."

Chandra turned to Kyle, "I believe there was one more thing left for me."

"Yeah. Sure." Kyle blinked, still staring at the guns and hand grenades.

Chandra snapped the case closed.

"Right. Yeah, they're over here behind the service cart." He ran up the stairs and came back down with two brown paper shopping bags, carrying them by their handles. He handed one to Chandra and the other to Tara.

She looked inside the bag and discovered a black foam neoprene wetsuit with red stripes across the upper biceps and booties. Also inside were a Special Forces assault vest and a black, hard plastic thigh holster for the Beretta.

"You can change upstairs or in the port-a-johns, if you want," Kyle offered.

She dropped the bag to the deck and stripped out of her oversized, gray NYPD sweatshirt and baggy blue sweatpants, glad to discard them. The evening was too warm for such heavy clothing. Modesty and inhibitions were never a concern for her. Stripped down to her bra and panties, she pulled the neoprene wetsuit from the bag and wiggled into it, pulling the zipper up her front from her waist to halfway between her breasts.

By then, Chandra had begun to do the same.

"You two are hardcore, huh?" Kyle asked. "Please tell me you use your powers for good?"

Neither one of them answered.

Tara strapped the holster to her leg and pulled on the vest. Fastening it, she returned to the case, opened it, and deposited two hand grenades into separate pouches on the vest. Then she grabbed a Beretta, slipped a loaded magazine into it, and racked a round in the chamber. She holstered it and dropped two more magazines into the other pouches in the vest.

She looked at Kyle. "I could use something to tie my hair back with."

"Yeah. Sure. We should have something." He jogged up the steps and went back into the shop.

"You don't need to do this, Kamal," Tara said as Chandra finished gearing up. "This isn't your fight."

He slipped his loaded Beretta into his holster and dropped the last two grenades into his vest pouches. "He kidnapped my family, Tara. Terrorized them. Threatened to kill them. When he did that, he made it *my* fight."

Kyle returned and handed Tara a handful of heavy-duty rubber bands. "Will these do?"

Tara took three of them. "Perfect."

She gathered her loose black hair into a ponytail and wound the elastic bands around it. She gave Kyle an encouraging smile. "Thank you for your assistance, Kyle. But we need you to do one more thing."

"Name it. I guess."

"Don't tell anyone we were here," she said. "What we're doing." She looked at the now-empty rigid plastic case. "Not for at least a few more hours anyway. We can't risk anyone knowing what we're about to do."

"What are you doing?" He looked at Chandra. "Your man assured me it was legal."

"It is," Chandra said.

"We work for Homeland Security." Tara didn't elaborate further than that. "You'll know what happened soon. And you can feel good knowing you helped stop something really, really bad from happening."

"Okay," he said, but still appearing less than convinced.

"Trust us, Kyle," she said. "Please."

"Okay." He stepped back. "Good luck, I guess."

To Chandra, she said, "I need to let Grayson know what we're doing."

He handed her his phone.

She walked to the far end of the dock. When the call went through, she updated Grayson.

"You're positive the railgun's on that boat?" Grayson said.

"No," Tara admitted. "But I'm pretty sure it is. I can't think of any other reason Ghaazi and Denikin would remain anchored where they are after last night."

"It does make sense," Grayson agreed.

"Either way, whatever my brother is up to, I will stop him."

"Brice and John are in the air. They're on their way down to assist you." She gave Tara a quick rundown on what Bannon, McMurphy, and Kayle had been through. "Let's hope they're in time."

"We can't wait for them."

"I know. Do what you need to do, Tara, and Godspeed."

Tara disconnected the call and handed the phone back to Chandra. "Let's go."

He looked skyward. "Patience, *mushkil ek*. It is not dark enough yet."

Reluctantly, Tara admitted he was right, but that did nothing to calm her jittery nerves. Adrenaline coursed through her body as she paced, trying to burn it off. They'd have to wait at least another hour before the sun set low enough that they might have a chance to approach the yacht without being detected. She fisted her hands, then released them.

"I need to do something," she said. She glanced at the stainless steel food cart. "Kyle, any chance you've got keys to that thing?"

"Sure. Why? You hungry?"

"Thirsty."

He opened the cart and dug three frosty Budweiser cans out of the deep ice.

They silently drank and watched the sun dip lower and lower in the sky. Tara finished her beer and thought about a second one, but decided against it. Not on an empty stomach. Having not eaten since the night before, she did accept the bag of barbeque potato chips Kyle offered her.

"It's time," Chandra said, finally. He shook hands with Kyle and thanked him for his help.

He and Tara climbed down the wooden ladder and boarded the hydrofoils below. With a twist of the key, the water behind the outboard motor bubbled, and the hulls lifted slightly. Besides a soft hum and vibration, Tara heard nothing of substance from the electric motor.

She smiled. Perfect.

She nudged the personal craft forward, then goosed the throttle control on the steering wheel. The hydrofoil leaned into a biting left turn. Chandra pulled out behind her. They gave Kyle, who remained on the wharf watching them, a wave.

He offered them a thumbs-up. And they were off.

CHAPTER **THIRTY**

NOT LONG AFTER TARA Sardana and Kamal Chandra arrived at the *Upper Bay Jet Ski Tours* and before they roared off down the Hudson River toward Manhattan's Upper Bay on their sleek personal hydrofoil boats, Bannon was on the phone with Elizabeth Grayson.

Kayla and McMurphy crowded around him.

He held the phone out with it on speakerphone, but with the call volume on low.

"I just got off the phone with Tara," Grayson said. "She's been through an ordeal, but she's fine. Perfectly fine." The group didn't interrupt but glanced among themselves. Their relief was apparent in their expressions.

Grayson went on. "But the situation is far worse than we imagined. Tara succeeded in tracking down her brother with the help of an old friend of hers, someone you all are familiar with, Kamal Chandra. Ghaazi's been posing under an assumed identity, pretending to be a diplomatic delegate attached to a humanitarian project to benefit Syrian refugees. The effort is being spearheaded by Pyotr Denikin."

"The former Russian ambassador?" Bannon asked.

"Correct. They arrived in the country on a superyacht called the *Morskoy Skat*."

"What the hell's a *Morskoy Skat*?" McMurphy asked.

"It's Russian for stingray," Bannon informed him.

"And owned by a Russian billionaire," Grayson said, sounding annoyed at the interruption. "A civilian," she added. "According to Russia's public affairs people, the yacht is on loan to Denikin specifically for this diplomatic mission."

"It's all a cover," McMurphy said. "It's got to be."

"Of course it is, John," Grayson said. "Tara managed to get on board the yacht last night. She confronted Ghaazi, who teased his plans to her but didn't give her specifics. She was forced to abandon the yacht before she could get further details."

"Is there anything else?" Bannon asked.

"Tara believes the railgun is actually on the *Morskoy Skat*, and I agree. They're currently anchored in Manhattan's Upper Bay but can head for open water at any time. And here's where the news goes from bad to horrifying. Ghaazi claims to have three VX-loaded warheads designed to be fired by the railgun."

"Nerve gas?" McMurphy asked. "Like normal munitions ain't enough for this madman."

Grayson went on. "We know these railguns have an effective range of fifty miles—"

"The target could be anywhere in New York City," Bannon said. "Or the Jersey shore."

"Oh, Brice," Grayson said. "We know exactly what the target is, and it's terrifying.

"Tell us," Bannon urged.

"Yankee Stadium. And we believe it'll be during tonight's game."

Bannon, Kayla, and McMurphy were left with their mouths hanging open.

McMurphy said, "They're playing the Red Sox tonight."

"The stadium will be at maximum capacity," Bannon added.

"Forty thousand people," Grayson said.

"Can you imagine what the yield from three warheads will be?" Kayla asked.

"You need to get us down there," Bannon said into the phone. "Now."

"I've already made arrangements," Grayson said. "There's an Air National Guard Blackhawk helicopter waiting for you at the Laconia Airport in Gilford. Flight time to Manhattan is an hour and a half. Get on it and get down there."

"Yes, ma'am," Bannon said. He pocketed the phone and looked at his team, his friends. "You heard the lady. Let's move."

Kayla called out to Leslie, who stood talking to one of his sergeants. "Lieutenant, could you arrange a lift for my friends here? They're in a bit of a hurry."

He strolled over. "It'll be my genuine pleasure. Where do they need to go?"

"Laconia Airport. They need to catch a flight."

"Right this way, boys." Leslie headed for his patrol car.

Bannon and McMurphy started to follow, but Bannon stopped when he noticed Kayla wasn't joining them. "What about you?"

"Someone needs to stay and babysit that." She pointed at the railgun. "We can't take the chance of losing it."

"Surely, Leslie and his people—"

"No, Brice. We can't risk it. I need to stay."

"We could use your help," he said.

She smiled. "Next time."

"Okay." He hugged her.

"Be safe." Kayla glanced over at Barnes. "What about her?"

Bannon gave her a sardonic grin. "Oh, she's coming with me. Like you with the railgun, I'm not letting her out of my sight."

He walked over to Barnes and grabbed her by the arm.

"Hey."

"You're going for a ride." He pulled her toward the waiting patrol car. She tried to shake her arm loose but couldn't. Bannon's grip was like a vise.

"What are you taking me?"

"New York City." He pulled her toward the state police car. Leslie sat behind the wheel with the engine running, waiting. McMurphy stood with the back door open.

"Why?"

"For a reunion with your old friend Ghaazi."

"Oh, hell, no." She succeeded in shaking off his grip. "He'll kill me for betraying him."

Before she could get away, McMurphy grabbed her around the waist and lifted her off the ground.

"We're on a tight timetable, sweetheart," he tossed her into the backseat, "and got no time for nonsense."

He climbed in the back with her.

Bannon jumped into the front seat with Leslie. "Appreciate the lift, Lieutenant."

"My pleasure, Commander. After what you guys stopped here, it's my absolute pleasure."

He flipped on the lights and the siren and pulled a large, looping U-turn through the dry grass and dirt. He straightened the cruiser out, got it back on the pavement, and sped off down the road like the devil himself was on their tail.

Ten minutes later, Leslie slammed the patrol car to a stop on the tarmac a hundred feet from a waiting Sikorsky Blackhawk helicopter. Its blades were lazily rotating as McMurphy, Barnes, and Bannon got out. With a final wave to the cop, they bent low and ran for the chopper.

The cabin door was open. Bannon and Barnes ran for it, while McMurphy reached up for the cockpit door. A female pilot in a green flight suit glared down at him as he pulled the door open.

She pointed a thumb toward the back. "You're in the back, big guy."

"Um, no. I'm a pilot."

"I don't care if you're both Wright brothers rolled into one and returned from the grave. Passengers ride in the back."

"I think you misunderstand, young lady," McMurphy said. "I don't do passenger. I'll be piloting this bird."

"Like hell, you are. My ride. I drive." She stared down at him with serious, dark brown eyes. "Either get in the back or I'm shutting this chopper down."

Bannon leaned out the open side door. "We don't have time for this, Skyjack. Get in."

"And that's Captain Garcia to you, Chief," the pilot said. "Not, young lady."

McMurphy frowned, looking like a child told he couldn't ride his favorite amusement park ride. "But I—"

"Get in," Bannon insisted.

McMurphy climbed in and plopped down in a seat and strapped in. "Skyjack McMurphy does not ride in the back with the... " He looked at Bannon, then focused on Barnes. "With the riffraff."

Bannon pulled his mike down to his mouth and told the pilot they were good to go. "What's your name, Captain?"

"Garcia, sir."

"Thanks for the lift, Garcia. Now, hit it."

The chopper lifted off, dipped slightly forward, then sped off. As it did, the pilot muttered something less than endearing about puddle pirates, but the rest of it got lost to the thump-thump-thump of the main rotor and roar of the chopper's two powerful turboshaft engines.

"Why are you taking me along on this little joyride of yours?" Barnes asked. "I did my part."

"And you'll keep doing it until I say otherwise." Bannon sat across from her with McMurphy on the other side, watching the ground pass underneath them through the open cabin door and sulking.

"Why didn't you tell Grayson about Lynch's summer camp?" Bannon said. "We could've raided it and recovered that railgun without all these games. Without bloodshed."

"Because I didn't know anything about it. You think I wouldn't have said something if I knew? What part of 'cooperate fully or you get a lethal injection' do you think I don't understand?"

"I don't know what you do or say," he said. "Everything I've heard out of your mouth's been a lie. No reason I should expect that to change now."

"Talk to Grayson about that. The plan was hers. Not telling you was her idea."

"Oh, I will. Believe me."

"I've cooperated fully with Homeland Security, with the FBI, with Grayson. Told them everything I know. Josh's property was way further north, in Clarksville, near the border. The FBI raided the place three days after you took me into custody. Why? Because I told them about it. Everybody had cleared out already. There was nothing there. Ask Grayson if you don't believe me."

Bannon glanced out of the open door. He checked his watch. They were flying low but making great time.

He called out. "Skyjack."

McMurphy turned.

"You okay? You seem preoccupied."

"Tough couple of days. You remember that kid, Tommy? Mary and Andy's kid? He plays on the—"

"Penguins, sure," Bannon said. "How'd you guys do, by the way?"

"We won. They did great. But here's the kicker. Tommy's gonna be at Yankee Stadium tonight. His camp. They do this end-of-summer field trip thing. He and a whole camp of little kids are gonna be at that game tonight."

Along with forty thousand other people. Bannon gave his friend his most encouraging look. "It'll be okay. We're going to stop this."

McMurphy nodded but silently returned to looking out at the ground below.

Bannon's phone rang. It was Grayson. He pulled his headphones from his ears, answered it, and cupped his other ear to block out the roar of the wind and the thrumming rotors overhead.

"I've spoken with Tara again," she said. "She and Chandra have commandeered a couple of personal hydrofoils and are making their way toward the *Morskoy Skat*."

"Hydrofoils. Smart." Fast, nimble, and damn near silent upon approach. The girl was resourceful. Bannon gave her that. "What kind of weapons do they have? Anything?"

"I don't know," Grayson said. "She didn't have time to go into a lot of detail, but from the reports and intel I've received regarding the incident from the night before, what they're racing into is a well-armed fighting force."

"The stadium, have you begun evacuating it?"

"Too late for that. It would be impossible to even try without creating a panic. The stampede alone would kill more people than we could save. We need to stop this at the source."

"Understood." Bannon checked his watch. "We're ten minutes out."

"Brice, I've consulted the President. He's scrambling two F-15s. The military's advising him to sink the *Morskoy Skat*."

"A civilian-owned Russian superyacht in American waters?" Bannon asked. "With Russian diplomats onboard? That'll start World War III."

"And if we don't, they will."

"Give us time to get there. Assess the situation."

There was a pause on the other end. Long enough, Bannon feared they'd lost the connection. Then, finally, Grayson spoke. "I'll buy you what time I can."

"Roger that." Before he disconnected the call, he added, "Thanks."

"Brice, one more thing. I'm texting you the GPS location and schematics we have on the *Morskoy Skat*. I hope it helps. Good luck."

As soon as he hung up, the phone pinged. He called up the schematics. After giving them a once over he handed the phone to McMurphy for a look-see.

"What have we got in the way of weapons?" Bannon pulled out the .45 Kayla had given him. He'd only fired one shot. He had six rounds left.

McMurphy said, "I've got a Beretta and a Smith & Wesson. I'm light one or two rounds in each."

"Will have to do."

McMurphy said, "I know that look."

215

"What look is that?" Bannon asked.

"That I'm going to do something wild and crazy, look. I think I know what it is, too."

"You know me too well." Bannon replaced his headphones and activated his mike. "Garcia, change of plans. We need you to take us directly to the *Morskoy Skat*."

"No can do. My orders are to drop you on the helipad on the *Intrepid*."

"Your orders just changed, Captain," Bannon said, his voice curt. He nodded to McMurphy.

McMurphy got up and headed to the cockpit with the schematics on the phone.

"There's a helipad on that yacht," Bannon said. "Skyjack's giving you the schematics and GPS coordinates. If you can't complete your mission, I've got the pilot who can."

"You need to do better than that," Garcia said. "Sir."

"I'm speaking with the direct authority of the President of the United States, Captain. You really want to risk defying a direct order from your Commander-in-Chief?"

In the pause that followed, Bannon could almost feel her anger and indecision. When she came back on the air again, she said, "Sit tight. Next stop's the *Morskoy Skat*." Then she added under her breath, "Damn, puddle pirates."

McMurphy returned to his seat and strapped in. He looked at Bannon and smiled. "Here we go, cowboy."

CHAPTER **THIRTY-ONE**

TARA AND CHANDRA SPED past the southern tip of Manhattan, the dark skyline against the purpling night sky beginning to glow as more and more lights came on to combat the gathering darkness of night. To their right, the Statue of Liberty stood, holding her torch lit high and bright overhead. A beacon of freedom that had so often been ignored of late.

A bracing wind blew in Tara's face, chilly after the day's humid heat. She pushed the hydrofoil to near its maximum speed, pleased at how well the craft maneuvered. Stable yet nimble, she thought with a smile, having fun driving the thing despite the deadly seriousness of the mission.

Chandra kept pace, riding just a few feet behind and off to her right.

Ahead, the *Morskoy Skat* remained anchored where it had been the night before. This side of the Verrazano-Narrows Bridge which connects the boroughs of Brooklyn and Staten Island. Not quite dark yet, the bright lights of the span sparkled against the purpling sky behind it. Headlights traversed the roadway, drivers and passengers going about their lives, blissfully unaware of the danger that lay below.

Holding a position where the narrow channel connected the upper and lower bays, the yacht sat with its running lights off. Dim interior lights inside the accommodation section that housed the spacious ballroom, dining hall, and guest cabins left it visible. The bow of the ship pointed more or less toward Manhattan.

Tara swung the hydrofoil in a wide arc, moving closer to the Jersey side of the river as they swung around the stern of the yacht. She and Chandra ran without running lights as well. They kept to the same route the Staten Island Ferry ran. To anyone on the yacht who might notice them, Tara hoped they'd assume the two of them were heading into the terminal facility where they could dock, go enjoy the community garden, walk along the piers and dock, or grab something to eat at the River Dock Café or the Dairy Queen Grill & Chill.

Of course, they didn't go that far.

They slowed. It was getting dark, but Tara wanted to give it a little more time. A little darker and they could swing around to the superyacht's stern, and with luck, pull right up the rear swim platform unseen, disembark, and set the hydrofoils to drift with no one being the wiser.

Chandra swung around beside her. They exchanged glances and nods. Both were ready.

Once they completed their turns, they made their starboard approach. Tara stayed in the lead.

As they got closer, Tara could make out two guards clad in black pants and black, long-sleeved turtleneck sweaters. Curse her luck. They were standing on the swim deck. Each was armed with a rifle strapped over their shoulders. Relaxed, not expecting trouble. One smoked a cigarette. They conversed in Russian. The end of the cigarette flared.

Tara pulled her Beretta, lined the silencer up, and shot the smoker.

Her victim emitted a sharp cry and tumbled into the water. The splash made more noise than the silencer had.

The second one leaned over, looking at where his partner had fallen into the water. "Ilia?"

He slipped his rifle off his shoulder.

Chandra shot him, hitting him in the neck.

He pitched headfirst into the water, joining Ilia.

Tara pulled up to the swim deck. She twisted the ignition key, killing the hydrofoil's quiet engine, and kicked it away from the yacht as she jumped onto the swim deck. The two bodies lay face down in the water. They slowly floated away. She worried they might be spotted, but the time and effort to retrieve and conceal them posed a far greater risk.

Chandra pulled his hydrofoil to the deck and followed Tara's lead. He kicked his hydrofoil away and whispered, "An auspicious start."

They crouched low to stay below the stern's gunwale. Tara cautioned care. "It's a long way from here to the promenade."

"I know the malted scotch was good," Chandra said. "But we were just on the promenade last night. I saw no sign of a gun there then, not one such as you have described."

"When Ghaazi took me below deck, I saw a man guarding a room under the bow. At the time, I thought there was a meeting or a private party for VIPs going on. Later, I realized they could've retrofitted the area underneath the bow and stored the weapon there. The space is certainly large enough. It might even be how they brought it into the country."

Chandra nodded. "Retractable hatch covers. They use them on yachts such as this all the time. Usually used to cover swimming pools so they can create dance floors or basketball courts. One I was on—"

Tara gave him a look. "You spend a lot of time on superyachts, Kamal?"

He smiled. "It is difficult work, but someone must do it."

She shook her head. "And here I am spending all my time in a dive bar on the seacoast."

"I am sure Brice would not appreciate the Keel Haul being called a dive bar."

"What he doesn't know," she said, but smiled. She loved the Keel Haul. Nowhere had she ever felt more at home than when she was there. Even after only a few weeks, she missed it. Even Captain Floyd, that crazy old coot.

"Come on," she said, pushing the thoughts away. "We don't know how much time we have."

She crossed to the portside gunwale. The cross-through had been left open by the recently dispatched guards. Crouching low, she slowly came up far enough to see over the gunwale and across the helicopter landing deck. With most of the lights on the boat off, it was hard to say for certain, but she didn't see any other guards.

With a hand wave to Chandra, she crept up the four fiberglass steps and onto the helipad, the Beretta held tightly in her hand. She sensed Chandra emerge behind her. Ahead of them, across the open expanse of the helipad, the yacht had a three-level accommodation section, with the top level housing the yacht's bridge, navigation, and communications.

She scanned the upper deck and again saw no one.

Once she made sure Chandra was ready, Tara jogged along the portside gunwale, staying low and on the lookout for any movement or sound. Chandra kept close behind her.

Just when she thought they were in the clear, someone shouted, "Hey! Stop!"

The command came from the upper deck, the bridge level. She glanced up. A figure who hadn't been there a second ago stood, aiming a rifle at them. He shouted again and fired.

Bullets pitted the fiberglass gunwale.

Tara ran but stopped when she heard Chandra cry out in pain. His body thumped to the deck. She turned. Her friend was on the deck, propped up on one elbow. One leg was stretched out to his side. The other he grasped with his hand. He'd taken a round in the thigh.

She started to go back for him, but he waved her back. "Go!"

"No."

"It hit my femoral artery. I'm already dead. Go." He already sounded weak.

The gunman continued shooting from above. Bullets chewed through the deck and gunwale. The gunfire echoed loudly across the bay.

Gripped with indecision, Tara hesitated.

Two more rounds ripped into Chandra. Another in his leg and one in his side. He grunted and shouted hoarsely, "Complete the mission."

Chandra pulled his two grenades from his vest pouches. He pulled the pin and lobbed one up onto the upper deck. It hit with a hollow thunk and exploded. The blast propelled a gunman over the railing. He landed with a thud on the helipad, his neck broken, among other things.

Chandra threw the second grenade in Tara's direction.

She twisted around in time to see a group of armed men running toward her down the port side deck. They screamed into their shoulder mics. She heard a mix of Russian and Arabic. The grenade hit the deck and rolled toward the charging men. Tara ducked to the right. The grenade exploded and sent one man over the gunwale. His body splashed into the water. A second man was thrown against the accommodation section bulkhead. He screamed as he slid to the deck, wriggling in pain.

Chandra's strength gave out, and he collapsed to the deck.

Tara ran to the back of the accommodation section. Through the large windows, she could see the dining room. She grabbed the brass handle of the doors and started to pull but stopped to look back at Chandra again. Tears welled in her eyes.

"I am so sorry, Kamal." She started to promise his sacrifice would not be in vain. Instead, she said, "I'm going to kill him, Kamal. I promise."

CHAPTER THIRTY-TWO

GHAAZI ALVI STOOD ON the promenade deck. At anchor, they faced the southern tip of Manhattan. In the gathering darkness, the Freedom Tower glowed brightly over the lower skyline. Ghaazi turned away unimpressed. He wore a charcoal gray Armani suit, a white Brioni dress shirt with a red paisley tie, a matching pocket square, and black Ferragamo loafers. The Americans knew how to dress with style. That he would give them.

Pyotr Denikin stood beside him, looking nervous.

"You did not need to remain onboard, Pyotr," Ghaazi told him.

"And where would I go once you do this thing?" he asked. A shorter man than Ghaazi, Denikin had to look up at him. "Every airport, rail station, and shipping port on the East Coast will be shut down. I would be arrested by the TSA before I could get my shoes off for the security scanners."

"The Americans will be too busy counting their dead."

"I think perhaps you underestimate the Americans."

Ghaazi stared down at him with angry eyes. "And I think you would be wise to mind your tongue."

Denikin snapped his mouth shut without reply.

They returned their attention to the deck in front of them as it began to split in two. The halves rose on hydraulic hinges until they were vertical, like walls on either side of the now open pit into the decks below. With a whine of machinery, the two halves then began to descend into the well below as a platform rose from the ship's interior.

It took several minutes, but soon the empty deck was replaced with a metallic platform upon which sat the remaining railgun.

Ghaazi smiled. A thing of beauty.

Comprised of three major components, the weapon had a pair of parallel conductive metal rails, fifteen feet in length. They resembled the barrel of a very large gun. There was an armature that bridged the gap between the rails, basically a carrier that housed the projectile that would be fired. And finally, a large electric generator, one of two sources of power needed to create the massive electric current needed to create what was known as a Lorentz force, necessary to fire the projectile. The other source of power would come from diverted electricity siphoned from the superyacht's overpowered two gas turbines and two diesel engines.

Several technicians in black coveralls rode the platform upward. They worked around the base of the gun and had the generator compartment open as they consulted tablets and checked settings, conducting final preparations for the gun's imminent firing.

"Is it not magnificent?" Ghaazi asked.

"As far as guns go, I suppose," Denikin said. His tone lacked conviction.

Ghaazi glared down at him. "You are on the cusp of history, Pyotr. Enjoy the moment."

"I will when it is done. When we are on our way. When I can be reasonably assured I will not spend the rest of my life rotting in an American prison. I understand Gitmo is a most unpleasant place to retire to." He glanced at his watch. "How much longer must we wait?"

Ghaazi said, "Not very long."

He looked over the deck at the people busying themselves around him. A young man, whose name he did not know, passed them. Ghaazi stopped him. "It is nearly the bottom of the hour. I would like to listen to the game."

"Of course, sir." The young man pulled out a cell phone. After a minute of fiddling with it, the sound of the Yankee telecast filled the night air. The young man propped the phone on the sill of the accommodation section's slanted window behind Ghaazi and Denikin and quickly continued on his way.

"After a scoreless top of the first inning," the announcer reported, "the leadoff batter for the Yankees will be… "

"Is that necessary, Ghaazi?" Denikin asked.

Ghaazi ground his teeth. He imagined shooting Denikin in the head, and that calmed him. "Yes, Pyotr, it is. Final preparations are underway. It won't be long now."

Ghaazi cared nothing about the game, of course. What he wanted was to hear the announcers as they realized something was wrong. Listen as death and destruction rained down on the stadium, sending the spectators and the players into a panic. He wanted to hear the broadcast switch as a news agency broke in to report what was happening. He was almost gleeful with the anticipation.

The Yankee batter hit a single. On the very next pitch, he successfully stole second base. The announcer shouted, "Safe at second! A stolen base! Yes, sir, this is going to be one for the record books. I can feel it."

"Yes," Ghaazi said with a satisfied smile. "Yes, it will be."

Then he frowned, his confidence shaken for the first time at the sound of gunfire coming from the back of the yacht.

"What is that?" Denikin asked.

"Gunfire, you idiot." Ghaazi pulled a walkie-talkie from his belt. "What is going on? Report!"

"Keep them working," he said to Denikin, pointing at the men buzzing around the railgun. "Stop for nothing. That gun fires on schedule. No matter what."

Ghaazi ran down the port side deck. His smooth-bottom loafers slipped on the wet deck. He grunted in irritation as he grabbed for the railing to keep from falling. They were so close. So damn close.

The night air exploded. This time, from the sound of a detonated hand grenade.

Ghaazi pulled his small, Russian-made Makarov .380 and chambered one of its eight rounds. A second grenade exploded ahead of him. "Damn them to hell."

He stopped short as one of his men went sailing over the yacht's side ahead of him. Screaming, another man slammed against the accommodation section's wall. The men behind them fell back in time to avoid the blast.

Ghaazi reached them and pushed them forward. "Go! Go! This attack must be stopped."

They stepped over the dead body on the deck. Ghaazi took only a minute to register the man's burned face. Bloody and raw. It fueled his anger and propelled him forward. When the men ahead of him reached the helipad, they spread out and moved in crouched formation to secure the deck.

Two guards stood sentry on the upper deck. He waved to them. "Lights!"

Powerful spotlights snapped on and illuminated the helipad in white, glaring brightness.

Ghaazi rushed to the body clad in a wetsuit, face down on the deck. He noted the bullet holes ripped through the neoprene, two in the man's leg and one in his side. Under him, a large pool of blood spread outward across the smooth deck. He had quickly bled out from his wounds.

Still grasped in the man's hand, a silencer-equipped Beretta. Ghaazi kicked it away and turned the body over.

"*Abn eahira!* Chandra." Mildly surprised, he'd half expected the body to be Bannon or that of the insufferable Skyjack McMurphy. He looked up at his men standing around him.

Ghaazi came to his feet. "The other one. Find the other one!"

"But, sir," one brave yet foolish man said. "There is no one else. He was alone."

Ghaazi knew better. If Chandra was here, it meant Tara had come aboard with him. Angry and frustrated, Ghaazi shot the man in the face. The others blinked and stepped back.

Ghaazi grabbed the back of the neck of the closest man and pulled him to the gunwale. Holding him, he called to the upper deck. "Put the spotlights on the water."

The bright beam panned across the water. It picked up two floating bodies. They wore the black uniforms of the Federal Security Service. A few feet further away, bobbing on the gentle waves of the dark Upper Bay, were two personal watercrafts.

"Look!" Ghaazi pointed at them and shook the man's neck, focusing his attention like one would push a puppy's nose at the accident it made on a carpet. "Do you think this man arrived on this boat alone? Or no?" He looked back at the guard he'd shot in the face. "Think carefully before you answer."

"No, sir. There must be two intruders."

"My sister is on this vessel." Ghaazi shoved the man away. "Find her!" He waved his arm angrily in the air and stomped around in his Ferragamo shoes. "All of you. Find her!"

They left him, organizing into small two- and three-person search details. As updates were called in over the radio, the crackle of static irritated him. Ghaazi stared out over the water. The New York City skyline ablaze with decadent excess. How he hated this city, this country. He despised the arrogant Americans and their damned patriotic exceptionalism.

He threw his walkie-talkie out into the water as hard as he could and screamed in rage. It plopped into the dark water too far out for him to see.

"Sir!" The voice called out to him from the upper deck. A single sentry remained by the rail, his rifle at the ready. "The bridge is reporting an approaching aircraft."

"What kind of aircraft?"

"A helicopter, sir. From the radar signature, they believe it to be military."

Ghaazi stared out over the Upper Bay, over the glowing landmass of lower Manhattan ahead and to the ports in nearby

Bayonne, New Jersey, to his left. He scanned the dark sky for any sign of the helicopter. He saw none.

Many of the city's buildings had helipads on them. Heliports littered the docks on both the East and Hudson Rivers. The presence of a helicopter flying around lower Manhattan was no reason for concern.

He glanced in the general direction of the city's two major airports, LaGuardia and JFK. They were two of the busiest airports in the world. As he stood and stared out at the night sky, he did notice something strange. Not the approach of threatening aircraft. Not even an increase in air traffic. What he noticed was quite the opposite. There were no lights in the sky indicating flights either in or out of the airports. None.

On a Saturday night, in the waning days of summer, to have no activity at all?

Now, that was something to worry about.

He rushed back toward the promenade and the railgun. As he ran, he called out to the sentry. "Track that helicopter. If it comes within firing range, blow it out of the sky."

CHAPTER THIRTY-THREE

McMURPHY STOOD AT THE opening between the cockpit and the cabin. His hands gripped the seatback cushions. Bannon noticed him squeeze them tightly. Without looking back into the cabin, he said, "Well, that can't be good."

"What?" Bannon asked.

McMurphy glanced over his shoulder. "I've been watching that Russian garbage scow as we approach. They're anchored under the Verrazano Bridge and have been operating with no running lights, just with a few cabin lights on. We're still too far out for me to tell what's going on, but the back end of that yacht just lit up like a Christmas tree. Either they're putting out the welcome wagon for us, or—"

"Something's wrong." Bannon climbed to his feet and looked out over the big man's shoulders.

A spotlight panned across the water's surface. He saw objects in the water but couldn't tell what they were. "Looks like debris."

"Yeah. Strange."

"Commander, you sure you want me to try and land this bird on that boat?" Garcia asked.

"We don't have another option, Captain."

Garcia continued flying toward the yacht, bringing the chopper lower as she flew. "Mind if I ask what's so important about that boat?"

McMurphy and Bannon exchanged glances.

"She deserves to know what she's flying into," McMurphy said.

She looked at them, apprehension in her brown eyes.

Bannon nodded, agreeing, "How many combat missions have you flown, Garcia?"

"Thirty-seven."

"This'll be thirty-eight." Before she could reply, he said, "There's a weapon on board that yacht capable of killing and seriously harming upwards of forty thousand people."

"And it's in the hands of a certifiable psychopath," McMurphy added. "I never did like that guy, by the way."

"That's what's at stake if we don't stop it," Bannon said, "and quite possibly the start of World War III."

"You're exaggerating," she said. "And if you're not, why not just shoot it out of the water? That'll neutralize the threat."

"That yacht's owned by a Russian billionaire. Other Russian diplomats and civilians may be on board. If we fire on it unprovoked… "

She nodded. "I get it. We're at war with the Russians long before we could prove they had aggressive intentions against us. After that, who started it won't matter."

"Exactly."

"We're three minutes out. Better take your seats."

"You have a weapon?" Bannon asked.

"Just a Sig Sauer P226 in my pouch." She glanced toward her door.

"It'll have to do," Bannon said. "We have two friendlies onboard. A man and a woman." He gave Garcia brief descriptions of Tara and Kamal Chandra. "Anyone else, shoot to kill."

"Except us, doll," McMurphy said, backing into the cabin.

"Call me doll again, puddle pirate, and you're getting one in that Neanderthal skull of yours."

McMurphy roared with laughter. "This one reminds me of Blades."

Once he retreated to the cabin, Garcia looked questioningly at Bannon. He shook his head. "Never mind him." He clasped her on the shoulder and squeezed. "No unnecessary chances, but we need to be on that yacht ASAP."

"Then you will be." She checked her instrument panel. "We're two minutes out, Commander."

He returned to the cabin and sat in the seat across from Barnes. Everyone was strapped in, unsure how the next couple of minutes would play out. McMurphy sat in the seat across from them, staring out the open cabin door.

"Give me a gun," Barnes said.

"No," Bannon replied without even looking at her.

"Our reception committee's going to be armed to the teeth. I deserve to be able to defend myself." When Bannon didn't reply, she said, "I can help. Three's better than four."

"We've got three," Bannon said. "Garcia's armed. And her I trust."

"Four's better than three, damn it. You're going to get me killed."

Bannon looked over at McMurphy.

His old friend shrugged. "She didn't kill me. Could have."

"Now there's a ringing endorsement if I ever heard one."

"I didn't kill you either," she reminded Bannon. "Could have."

He nodded, and McMurphy tossed her the Lady Smith. She caught it. A revolver, she checked the chamber, spun it, and slapped it closed.

"Hold on," Garcia said. "I'm going to come in fast. Our guests are waiting for us."

Bannon wasn't surprised. They'd have heard the chopper approaching. Without time to come up with a stealthier way onboard, there wasn't much else they could do. Land hard and fast, risk the small arms fire they'll take, and hope they land before either the chopper or the passengers took too much damage.

"I'm going to swing around so the bad guys are on our right. I suggest you plan on exiting stage left. Use the Blackhawk for cover once you hit the deck."

"Understood," Bannon said.

McMurphy unstrapped and stood between Bannon and Barnes on the chopper's left side. He grabbed hold of an overhead strap in case the landing got bumpy, then leaned out as Garcia made a wide turn around the back of the yacht. Flying south, it would appear to those on deck that the Blackhawk was passing them by. Garcia played it like they were doing reconnaissance with no orders to engage the yacht.

If it worked, it might buy them a few seconds by putting the crew at ease before she completed her turn, doubled back, and dropped the Blackhawk before Ghaazi's forces could gather their wits about them.

That was the plan anyway.

Bannon took in as much detail as he could about the yacht. He began rattling off his observations. "Looks like a length of about two hundred seventy feet with a thirty-four-foot beam," he estimated. "The accommodation section has four levels above the deck, including the bridge. The stern deck is clear for landing."

McMurphy said, "Yacht that size is gonna have a crew of around twenty. Who knows how many Ghaazi goonies on top of that?"

"The railgun's mounted on the bow. It's too dark for me to see if it's operational yet," Bannon said.

The Blackhawk completed its arc. As it spun, those in the cabin lost sight of the ship. As Garcia put the right side of the Blackhawk to face the yacht, the helipad would be directly below them. True to her word, she roared the helicopter forward, nose down, and then quickly leveled off.

It was about to get real. The chopper began to drop altitude.

Bannon leaned out the open door but couldn't see the boat underneath them. It wouldn't be visible to them until they were practically touched down. He had to take it on faith Garcia had them positioned correctly to land on the stern helipad. He believed she did.

"She's good," he said to McMurphy.

Reluctantly, he nodded his agreement. "Maybe after all this is over, she'll give me her number."

Bannon grinned. "Dog."

The helicopter rocked.

"We're taking fire," Garcia shouted over the comm system seconds before bullets began pinging against the chopper's metal skin. The chopper continued to descend but wobbled badly.

Bannon tensed, tightening the grip on his .45. This was the part he hated. The time it took to land. There was nothing they could do but hold on and ride it out. He thought about directing McMurphy to the other door to return fire, but they'd be on the pad before he'd have time to get into position.

All they could do was wait it out. Seconds turned into forever.

"Oh, that's not good," Garcia said. Before Bannon could ask, she added, "RPG. Incoming!"

She banked the chopper hard to the left. It felt like the floor had dropped out from under them. McMurphy stumbled but held tight to the strap he had wrapped around his wrist. The nose dipped, and Bannon's stomach did a somersault.

He glanced out the open cabin door to see a smoke contrail streak under them before the chopper wobbled back into position and continued to drop.

Seconds. They were seconds away from landing.

Garcia called out again. "Another one!"

They were too close. No way Ghaazi's men would miss with a second missile attack.

Bannon called out, "Bail!"

McMurphy unwound his wrist.

Bannon slapped open his five-point harness release and stood up.

Panicked, Barnes fumbled with her release. She couldn't get it to release.

Bannon reached out and tried to slap the mechanism open.

"No time!" Barnes shouted. She shoved Bannon hard in the chest with the heel of both hands. Over the roar of wind and thrumming rotor blades, she shouted, "Go save the world, Boy Scout!"

Her shove sent Bannon stumbling toward the open cabin door. McMurphy tackled him, completing the task of driving Bannon from the chopper. The impact of his friend's body slam propelled them both out of the chopper. They tumbled from the chopper. Their pant legs rippled in the wind like they were skydiving.

The fall didn't take nearly that long.

When the second RPG had fired, Garcia had read the writing on the wall. She goosed the Blackhawk to the left, placing the chopper closer to the stern, giving her passengers the chance they needed to leap into open water rather than slamming onto the deck where they risked injury, capture, or just getting dead.

As Bannon and McMurphy plunged toward the water, time seemed to stand still, seconds again stretching into infinity. Bannon saw they'd clear the yacht's swim deck by about five feet. He also saw five gunmen lined up on the upper deck behind the bridge. There was where the marksman with the RPG stood, grinning.

He would not need to fire a third round.

Bannon and McMurphy impacted with the cold water below.

The Blackhawk exploded in a fiery burst of flames and black oily smoke. The explosion was deafening. A rolling fireball blasted from the open cabin doors, killing Barnes instantly. A secondary explosion blasted the cockpit windows outward, eliminating any chance Captain Garcia had to survive the explosion.

The chopper's blackened, burning shell wobbled and pitched forward. With a high-pitched whine, it plunged into the water, clipping the corner of the yacht's stern. The whirling blades cut through fiberglass and metal. It sounded like someone had thrown a fistful of stones into an industrial-size fan. The bow lifted skyward. The yacht rocked violently, listed to port, but remained afloat.

Bannon and McMurphy hit the water while gunmen opened fire on them with automatic weapons. Bullets pinged in the water around them. The two experienced swimmers dove deep.

They kicked and swam hard to put distance between them and certain death.

CHAPTER THIRTY-FOUR

ONCE SHE'D CRASHED THROUGH the doors from the helipad, Tara crossed the wrecked dining room. It appeared as if no one had attempted to set right the damage caused by her hasty retreat from the night before. Tables and chairs were still overturned. Tablecloths, linen napkins, and broken dinnerware littered the floor. The carpet was damp in spots from spilled water and wine.

The acrid smell of something burning hung in the air.

It wasn't until Tara reached the kitchen that she discovered the cause.

The industrial-size chrome stove was a blackened, charred, and white fire-retardant-foam-covered mess. The result of a grease fire. A rather large one from the condition the stove and surrounding area were left in. Pots and pans and spilled food littered the floor back here as well. A hasty retreat had been made by all, it seemed.

A large explosion startled her.

She ducked and looked around, realizing the blast had come from behind her. She turned. The railgun was on the bow, so it hadn't been that. Before she could give it much thought, the deck under her feet lifted and sent her cartwheeling into the stainless steel kitchen island. She banged her hip on the edge and fell to the deck. A shooting pain rocketed through her leg. She winced. Pots and pans and cooking utensils slid across the deck, crashing into her and the rear bulkhead. Spilled soup slicked the red tile floor.

She pulled herself to her feet just as a secondary explosion followed the first. Tara didn't know what was going on and couldn't waste time figuring it out. Dismissing it all, she needed to stay on task, remain mission-focused.

Ghaazi could fire the railgun at any moment. That couldn't be allowed to happen.

Tara hit the call button for the elevator as the boat righted itself. She stood off to one side, aiming the AK-47 she'd lifted from one of the dead guards. Tense, she waited for the elevator to arrive.

In the quiet stillness, her thoughts turned to Chandra. Why had he insisted on coming with her? Why had she allowed it?

"It wasn't your fight," she said under her breath.

The elevator didn't ping, signaling its arrival. The doors simply slid open.

Tara tightened her finger over the trigger, but the elevator car was empty.

She stepped inside, hit the button for the next deck down, and faced the doors as they closed.

A few seconds later, the elevator doors reopened.

She stood to one side with the AK-47 at the ready. Again, there was no one to shoot. Tara was getting frustrated. She needed to purge the pent-up anger and adrenaline in her system. What she needed to do was avenge Chandra's death. Someone had to pay for that.

Tara counted to five, then stepped to the threshold of the open doors. She glanced right, then left. The corridor in front of her was clear.

The elevator doors closed behind her. She stood, listening. She found herself in a short service corridor between two passageways. This was the same level Ghaazi had taken her to the night before.

The first indication of trouble came from the soft slap of a metal buckle carelessly hitting against the plastic stock of a rifle. The sound came from the passageway to her right. She ducked behind a food service cart, the same kind they used on commercial airplanes.

A second passed before a dark-skinned guard dressed in black pants and a black turtleneck sweater appeared in the opening and sprayed the corridor with bullets. The rat-a-tat-tat of the automatic fire was deafening in the cramped space. Bullets pinged off metal and chewed through the wooden façades of the bulkheads.

Tara covered her ears and waited for the shooting to stop. When it did, and before the guard could retreat to safety, she fired a single well-placed bullet from around the side of the cart. It turned the man's left eye into a gory, blackened hole. He screamed and fell back. His weapon clattered to the floor.

She waited for more gunfire, but none came.

Had he been a lone gunman? Or were others waiting? If they were, they demonstrated a greater patience and discipline than the first one had.

When she felt she couldn't wait any longer, she darted from her place of cover toward the intersecting passageway behind her. She charged through the opening and immediately realized her mistake. At the end of the passageway came seven gun-toting guards.

They were all fair-skinned. That would make them from Russia's Federal Security Service.

Tara skidded to a stop and turned back, only to see four more guards advancing on her from the far end of the connecting corridor. They were Middle Eastern, like the one she'd just put down. National Defence Force.

Fine, she thought. The odds were overwhelming, but she'd wanted an enemy to fight, someone to pay for Chandra's murder. Here they were. She'd fight her way out of this. Kill them all or die trying.

She fired a short burst of gunfire at the advancing Russians, then ran back to the connecting corridor. For a second, she considered the elevator. Even if the lift remained on this level, she'd never get the doors open and get inside before they cut her into ribbons.

Tara sprayed a burst of automatic fire at the four NDF guards facing her.

They ducked and darted to the left and right.

Tara kicked the cart she'd hidden behind at them. It rumbled across the space and caught one of the guards in the leg. She ran after the cart, using it for cover as she closed the distance between her and the four men. She squeezed the AK-47's trigger until the weapon ran dry.

She ducked behind the cart.

Two gunmen were to her left. The other two were on her right.

Like a wild woman, Tara swung the butt of her empty assault rifle and clipped one man to her left in the jaw. He fell back with a grunt. She hit the second one in the gut with a side snap kick. He made an oomph sound and crashed into the left wall.

She spun, dropped the empty weapon, and slipped the second AK-47 she'd confiscated from her shoulder. She shot one of the two men to her right in the chest. He collapsed into a pile on the floor. Dead. She fired two shots at the guard next to him, but he was too quick. He ducked under her fire and remained unscathed.

The guard she'd clocked across the jaw was back on his feet. He faced her with his rifle at the ready. She ran straight at him, surprising him. He backed up. She executed a perfect pirouette, slamming her back into his chest as she wrapped her arm around his gun arm. She pinned his hand around the pistol grip and squeezed, firing the gun from under her armpit at the Russian guards who appeared at the far passageway opening, brushing them back.

She tugged the guard's arm and mowed down the remaining two guards with his—their—automatic fire. A line of bullets stitched across their chests, opening them up like a can opener.

Three down.

The guard she'd had her back pressed against pulled his hand from the gun, ending the barrage of bullets rattling through the chamber. Tara could barely hear and feared permanent ear damage. A worry for a later time, she reminded herself, like once she knew she wouldn't die in the lower decks of a Russian billionaire's superyacht.

She twisted around and drew her silenced Beretta and shot the guard in the gut, twice. He grabbed his bleeding stomach and dropped to his knees. She put a third bullet through his temple.

Four down. Seven to go.

They appeared in the passageway opening again, automatic guns a blazing once more.

Tara dove for the safety of the rolling food cart once more. She felt a bullet tear through the neoprene of her wetsuit and rip across her upper arm, just below where she'd cut herself the night before. She grabbed for the wound and ducked further down.

With her hands over her ears, Tara remained behind the bullet-ridden food cart. On the floor around her were broken plates, trays, cups, and glasses, and those silver dome things hotels use to cover the plates of food to keep it hot. She worked to regulate her breathing. The bullet wound in her arm stung. Though only a graze, the pain distracted her as she struggled to listen. Unable to see them, she wanted to hear if the men were advancing on her. That her ears still rang after the close-range gunfire in such an enclosed space didn't help. Add to that, the Russians demonstrated a high level of sound discipline.

She didn't know how many rounds remained in the AK-47, but she was certain it hadn't run dry yet. She still had her fully loaded Beretta, now back in her thigh holster, and the two hand grenades in her vest. Tara considered using them, but she had something else in mind for them.

Besides, this would be so much more fun.

She started wildly flinging trays and plates and glasses, anything she could reach, over the cart at the advancing men.

If she was resorting to grabbing whatever she could to use as weapons, surely, they'd assume she was out of ammo.

She wasn't.

They whispered. In Russian, so she couldn't understand them. But she didn't need to. It was the sound, not the words, she needed to locate them.

They slowly advanced on her. She counted down from ten.

At one, she kicked the cart forward and leaped over it. The startled guards were in a three-by-three formation with the leader in the middle, hanging back. She dropped kicked one in the chest, sending him reeling backward with a grunt. He stumbled into the two men behind him.

Then she dropped low in front of the ones on the other side. She slapped a rifle to the side and drove her fist into the groin of the closest one. He cried out, dropped his rifle, and cupped himself as she brought her knee up and crushed his manhood a second time.

Tears leaked from his eyes as he stumbled to the ground.

Tara twisted to face the two guards still on their feet. She pulled the Beretta from her holster, the silencer still attached. She shot them in their throats. Two quick spits of sound and blood spurted from their necks like macabre water fountains for vampires.

The other three were struggling to get to their feet.

She shot each of them in the head. She looked at the last one still in the passageway. He looked ready to run.

"This is for Chandra." Tara shot him in the forehead, ending him. He twisted like a cork and dropped to the floor.

Tara looked at the carnage around her. She was breathing heavily. She took no pleasure in killing them, but tens of thousands of innocent lives were at stake. Nothing mattered more than that. Not even the stain on her soul.

The bullet wound stung. She used her fingers to peel back the torn neoprene wetsuit from around the wound. It was deep and bled profusely, but it was only a graze. A flesh wound.

She returned to the overturned food service tray and grabbed a white linen napkin from a spilled stack. She wrapped it around her arm, tied it, and used her teeth to cinch the knot tight. She swapped her AK-47 for a fresh one from one of the dead. She made sure it had a full 30-round box magazine, then she stepped back into the passageway. Unopposed, she had her eye on the prize. "Now to see what's behind door number one."

CHAPTER **THIRTY-FIVE**

BANNON KEPT McMURPHY IN sight as they dove into the inky black waters of Manhattan's Upper Bay. The two men had worked together for so long, even barely able to see one another; they leveled off their dive at the same time and began to head for the surface, hoping they were far enough from the yacht to surface without getting their heads blown off.

They slowed their ascent before soundlessly piercing the surface, tipping their heads back so only their faces were above the surface. They gulped air and tread water, remaining submerged up to the bridge of their noses, giving them a chance to assess their situation.

The wrecked helicopter's tail section hung at an angle from the stern's gunwale, causing the yacht to list to port. The oily black water around it was on fire. Scattered wreckage floated on the surface: a rotor blade, a seat, canvas netting, sections of the Blackhawk's metal skin.

Bannon said a silent prayer for Barnes and Garcia, promising to not let their deaths be in vain.

Bright white spotlights crisscrossed over the surface of the water. There was a flurry of activity on the helipad as the crew worked to keep the fires on deck from spreading. Others tried to disengage the remains of the helicopter, weighing down the back end of the yacht. While other armed men raced from port to starboard, searching for Bannon and McMurphy.

They bobbed in the water, just outside the reach of the powerful spotlights swinging back and forth over the surface. They could return to the yacht undetected by swimming underwater, but it would be impossible to climb on board without getting shot to pieces.

"We need a plan, brother," McMurphy said.

"I have one." Bannon had spotted the two floating hydrofoils nearby. "Any chance you could hotwire one of those?"

McMurphy snorted. "Any chance you own a bar in New Hampshire?"

They slipped underwater and swam quickly to the closest of the two hydrofoils.

As they resurfaced on the far side of one, McMurphy said, "These are sweet."

Designed to accommodate two, he slipped into the front seat and grinned. As Bannon climbed into the seat behind him, McMurphy said, "No hotwiring required. Someone left us the keys."

"That someone would be Blades."

McMurphy twisted the key. The machine fired right up.

Impressed by the quiet smoothness of the engine, Bannon could feel the vibration of the hydrofoil's propeller spinning underneath them. They sat low in the water outside where the spotlights continued to crisscross over the dark surface.

"Now what?" McMurphy asked.

"How are you at waterski jumping?"

McMurphy followed Bannon's gaze.

Together, they looked at the yacht. More specifically, they were looking at the tail section of the helicopter caught on the swim deck. Bannon estimated it to be at a thirty-degree slope. The oil-slick water around it burned hot and bright. Armed guards patrolled the helipad, while others tried to figure out how to disengage what Bannon saw as an ad hoc ramp.

"How do you afford life insurance?" McMurphy asked in wonderment.

"Can you do it or not?"

McMurphy leveled him with a stern look. "When are you going to stop asking me ridiculous questions like that?"

Bannon patted his shoulder. "Then what are you waiting for?"

"Hold on."

McMurphy grabbed the hydrofoil's wheel and spun it in a circle away from the yacht, giving them the extra distance they'd need to gain maximum momentum. As they gained speed, the hull lifted out of the water. McMurphy pushed the hydrofoil to its limit. The electric motor made a low, humming noise.

Bannon held tight to the grip of his .45.

The beam of a spotlight passed over them just a few feet from where the water burned and lapped around the helicopter's tail section. It stopped and snapped back, illuminating them. That was followed by a lot of shouting from the helipad and upper deck.

"Here we go!" McMurphy warned.

Bannon raised an arm to shield the light from his eyes.

Then the gunfire started.

The hydrofoil rode over the flames around the helicopter. The heat from the burning oil was intense, but they weren't over it for very long.

The foils hit the dark green skin of the tail section. The impact rattled Bannon's teeth. The foils skidded up the metal ramp, made a piercing, screeching noise, and sent out a fan tail of sparks behind them. The spinning propeller hung low under the hull. It hit the tail section, clicking, making a metal-on-metal spinning noise. Several fins snapped off.

The spotlight still in his face, Bannon fired blindly at the cluster of guards shooting at them.

The hydrofoil continued its upward trek. The engine emitted a high-pitched whine.

They reached the end of the tail section, and momentum sent the hydrofoil sailing in an arc over the helipad.

"End of the line!" McMurphy shouted.

They leaped from the watercraft.

McMurphy pulled the Beretta from his waist and started firing as he jumped awkwardly away from the hydrofoil. Bannon leaped to the right, shooting as he tumbled through the air.

Two gunmen collapsed to the ground.

Bannon tucked his shoulder and hit the helipad deck hard. He rolled. Momentum sent him spinning across the smooth surface like a log rolled down a hill. The hydrofoil crashed onto the deck and blew apart. Pieces flew in a hundred directions as fiberglass and chrome and the metal foils snapped and broke apart.

Bannon scrambled to his feet and ran for cover to the starboard side of the helipad. He pressed his back to the bulkhead of the accommodation section, under the upper deck overhang. He counted three gunmen gathered at the yacht's stern. He spotted McMurphy lying against the gunwale, holding his ankle and aiming his Beretta at the upper deck. He popped off several shots.

Bannon grabbed the wrist of his gun hand and steadied his aim. Like ducks in a shooting gallery, he picked off the three men on the stern deck. One. Two. Three. Each shot was followed by a sharp cry of pain. Each enemy combatant jerked once and crumpled to the deck.

With that threat eliminated, Bannon ran to his friend, pinned down by gunfire from gunmen on the upper deck. He shot one-handed behind him and up as he ran, more to brush the shooters back than anything else.

He reached McMurphy and crouched beside him. "What is it?"

"My ankle," McMurphy said. "Must have twisted it when I jumped. Awfully clumsy of me."

Crouched where they were, they were exposed.

Bannon draped McMurphy's arm over his shoulder and lifted him. Half carrying, half dragging him, they ran back across the deck, continuing to shoot at the upper deck gunmen, keeping them at bay. Their guns ran dry, but they made it to the overhang without getting shot, so that was something.

Bannon eased McMurphy to the deck, sitting him up so his back was against the wall.

"It's just a sprain," McMurphy said, more to convince himself than as a statement of fact. He leaned his head back against the wall and squeezed his eyes against the pain. His face was coated with sea spray and sweat. "No big deal, right?"

Bannon looked down at McMurphy's leg. It was a lot more serious than a sprain. Blood soaked his pant leg. His tibia was broken. The bone stuck out through his skin and a rip in his pant leg. Bannon didn't answer. Instead, he darted back across the deck to where some of the dead lay. He grabbed three of their weapons and ran back. He handed McMurphy two AK-47s and kept one for himself.

"That bad, huh?" His friend pushed himself up into a straighter sitting position. He looked at his leg. "Son of a—"

"Don't move. I'll get something—"

McMurphy grabbed his arm before he could stand. "No. There's no time. Ghaazi's gonna fire that gun any minute. Go find Blades." Bannon could read the deep concern in his friend's expressive eyes. "Get our girl and end this."

Before Bannon could respond, McMurphy picked up one of the AK-47s from the deck next to him. He fired it at the boat's swimming platform. Bannon snapped around to see a guard flung back from the impact of the shot.

"Go," McMurphy insisted. "I've got this."

Bannon patted his old friend's shoulder. "I won't be gone long."

He stood up and ran for the bow of the ship.

CHAPTER **THIRTY-SIX**

BANNON RAN TOWARD THE side deck that ran the length of the accommodation section. Through the windows, he saw a large dining room that looked like it had been through hell. At the gunwale, a body in a black wetsuit lay on the deck. Fear gripped him as he noticed the bullet wounds. Two in the man's leg. One in his side.

Bannon rolled the man over.

Kamal Chandra. Damn it. And what did it mean for Tara?

He hadn't seen or heard from his old friend in many years. To find him there, like that—a wave of grief hit him that was almost painful. With it came a debilitating sense of fatigue, too.

So much bloodshed. So many deaths. When would it all end?

Again, Bannon said a silent prayer for a fallen friend, then vowed to make sure his sacrifice would not be made in vain. It was a vow he was getting damned tired of making.

Bannon stepped over Chandra's body and had only taken a few more steps before he came across another dead body.

This one sprawled across the side deck with his back propped against the hull. His face was burned—red, angry, and raw. One of Ghaazi's men, thankfully.

Under him, the teak wood deck was scarred with exploded black gunpowder. Bannon recognized the pattern immediately. It was the telltale signature of a hand grenade.

With a grim smile, Bannon saw this as hope for Tara. Hope she was still alive. Hope she was somewhere trying to put a stop to Ghaazi's ghastly plan.

At the forward section of the accommodation section, Bannon stopped. He leaned his back against the wall. He heard talking, a mix of Arabic and English. More importantly, he recognized one of the voices. It was the man he knew as Ghaazi Alvi. The so-called *munaqadh*. Along with the voices he heard on deck, he could hear the baseball game's announcers calling the play-by-play.

The Yankees scored in the bottom of the third. They were up one-nothing.

Bannon crouched low and risked a peek around the corner, confident the surrounding darkness would keep him from being seen.

The sight of the railgun chilled his bones. It appeared ready to fire.

A technician stood by a podium to the right of the gun. The computer screen glowed blue in the darkness. Two men were gingerly lifting one of three projectiles from a cradle beside the swivel base of the gun. Bannon watched as they loaded the projectile into the breech end of the armature. Ghaazi and a shorter man stood overseeing the process. Bannon assumed the other person to be Pyotr Denikin. Ghaazi held a walkie-talkie in his hand, but it was silent at the moment.

From his experience on the *Oceanic Princess,* Bannon knew once the railgun was loaded and the firing process began, it would only take the weapon milliseconds to generate the current it needed to create the Lorentz force it needed to fire the projectile.

His pulse raced. They were seconds from that happening.

The technician at the podium tapped commands using the keyboard under the computer screen. He turned to Ghaazi. "We have target lock. All systems are operational."

Ghaazi nodded. "Very good, Makeen. Very good indeed."

Not giving Ghaazi the chance to give the order to fire, Bannon spun around the corner of the accommodation section and shot the technician in the head. The man took two steps back, and with a surprised expression on his face, he collapsed to the deck.

Ghaazi and Denikin ducked. The men operating the railgun climbed around to its far side, putting the gun between Bannon and them. Bannon swung the barrel of the AK-47 toward Ghaazi. He lined up a shot but was stopped short when he felt the hard metal of a gun barrel press into the back of his neck.

"Drop it," the heavily Arabic-accented voice said. "Or die."

Bannon considered sacrificing himself to kill Ghaazi, and he would have in a heartbeat, except he had no guarantee Ghaazi's death would stop the madness. Would they fire the railgun even if he killed the madman? Would Denikin step up and complete their mission?

The only way to know for sure was to destroy the railgun. Bannon couldn't do that if he were dead. He lowered the AK-47 and raised his hands in surrender.

Ghaazi and Denikin slowly rose from where they crouched on the deck as Bannon was marched out at gunpoint by Ghaazi's fatigue-clad henchman.

The guard stripped Bannon of both his stolen AK-47 and the .45 tucked in his belt.

Ghaazi pulled a compact Makarov PM .380 and pressed it to Bannon's forehead. "Tell me why I don't just end you this instant?"

"Old times' sake," Bannon quipped.

Ghaazi stepped back but kept the gun trained on Bannon. To the guard, he nodded his head toward the dead technician. "Well done, Tarik. Have someone take care of that mess and get Safar up here immediately." To Bannon, he said, "Did you seriously think I'd have only one person capable of firing the railgun?"

"I was hoping," Bannon admitted.

"You always were naively optimistic."

"Beats the alternative," Bannon said. "You were one of the good guys, Ghaazi. Once. What happened to you?"

"Good guys?" Ghaazi said and barked a laugh. "There is no such thing."

If Bannon could keep him talking, maybe he could buy some time. Keep him from ordering the railgun fired. That was the theory anyway.

Tarik snapped his fingers and ordered two men to deal with the dead technician.

"Take him to the stern," Bannon suggested. "Throw him on the pile we've got started back there."

Tarik ignored him, but Ghaazi shook his head, like a father needing to deal with a disappointing son. "It is over for you, and yet, you joke."

"Who says it's over?"

"I do, old friend." He sneered. "That has always been your problem."

"What's that?"

"Your cocky overconfidence. You and your countrymen and their infuriating arrogance."

Bannon shrugged. "Better that than being a megalomaniacal blowhard with delusions of grandeur. You always were a bit grandiose, Ghaazi, but *munaquadh?* The savior. Really?"

"That's funny coming from you, Bannon. You and your American exceptionalism. Above the law, superior to the rest of the world. Your nauseating truth, justice, and the American way that you seek to impose on the rest of the world."

"We're not superior, Ghaazi, and we don't try to impose our will on everyone else, contrary to popular extremist propaganda. But when we see wrong in the world, sure, we try to do something about it. And sure, we don't always get it right. But we try. You hate us for our patriotism, but the truth is—"

"You're invaders!" Ghaazi shouted. "Destroyers of lives."

"Says the guy about to unleash a horrible death on forty thousand innocent people. There's no justifying that. It's mass murder, plain and simple."

"To stop a war," Ghaazi insisted. "To save hundreds of thousands. Maybe millions."

"Said every madman throughout history ever. That's not how these things work out."

"It will. This time."

"Do you really think you can murder tens of thousands of American citizens on U.S. soil and expect America to suddenly lay down its arms and give up?"

"Ultimately, the price of interference will be too high. Your populace will rebel."

"Hasn't happened yet," Bannon said.

"This time it will. The cost of retaliation will be war with Russia, then China, and then half of the Middle East. That is a conflict America cannot hope to win."

"The war to end all wars," Bannon said. "I'm sorry to say, but it's been tried before. Didn't work out so well then, won't work out for you now. We will fight. We will stop you. If not today, then tomorrow, or the next day. But we will never stop fighting. And, ultimately, we will win. That's the spirit you're trying to crush, and you can't. Not today. Not ever."

Ghaazi smiled. "And there it is again, that nauseating Yankee optimism." A roar came from the baseball game still being broadcast following another Yankee home run. "Ironic, don't you think? Or is it poetic? I always get those two confused."

"What happened to you? The man I knew wouldn't do this."

"On that, we can agree," Ghaazi said. "That man was weak, stupid. Gullible to the lies of the West." He slashed the air with his hand. "But no more. Now I am a man who makes a difference. I am a man of change. I am the *munaqadh*."

"Please, you're a man with no grasp on his own sanity."

Tarik returned with a dark-skinned man wearing thick, black-rimmed glasses and dark coveralls. A young man in his twenties, he did not look happy about being there.

"Safar," Ghaazi said. "Makeen has met with an unfortunate accident. You will have to complete his work."

The man pushed his glasses up the bridge of his nose. "What happened to...?"

He looked at the blood-stained platform below the podium where the man had been working. He swallowed hard.

"The situation has been corrected, Safar." Ghaazi glared at Bannon. "Trust me. It is safe for you to conduct your work."

The man took tentative steps toward the railgun's control panel.

"I'll stop you, Ghaazi," Bannon said. "You know I will."

"How?" He gave Bannon a pitiful look. "If your government were going to fire upon us, they would have done so by now. Either they have not been alerted to the full danger they face, or they fear starting a war with the Russians. Thanks to my good friend Pyotr Denikin and the use of his countryman's superyacht." He drew in a breath and kept going. "Chandra's dead. That oafish Skyjack you're so fond of is badly injured. He cannot so much as crawl across the deck."

At Bannon's surprised expression, Ghaazi held the walkie-talkie up. "I've been getting updates. As for Tara, my dear, dear sister, she's below deck being dealt with as we speak."

Bannon advanced on him. Gun or no gun. "If you've hurt them, so help me—"

Tarik had circled back around him and now grabbed Bannon by the arms. He pulled him back, locking Bannon's arms behind his back.

"Hold him," Ghaazi said. "Safar, are we ready to proceed?"

"Momentarily," he answered, tapping the computer keyboard. "With the yacht tilted this way, Makeen's targeting calculations are way off."

Bannon watched the computer screen as bullseye circles moved around a satellite image of New York City. In response, the railgun rotated its position, turning left in a more northerly position. The hydraulics of the platform made a whirling noise as the gun repositioned itself. The rails rose several degrees.

"Don't do this, Ghaazi," Bannon said, struggling in Tarik's grasp. "It's madness."

"Silence him," Ghaazi commanded.

Bannon tried to break free, but Tarik held him tight.

"Target is acquired," Safar announced. "Current is building nicely."

Visible through the windows behind them, the lights flickered and dimmed inside the accommodation section. Running lights along where the gunwale and deck touched also flickered and died out.

"Ghaazi, don't," Bannon said, panic in his voice.

The terrorist ignored Bannon's plea. "Fire!"

Safar hit a key. For a second, nothing happened. Then all the lights on the yacht went out completely. The bow was plunged into darkness, and then the railgun emitted an ear-popping bang. An explosion of white-yellow fire and black smoke consumed the base of the twin rails and the bow of the yacht. The sound was like the loudest Fourth of July fireworks display ever done.

Denikin clapped his hands over his ears.

Ghaazi stared at the gun and smiled.

A fiery contrail of white smoke shot from the muzzle of the gun.

The VX nerve gas-loaded missile streaked northward toward Yankee Stadium. Traveling at five thousand three hundred seventy miles per hour, it raced toward forty thousand innocent lives at Mach 7. Seven times the speed of sound.

CHAPTER THIRTY-SEVEN

TARA REACHED THE DOORS she'd seen so heavily guarded the night before. They were high-quality, solid red oak and had raised arch panels and highly polished brass hardware. She pulled on the handles, surprised to find the doors unlocked.

She stepped inside and swept the room with her assault rifle, but the room was empty.

In front of her were two large crisscrossing scissor lifts extended up to the ceiling. As she'd suspected, the railgun had been mounted on a platform in the bowels of the yacht. The deck above had a retractable floor. The railgun had been raised and was now in position to be fired.

Her pulse raced. Time was running out.

While she had an idea, it was a crazy one.

But before she could put her plan in motion, disaster struck.

The lights in the room blinked out. Only a few console lights remained illuminated. A thunderous boom overhead quickly followed the blackout. The yacht pitched violently. Lights winked on, then off again. There was the loud sound of metal banging. Tara grabbed the bulkhead behind her to keep her balance. She remained upright, with a gut-wrenching sourness in her stomach. She knew what that noise was.

He'd fired the railgun. Goddamn him to hell, she raged silently.

The lights came back on. Frantic, she looked around the room, angry at herself for being too late.

There was nothing she could do about what was done—easy to say—but unless Ghaazi was exaggerating, he still had two more VX-loaded missiles. Who knew how many conventional missiles he might have and could still fire with the railgun? She had to stop him from firing the damn gun again.

Whatever it took, the gun had to be destroyed.

She spotted a workbench in the back corner of the room. She pawed through the tools and rags, and other items littering the greasy metal surface. But it was underneath, on a bottom shelf, she found the items she was looking for.

A six-hundred-foot spool of three-strand, twisted, polypropylene safety rope, yellow and black striped, a quarter-inch thick. Perfect. Next, she found two red plastic gasoline cans. She swished them around. Each was less than a third full, but that would be plenty. Might even work out better, she thought. Lastly, she found what all good shops had: a roll of silver duct tape.

Tara knelt at the base of one of the two scissor lifts. There, she used the duct tape to secure a hand grenade to the lift's hydraulic piston, careful to tape under the spool. Then she repeated the process at the base of the other scissor lift. She cut two lengths of safety rope, measuring one out to a length of fifteen feet, and the second one she cut at twelve feet long.

She soaked the rope in the gasoline, then put the cans at the base of the scissor lifts. She carefully tied the safety rope around the taped grenades, this time tying down the spools of each grenade. With the ropes good and soaked with gasoline, she laid them out on the floor, leading from the grenades out to the door of the room.

One last thing to do.

Holding the grenades carefully, her thumb on the spools, she pulled the pins from each grenade. Each time, she held her breath until she was sure the ropes would hold the spools down.

Tara exhaled and returned to the kitchen. There, she found a box of wooden matches.

Back at the doors to the mechanical room, she knelt where her ad hoc fuses ended. She lit them with the matches. She waited long enough to make sure they would stay lit.

The flame raced quickly across the ropes. Maybe too quickly.

The room smelled of burning asphalt and gasoline.

She wrinkled her nose and ran as fast as she could away from the room. Down the passageway, she ran into the stateroom Ghaazi had held her in the night before. She ducked behind the door. If her plan worked, the flames would burn away the gasoline-soaked rope, melt the polypropylene until the ropes weakened around the grenade spools, causing them to pop off.

The varying length of cord would cause the blasts to follow, one after the other.

Once the grenades exploded, the vapors trapped inside the gas cans would create secondary flashback explosions. Hopefully, the blasts would be large enough to destroy the scissor lifts and bring the railgun crashing down into the bowels of the ship once more.

That was the theory anyway.

With a held breath, she crossed her fingers and was quickly rewarded. The first grenade exploded and set off a quick chain reaction of explosions. BOOM! BOOM! BOOM!

The yacht shook from the blasts.

Fire alarms blared. Bright white emergency lights flashed in the room.

Tara raced back to the mechanical room to inspect her handiwork. The main lights in the corridor went out again. She covered her nose with the crook of her arm. The acrid stench watered her eyes.

The red plastic gas cans had been shredded into hundreds of pieces. They were scattered across the deck. Pools of gasoline on the floor burned bright blue and white. The crisscrossed scissor legs were bent and crumpled, unable to hold the overhead weight once the extended hydraulic pistons were blown. The metal was blackened. The platform had not come completely crashing down as she'd hoped. It tilted to the left, wedged at an angle between the opening, the bulkheads, and the support of the less damaged right lift.

"Will have to do," she said.

A space had opened up between the upper deck and the platform. Narrow, but she could squeeze through it. Step two to stopping this insanity permanently was to get to the upper deck. Get to Ghaazi and finish this forever.

She feared she was already too late. He'd gotten one round off. How many people had it killed? How many people would pay the price because she'd been too slow to stop it? To stop him?

Thinking about it made her sick to her stomach. She pushed the thoughts away and began to climb the scissor lift instead. One way or another, this madness ended now.

CHAPTER THIRTY-EIGHT

BANNON STARED INTO THE sky. He watched the contrail of the missile fly over the city's bright skyline before getting swallowed up by the night sky. But oddly, a smile spread across his face. What happened next took less than ten seconds to occur. Which was a good thing, because traveling at Mach 7—seven times the speed of sound—the missile would've reached Yankee Stadium in seventeen point nine zero four seconds.

Instead, high over the Bronx Terminal Market, above the Harlem River, seven seconds short of its target, the missile exploded in spectacular fashion.

Everyone on the bow of the yacht blinked as the missile turned into a bright yellow fireball. Seconds passed before they heard the explosion. It took several more seconds for Ghaazi, staring at the fiery failure of his plan, to react.

He dropped his arm. Pointed the gun he held at the deck as he took several stiff steps toward the railing. With an expression that shifted from concern to confusion, he turned. "Safar, what happened?"

The technician pounced on the computer podium. He frantically tapped at the keyboard and scanned the charts and fluctuating bars that appeared on the screen. "It seems the missile's payload... fired early."

"Premature detonation," Bannon said. "It's a real thing I hear... "

Ghaazi brought his gun up, pointing it at Bannon once more. His hand trembled with rage. "Silence!"

Tarik tightened his grip on Bannon's arms.

To Safar, Ghaazi shouted, "What! Happened!"

"Ask me. I'll tell you," Bannon offered.

"Fix it!" Ghaazi shouted at Safar. "Do it again. This time get it right!" Ghaazi waved his gun at the other technicians standing around. "What are you all standing around for? Load the next missile. Do it!"

Safar went to work, furiously tapping keys. The technicians jumped as if they'd been prodded with a stun gun and set to work loading the armature with a second missile.

He was losing it. Good, Bannon thought. "It's not his fault, Ghaazi. There's nothing for him to fix."

Ghaazi rushed at Bannon. He jammed the barrel of his gun in the hollow spot under Bannon's jaw. Bannon winced. "And there's nothing stopping me from blowing your head off, Bannon. Stop testing me."

"They blew it out of the sky, Ghaazi. Fighter jets armed with Sidewinder missiles. They were scrambled before I even came aboard. Surely you knew we could shoot it down. Didn't you?"

When he didn't answer, Bannon continued, "Your success depended on striking before anyone knew you were here. You lost that advantage when you let Tara slip through your fingers last night. Once that happened, the fight was lost before it even began."

"No!" Ghaazi shouted, but Bannon could tell by his expression he knew it was true.

"The only thing keeping them from blowing you out of the water before now was him." Bannon nodded his head toward Denikin. "A couple of Mark 84 general-purpose bombs from a pair of F16s would have obliterated any usable evidence of your intentions."

This had been part of Ghaazi's plans from the beginning. A superior tactician, he had all but admitted it earlier. "They couldn't risk the international uproar that would follow from the unprovoked sinking of a Russian yacht in American waters. The claim of a superweapon, without proof? That wouldn't have been enough to prevent the war you're so interested in stirring up. But now… "

He let the statement hang.

Denikin grabbed Ghaazi's arm. "He's right. We must go."

Ghaazi shook him off. "And go where, you fool?" He pointed off into the sky. "You saw how quickly they blew the missile out of the sky. You think we can outrun a Sidewinder missile in this?" He waved his arm around the yacht.

"What are we going to do then?" the former ambassador asked.

"Fire every missile we've got as fast as we can. We only need one to get through…Safar, are we ready to fire again?"

"Um, um. Yes. Yes, we are."

"Then what are you waiting for? Fire!"

Safar tapped a couple of keystrokes before stumbling away from the podium. The dull sound of an explosion vibrated upward through the platform. It bucked, then tilted the platform crazily to port. More explosions followed the first one. Amid the sound of rending metal, the platform bucked and shifted again.

Bannon took a step to the right to compensate as the yacht rocked. Fire alarms wailed below deck. Lights in the accommodation section snapped off before being replaced with bright halogen emergency lighting.

He smiled. Tara. He didn't know how she did it, but Bannon recognized her work anywhere.

Over the sound of rending, failing metal, the platform pitched further to port. The men on the deck started scrambling in that direction, crying out in surprise and fear.

Ghaazi shouted, "Fire the missile! Fire!"

Safar was on his hands and knees on the deck. Like a child learning to crawl, he climbed up the inclining deck.

Bannon shoved backward as hard as he could. Off-balance, Tarik stumbled. Bannon slammed him into the bulkhead behind them. The impact broke his grip on Bannon. He spun and faced the large Middle Eastern men.

Bannon threw two quick, closed-fisted punches, one left-handed. The other with his right. His fists landed solidly across the man's jaw. Able to take a punch, Tarik blinked and shoved Bannon back. Bannon pummeled several solid punches to the man's midsection. He *oofed,* but otherwise, they did little damage.

Ghaazi had fallen to his knees and was sliding toward the port side gunwale. He waved his hands in the air. "Stop him! Kill him! Fire the goddamn gun!"

Denikin had disappeared, no doubt making a run for parts unknown.

Tarik grabbed for his sidearm.

Bannon grabbed his wrist, wrestling him for the gun. He got his hands around it and body-slammed Tarik into the bulkhead again. The impact dislodged the gun from both their hands. It hit the deck and skidded toward the portside gunwale.

Tarik kicked his knee into Bannon's gut. The blow knocked the wind from Bannon's lungs. Tarik double-downed with two smashing punches to Bannon's face. Bannon dropped down to one knee. Tarik towered over him.

Bannon leaped up and drove his shoulder into the bigger man's stomach. With all the strength he could muster, he lifted Tarik off the deck and ran, half carrying the man over his shoulder. Tarik pounded his fists into Bannon's back. With the deck pitched downward, Bannon picked up speed, ignoring the sledgehammer-like fists beating into him.

With a loud grunt, Bannon slammed Tarik into the waist-high gunwale. He heard the bones in the man's back crack as they hit the railing. Tarik's torso arched backward. He cried out. Bannon grabbed the man's powerful thighs and pushed him the rest of the way over the railing. His screams were cut off by a splash.

Breathless and sore, Bannon turned from the railing only to once again find himself face to face with Ghaazi and his Makarov PM .380.

"Move a muscle, Bannon, and you die."

Over the terrorist's shoulder, Bannon watched helplessly as Safar pulled himself up to the computer console. Ghaazi twisted around to see the same thing. "Fire the damn gun, Safar! Fire it now!"

CHAPTER THIRTY-NINE

TARA CLIMBED THROUGH THE gap where the platform dipped below the overhead promenade, hoping neither the yacht nor the platform would shift again. There wasn't a lot of room to squeeze through, but she was thin and flexible. Of course, stopping her brother was a hell of a motivator.

Her hips got stuck. She had to twist and wiggle them to finally slip through. The wet neoprene helped with that, but she had to leave her AK-47 below. Breathless, she climbed to her hands and knees onto the top side of the platform. She found herself between the V-shaped bow and the massive railgun's turntable base. The two rails that formed the gun's barrel extended over her head.

Should they fire the gun at that moment, she'd lose her hearing for sure. And get incinerated in the blast, probably. Quickly, she pulled herself to the starboard side of the yacht. She heard Ghaazi's voice.

"Fire the damn gun, Safar! Fire it now!"

The gun began to pivot on its base. The machinery whined and clicked. The rails swiveled to the left, began to rise, adjusting to commands being fed to it.

Tara scrambled to get to the far side of it. Even with the platform tilted, the railgun's mechanism appeared unaffected. Damn, she couldn't catch a break.

The platform's pitch was walkable if she was careful. But a single slip would send her careening to the portside gunwale. She reached the starboard gunwale and grabbed the railing. With her arm hooked around the railing, she pulled herself to the gunwale.

If she didn't move fast, she'd be too late. Again.

There, only a few feet away, was the computerized control podium. A similar setup to the one Aziza Faaid had used in the attack on the *Oceanic Princess*. At the controls was a young man wearing black-rimmed glasses. He was having trouble keying in commands, holding on to the podium with one hand to keep from sliding down the incline, and working the keyboard with the other.

Tara didn't waste time with a warning. They were so far beyond that by now.

She raised the silencer-equipped Beretta and fired two shots. They sounded like firecrackers popping to her ears, which felt like they were stuffed with cotton. Her first round hit the young man in the side. He let go of the podium. His hand was over the wound when the second bullet entered his temple. It snapped his head to the side. He tumbled away from the control pad, hit the deck, and rolled down the platform.

Tara ran to the podium, grabbed it, and twisted around to see Ghaazi standing over Bannon with a Makarov PM .380 pointed at her friend's head. She aimed her Beretta with a steely gaze in her eyes.

"Drop it, brother," she said. "It's over."

"For him," Ghaazi said. "Unless you put down your weapon, sister."

"Remember our conversation last night?" she asked.

A flicker of confusion crossed his face. "What of it?"

She fired. The single bullet slammed into Ghaazi's cheek. Blood spurted. It splattered Bannon's face. Ghaazi fell into the gunwale as Tara's second trigger pull fell on an empty chamber. Didn't matter. One shot was enough.

Ghaazi slid down the gunwale into a sitting position. He dropped his weapon, and his head fell forward. His chin rested on his chest. Blood leaked from the wound in his face. It didn't pump. His heart had stopped. He was dead.

Bannon kicked the .380 from Ghaazi's hand as Tara joined him. They stood and stared down at Ghaazi. A friend. A brother. A terrorist.

"What did you say to him last night?" Bannon asked.

"I told him… if he did not stop this… insanity. One of the last things I said to him was 'brother or no brother, I will kill you, and I will spit on your dead body when I'm done.'"

She spit on Ghaazi.

She holstered her gun, crossed to the passageway, and leaned against the accommodation section's wall. She lowered her head. Bannon joined her. "I'm sorry, Tara."

"I lost him a long time ago, Brice," she said. "That man was not my brother."

"No," Bannon said. "He certainly wasn't the Ghaazi Alvi I remembered."

She looked at him, tears welling in her eyes. Not for Ghaazi, for the…

"He fired the gun," she said.

Bannon nodded. "An F-16 took it out with a Sidewinder missile over the Harlem River. With a whole seven point nine zero four seconds to spare."

She gave him a lopsided smile. "Doesn't even qualify as a close call."

"Tell my nerves that," Bannon said.

"Hey," a gruff voice called out.

They looked to the starboard gunwale.

McMurphy was there, holding Denikin by the scruff of his neck. Under his other arm, McMurphy leaned heavily on a wooden oar, using it as a crutch. He'd tied his work shirt around his lower leg, where he'd broken his fibula. It was blood-soaked. Tied to either side of his leg were two AK-47s, a makeshift brace.

"Please tell me those rifles are unloaded," Bannon said.

McMurphy gave him a look but didn't dignify the question with an answer.

"An oar, Skyjack. That's the best you could come up with?" Tara asked, beaming at the sight of him.

"Come on, Blades." He grinned back. "You ever know me to get caught up a river without a paddle?"

They all groaned at the joke.

"Anyway," McMurphy shoved Denikin to the deck. "Caught this one trying to jump ship like a scurrying rat. I'm guessing someone would wanna have a chat with him."

"I'm sure they will," Bannon said. He pulled his cell phone out.

McMurphy said, "Tell me you're ordering pizza. I'm starving."

"Calling Grayson," Bannon explained. "Figure I better let her know the situation's secure before the President orders a strike that'll blow this yacht to Kingdom Come."

CHAPTER **FORTY**

GRAYSON HAD HAD THE police and the Coast Guard on standby. Less than three minutes after she got the call from Bannon, the *Morskoy Skat* was surrounded by a white and red 45-foot response boat, three 25-foot port security boats, and two NYPD harbor patrol boats. They had spotlights trained on the yacht. Warnings were issued through bullhorns for those still aboard to lay down their weapons or suffer the consequences.

The senior Coast Guard officer was a gruff African American captain named Greer. He led a joint boarding party of Coasties and NYPD S.W.A.T. personnel. Within minutes they'd swept through the yacht and had rounded up the crew and over a dozen members of the Federal Security Service and National Defence Forces—those still alive anyway. Soon they were on the helipad. Zip ties were used to secure their wrists behind their backs.

Captain Greer turned Denikin over to a young woman wearing a dark-colored pantsuit. Greer said she was State

Department. Bannon suspected she was CIA. Either way, Denikin was their problem now and no longer his.

He, McMurphy, and Tara made their way to the dining room, where Tara and Bannon righted a round table, tossed a cloth over it, and set out five chairs around it. McMurphy found an unbroken bottle of eighteen-year-old Kentucky straight bourbon and four glasses.

When he sat down, he propped his leg up on the extra chair.

Tara glanced at the label on the bourbon. "That's an eight-hundred-dollar bottle of booze."

McMurphy cracked the top open. "Good. Because we earned it."

Bannon couldn't argue with that. He and Tara sat down while McMurphy poured four fingers of bourbon into three of the glasses. They clinked glasses and drank.

As they did, the police sergeant who had boarded with Greer emerged from the kitchen. He squeezed his shoulder mike and was talking into it as he walked past them on his way to the helipad. "We're gonna need coroners, medical examiner investigators, three crime scene unit teams, and detectives down here ASAP. Oh, and that refrigerated tractor-trailer, get that, too. We're gonna need it for all the dead over here. I can't even count the number of bodies we're finding. It's a goddamn bloodbath on this boat."

McMurphy and Bannon glanced at Tara. McMurphy asked, "What'd you do down there, girl?"

"Won."

Bannon raised his glass. "I'll drink to that."

McMurphy called out to the cop, "Tell 'em to send a couple of divers, too, Sergeant."

"What for?"

"There's a couple more bodies floating around out there. Also, there's two dead American heroes you need to recover from that downed Blackhawk."

The cop nodded. He squeezed his mic. "And some scuba guys. We're gonna need them, too."

McMurphy lifted his glass, saluting him before he left.

Before the door fully closed, Elisabeth Grayson grabbed it and pulled it open again.

She wore a dark pantsuit under a tan overcoat. McMurphy poured her a drink. She draped the coat over the chair McMurphy used to rest his leg. She looked at it as she sat down, taking a sip of her drink. "You should get that attended to, John."

"After my drink," McMurphy said.

Tara poured a second round. "I'll take over the bartending duties, Skyjack. You look about ready to pass out."

"After my drink," he said.

"I'm glad to see you're all relatively unscathed," Grayson said.

"Where's Kayla?" Bannon asked.

"Still babysitting the railgun in New Hampshire. DARPA's on site. They're supervising its secured shipment to their headquarters in Arlington." Grayson changed the subject. "Barnes?"

"Didn't make it," Bannon said. "She saved my life."

Tara raised an eyebrow. "Seriously?"

"Me, too," McMurphy said, his speech getting slurry.

Tara gave them both the strangest looks. "I leave you boys alone for a few weeks, and the whole world goes topsy-turvy. You're trying to tell me Bridget Barnes turned into one of the good guys?"

"I'm not sure I'd go that far," Bannon said.

"She tried to kill me. Several times, remember?" Tara said.

"She led us to the third railgun," Grayson said. "Stopped it from being used."

"She didn't kill me," McMurphy said with his eyes closed. "Could have."

"Or me," Bannon added, taking a sip.

McMurphy mumbled something that none of them could understand.

"You okay, John?" Grayson asked.

"He found some painkillers in the ship's infirmary," Tara said. "Clearly they're working."

"Ms. Sardana," Grayson said. "We'll need to discuss you leaving without permission and your other extracurricular activities before too long."

"Yes, ma'am." She looked down at her drink.

"I am sorry about Chandra," Grayson said. "He seemed like a good man."

"He was."

Bannon interrupted the silence that followed. "Madam Secretary, I need an explanation regarding Barnes and this charade you and she concocted. You damn near got me killed."

"Hardly, Brice," she said. "And for the record, Barnes had nothing to do with the planning of it. That was all me." She raised a hand, stopping him from speaking. "But you're right. I should have clued you in from the start. That was," she paused to take a sip of her drink, "a tactical miscalculation."

Damn it, Bannon thought. Grayson didn't make mistakes often, and she admitted them even less. He'd geared up for an argument, but it was impossible to fight with someone who agrees with you. He'd expected blowback from her. Not getting it, he felt let down.

Still, with a harsh tone, he demanded, "Then why didn't you?"

"Because there wasn't time to have this argument, first of all." She sighed. "And because you didn't trust her."

"And with good reason."

"Granted. But she was our best, quickest way to the location of the other railguns." Grayson's tone softened. "I didn't trust her either, Brice. But I couldn't let that stop me from using her, using whatever I had at my disposal to get the job done."

"I get that," Bannon said. "I really do. What I don't understand is why you played me. Why keep me in the dark?"

"Because," Grayson said, "once you got to Michigan, you'd never have let her go alone with Van Sistine and the others."

"I—"

She cut him off. "You wouldn't have. And for two very valid reasons. One, you didn't trust her, and secondly, it's not in your nature to let someone go it alone like that. Not even her. I, on the other hand, had no qualms about sacrificing her if it became necessary."

He tried twice to mount an argument, but he couldn't. She was right, and he knew it. He looked at the others around the table. They nodded in agreement. They knew it, too.

Conceding, he said, "Understood." He threw down the last of his drink and signaled Tara to give him a refill. "What happens now?"

Grayson sighed. "We sort it all out. The Justice Department, DoD, and CIA will go round and round to get what information they can out of Pyotr Denikin while we still have him."

"What do you mean, while we still have him?"

She frowned. "Ultimately, he'll be returned to the Russians. Unless he chooses to defect. Otherwise, he'll become a bargaining chip. State will eventually negotiate some kind of trade. Denikin for a captured asset we want back or to force the Russians into some other high-value concession."

"Just like the bad old days of the Cold War," McMurphy mumbled. He had his arms folded over his chest and his head down with his eyes closed.

"As for the rest of this," Grayson said, looking around the dining room. "We'll interrogate the prisoners we've got. Find out where Ghaazi's been for the past seven years. Dig through his network of friends, associates, and accomplices. Try to find out what else they might be planning. Hopefully, stop whatever we can."

"It never ends," Bannon said.

"It doesn't seem to." Grayson finished her drink and stood up. "We'll start the debriefs in the next day or two. In the meantime, get some rest." She looked at McMurphy, who had begun to snore. "And get him to a hospital."

She took her coat and folded it over her arm. When she reached the door leading out to the helipad, she turned back. "You did good work here today. Very few people will ever know about it, but this country owes you a great debt once again. As one of those grateful people, thank you."

Grayson left.

Bannon and Tara clinked glasses and drank.

271

"How are the renovations going at the Keel Haul?" she asked over McMurphy's heavy snoring.

"Almost done," Bannon said. "Cap'n Floyd misses you."

She smiled. "Strangely, I miss him, too."

SUNDAY

Yankee Stadium
East 161ˢᵗ Street, Bronx, New York

THE NEXT NIGHT, BANNON, Tara, McMurphy, and Tommy Pawlowski sat in the first four seats in the front row of section 17 B. They were on the first baseline of Yankee Stadium. Directly to their right was the Yankee dugout. The game hadn't started yet, but the anticipation in the sold-out stadium was high. The Yankees and the Red Sox were locked in a grueling battle for first place in the American League East with less than a month and a half of regular season play to go. The Sox had won the first game of the series on Friday night, and the Yankees had won in extra innings with a walk-off homer in the bottom of the tenth the night before.

Everyone in the stadium and most everyone in the world remained blissfully clueless to how differently the game almost ended.

Tommy stood at the rail and craned his neck, trying to see into the Yankee dugout as the team got ready to take the field. "Two games in two nights. This is awesome." He turned to McMurphy. "Thanks, Skyjack."

McMurphy sat in the aisle seat. He smiled. He had a splint and brace on his broken leg, which he extended into the aisle. His crutches were leaning against the side of the dugout. He wore a pair of blue jeans with the left leg cut off, exposing the brace, after spending the previous night and most of the day at the hospital. CAT scans and an MRI had shown McMurphy had done a remarkable job of realigning the two broken pieces of his tibia while still onboard the *Morskoy skat*. His efforts, no matter how ill-advised they would have been by a doctor, had prevented him from needing surgical screws, plates, or rods.

The pain of pressing his bones into alignment must have been excruciating. Bannon still winced just thinking about it.

Tommy turned around. "Too bad we couldn't get seats by the visiting team's dugout."

"Don't press your luck, bud," McMurphy said with a grin. Grayson had somehow secured the tickets but refused to tell anyone how. Simply saying they were a gift. "Bad enough you convinced me to let you wear a Red Sox cap."

McMurphy, on the other hand, wore a midnight blue T-shirt with the Yankee logo on it and an unbuttoned Yankee jersey, a large number 99 on the back. He'd demanded Bannon and Tara wear Yankee baseball caps, too. They were happy to comply.

Tommy plopped down on the seat next to McMurphy. He swung his legs and looked at the peanut shell-littered concrete floor.

"You okay, buddy?" McMurphy asked.

Tommy looked up at him. "What's going to happen to my mom and dad?"

McMurphy exchanged glances with Bannon and Tara. He put his arm across Tommy's shoulders. "Tell you the truth, bud—I'm not sure. They've made some mistakes. Did some things they shouldn't have."

"Are they going to go to jail?"

"They might," McMurphy said. "But here's the thing. They're accepting the consequences for what they did. You understand what that means, don't you?"

The boy furrowed his forehead, thinking. "Like when you get into a fight at school and get sent to the principal's office."

"Yeah," McMurphy said. "And what usually happens next?"

"You get detention or suspended."

"That's right. Why?"

"For fighting. You're not allowed to do that."

"Exactly. You break the rules, you've gotta be willing to face the consequences. Hopefully, the punishment teaches you to not break the rules again. It's the same with your mom and your dad."

Tommy nodded, thinking about it.

"No matter what happens to them, we'll support them. And regardless of how it all plays out, I'll be there with you. All the way. Deal?"

McMurphy held out his fist, and Tommy fist bumped him. "Deal."

"That's for tomorrow," McMurphy said. "Tonight, we enjoy the game."

Tommy grinned. "When the Red Sox crush the Yankees."

McMurphy playfully slapped the bill of his cap. "Stinker."

Bannon glanced over at Tara. "You've been unusually quiet today. You okay?"

She forced a smile. "Yes. Tired. It's been a long few weeks."

Ghazi Alvi was the last family she had. Her mom was an only child, and her dad had one brother who never married. He died two years before Tara's parents were murdered. Now with Ghaazi gone, she was alone.

"I wish we'd known Ghaazi had been alive," he said. "I can't help thinking we could've helped him. Prevented all this before it got this far."

She shook his head. "This was his path. Had been for a very long time." She reached out and clasped Bannon's arm. "He died a long time ago, Brice. I've already mourned his passing. That person yesterday, that wasn't my brother."

"But your whole family is gone now. That's got to be hard."

She smiled at him from under her Yankee hat. "Family isn't blood. You know that better than anyone, Brice." She squeezed his arm and looked past him at McMurphy. "This is my family. You and Skyjack and Kayla. Even, God help me, Grayson and Captain Floyd. It's all I ever wanted. All I'll ever need."

She leaned over and kissed his cheek. "Thank you for coming to get me. Again."

"Always." He smiled back. "But I'd say it was more like you saving my bacon again."

"Either way, can we take a break from saving the world for a while?"

"Sounds like a plan."

The stadium's loudspeaker crackled to life. "Good evening, ladies and gentlemen, and welcome to Yankee Stadium. Will you please rise and remove your caps for the singing of our National Anthem."

"Grab my crutches, would you?" McMurphy said to Tommy.

"Skyjack, your leg," Tara said.

"Stow it, Blades. There's no way in hell I'm not standing for the National Anthem." He waved at the crutches. "Tommy."

Tommy grabbed the crutches and helped McMurphy stand up. The big redhead leaned over the crutches and put his cap over his heart.

They stood, along with forty thousand other fans, and directed their attention to the American flag flying on the giant jumbotron over center field. With their caps and hands over their hearts, Bannon, Tara, McMurphy, and Tommy sang along to the Star-Spangled Banner.

After it was done, the stadium settled into their seats, anxious for the game to start.

Bannon sat down, grateful for his friends.

Smiling, he and the whole stadium waited for the umpire to yell, "Play ball!"

WANT MORE?
Join David's Mailing List.

https://www.subscribepage.com/daviddelee

Members receive information via e-mail about David's latest releases, special events, and exclusive content only available to subscribers.

If you enjoyed *Strike of the Stingray,*
Don't miss the next adrenaline-fueled Brice Bannon
Seacoast Adventure

THE
YAKUZA GAMBIT

Here's an exciting preview…

NIGHT.

A full moon hung large and bright in a cloudless sky over the tranquil Atlantic Ocean. Moonlight glimmered over the surface of the water. The light reflected off the gentle ripples like liquid diamonds.

Visible in the distance was the dark shoreline of Hampton Beach and North Hampton, New Hampshire. Yellow squares of lights from the expensive homes dotted the crest of the craggy seacoast like Christmas lights strung along a rooftop.

Water lapped against the fiberglass hull of the motionless twenty-two-foot ski boat as it bobbed alone in the vastness of the ocean. A mile from shore. Dark. Its engine silent. The running lights off.

Illuminated only by the pale glow of the instrument panel, Billy Palmer sat behind the wheel of his sixty-five-thousand-dollar boat, which he'd named the *Bottom Line*. He puffed smoke from a thick Cuban cigar as he and his friend Alex Riggi drank cold beers from longneck bottles and enjoyed a taste of the good life.

Alex sat in a stern seat with his long legs extended toward the seat facing him. Both men were in their late twenties. Best friends since elementary school, they'd decided to brave the late October cold in New England to take the *Bottom Line* out one last time before the marina was scheduled to pull it from the water for the winter.

"Mr. LaSala's sending us on another job," Alex said, breaking the quiet.

Billy sipped his beer. "So soon? Didn't you guys just pull a job a couple of days ago?"

"Yeah. Last week." Alex shrugged. "Bennie says there's a big shipment coming in. The boss needs some upfront cash."

Billy said, "Huh."

He left it at that. Finishing his beer, he held the empty bottle out to Alex. "Got any more in there?"

Alex took the bottle and dropped it into the case filled with empties at his feet. He dug through the ice in the cooler at his feet, pulled a fresh beer out, and handed it to his friend. Billy twisted the top off and flung the cap into the ocean. Alex finished his beer and grabbed another for himself. He took a sip and furrowed his forehead.

"You hear that?"

Billy did. He recognized it as the whine of a high-performance engine. It reached them from across the open water, sounding like a mosquito near his ear as it grew louder. Billy twisted around in his seat.

"There." He pointed, spotting a low, sleek racing boat skimming across the water to the south of them. It sped along at what Billy guessed to be close to sixty-five knots.

Like the *Bottom Line,* its running lights were off.

Billy shrugged, *idiot,* and turned back in his seat to enjoy his beer and his Cuban.

Alex kept a wary eye on the approaching speedboat.

As it got closer, the engine hum grew louder.

After a few minutes, Alex said, "Billy. You might want to turn on the running lights. I don't think that guy sees us."

Billy twisted around again. The racing boat was moving fast. Its deep V-hull slapped the water as it powered in a direct line at them. If he didn't know better, he'd think they were aiming straight for the *Bottom Line.*

This time, Billy verbalized his thoughts. "Idiot."

He snapped on the boat's running lights. Red and green sidelights and the white stern lights came on, glowing brightly.

The approaching speedboat showed no sign of either slowing down or deviating course.

Billy stood up. He grabbed the edge of the windshield to steady himself in the gently rocking boat. His lack of sea legs had nothing to do with the six-pack he'd consumed over the last hour and a half and all to do with the sudden fear that gripped him.

"They're slowing down," Alex announced.

Billy agreed. "Or changing course."

The racing boat was close enough that Billy could make out a single, silhouetted figure standing behind the wheel. It was too dark to see anything more than that.

"What does he think he's doing?"

"I don't know," Alex came to his feet. "You think maybe we should move?"

After a moment of indecision, with the racing boat still approaching at full speed, Billy twisted the key in the ignition. The big inboard four-hundred-and-ten-horsepower engine rumbled but failed to start.

Billy stared at the instrument panel. "Are you serious?"

"We've gotta move," Alex said, his voice trembling with fear.

Billy glanced at the approaching boat. It continued to skim over the water, coming at them fast. Billy swallowed hard.

He twisted the key again. "Come on. Come on."

The engines caught with a deep, throaty growl. The water behind the stern bubbled up white and frothy. The racing boat was nearly on top of them.

"You gotta get us out of here!" Alex shouted in a high-pitched panic.

Billy gripped the wheel and slammed the throttle forward. At first, nothing happened. Afraid he'd flooded the engine, Billy stole a glance at the racing boat. It was seconds from slamming broadside into the *Bottom Line*.

The big engine under his feet finally dug in. The bow lifted with a roar, and the *Bottom Line* surged forward as the racing boat swerved. Not to avoid a crash, but to initiate one. There was a loud bang as the boat slammed into the

Bottom Line's aft gunwale. The hulls scraped against each other with a horrific screech. Alex was thrown to the deck. Billy managed to remain on his feet only by clutching the wheel with a death grip.

The racing boat was knocked off its course, like a bumper boat at the amusement park.

The *Bottom Line* twisted. Its stern swerved toward port. Billy spun the wheel, digging them out of the spin. On hands and knees, Alex crawled up the center aisle to the space between the passenger seat and the dashboard. There, he used the dashboard and seat to pull himself to his feet.

Their dropped beer bottles rolled across the deck, spilling frothy beer to slick the fiberglass floor.

"You okay?" Billy asked, stealing a glance at his friend and thankful he hadn't been knocked clear out of the boat.

"Are they trying to kill us?"

Billy wasn't going to hang around to find out. He straightened the wheel and pushed the throttle full open. At first, heading out to sea, Billy made a wide arc south. Intending to make a run for the Hampton Harbor Inlet, return to the Hampton River Marina where he docked the *Bottom Line,* and report the reckless racing boat driver to the authorities.

After striking them, the reckless racing boat continued north.

Billy tried to convince himself it was just an accident, a drunk with no business being out on the water. But then the boat made a wide turn. It almost lay sideways in the water as it cut into the turn, the stern dug deep in the water, and the long, sleek bow rose high in the air.

The boat was longer than the *Bottom Line*. Billy estimated it to be a thirty-five-footer. Built to race, the cockpit only had space for two seats. As Billy glanced back, he noticed there was a second person in the co-pilot seat.

The racing boat completed its turn. It was once again pursuing them. Billy held out little hope they could outrun the faster racing boat. The most he'd ever gotten out of the *Bottom Line's* engines was forty-seven knots, about a third slower than what the racing boat could do.

Already, they'd cut the distance between them to a frighteningly short span.

Billy gunned his engines, but the race was already lost.

Their pursuers had almost already caught up to them, moving toward the *Bottom Line's* starboard side.

Billy glanced over his shoulder. The second figure he'd spotted earlier was leaning out around the windshield. He had something dark and long in his hands, but in the dark, that was all Billy could tell until the night was lit up with bright yellow muzzle flash.

Followed a millisecond later by the sound of gunfire.

"That answer your question?" he shouted at Alex. "Yeah, they're trying to kill us."

Bullets pinged off the windshield frame and dug into the fiberglass deck, gunwales, and seat cushions. Alex covered his head with his arms and dropped down to the space between the seat and the dashboard. Billy zigzagged the *Bottom Line* and aimed the boat for shore. A dangerous proposition. The seacoast shoreline was notoriously rocky.

Still, Billy would take ripping out the bottom of the hull and scuttling his pride and joy over getting shot to death or run over. Now, if only the driver of the racing boat wasn't crazy enough to chase them into the dangerous, shallow, rocky coastline. A big ask, considering he'd already used his boat to try and run them over. Yet, it was the only chance they had.

"Hold on!"

He aimed the boat straight for the rocky shoal. If they were lucky, they could get close enough to shore to jump ship before they ran aground on a rock. And if their luck really held, they could get lost in the dark and hide in the frothy, rocky outcroppings. But luck wasn't on their side.

Not unless one considered bad luck.

The *Bottom Line* almost immediately struck an outcropping hidden just below the surface. The boat angled up, like it had hit a ski jump, and slammed to a stop. At top speed, the momentum launched Billy over the windshield. He flew through the air and landed hard against the bow railing. He struck his head against the gunwale before tumbling back into the foredeck well, leaving a streak of blood from a deep cut over his eye across the bow seats.

Billy groaned.

The chasing boat slowed and gingerly made its way to the stuck *Bottom Line*.

As it moved up alongside, the gunman silently leaped onto Billy's boat.

Billy blinked blood from his eyes. Through his red, blurred vision, he believed he was seeing things.

Dressed entirely in black pants and a black tunic, with a black sash tied around his waist, the gunman wore a black hood and face mask that covered everything but his eyes. Billy could see the man was Asian, which was the only part of the senselessness that made sense. He'd watched "Duel to the Death" enough to know a ninja when he saw one.

Still, the thought defied logic. His boat was being boarded by a ninja.

A ninja carrying an assault rifle in his hands.

He made his way toward the bow.

The *Bottom Line's* engines had stalled upon impact with the rocky shoal. The only sound came from the idling engine of the racing boat and the gently slapping waves against the hulls of the two boats.

The ninja-gunman paused. He glanced down at the space where Alex hid.

"No!" Billy yelled.

The man shot Alex.

The gunshot was loud and echoed in the air like an explosion.

Billy jerked, almost as if he'd been shot himself.

The ninja-gunman grabbed Billy by the back of his shirt and pulled him to his feet.

"What do you want?" Billy's voice shook with fear.

Billy was pulled to the stern. As he passed through the cockpit, he glanced over at Alex's body. Curled into a ball, Alex's arms were wrapped protectively around his head. It had done nothing to stop the bullet that put a hole in the back of his skull.

Billy was shoved over the railing. He tumbled headfirst into the racing boat's cockpit deck.

The driver of that boat, also a ninja, took the assault weapon and held Billy at gunpoint while the first ninja tied a tow rope to the *Bottom Line's* stern cleats. Then he opened the boat's drains and returned to the racing boat. He covered Billy with the gun while the driver put the racing boat in reverse and tugged the *Bottom Line* from the rock it was perched on with a rending, nails-on-a-chalkboard sound.

Once it was free, they towed it about a half mile from shore.

There, they released the tow rope, letting the *Bottom Line* float free.

And they waited.

Billy sat in the co-pilot seat with his hands interlocked on top of his head. They watched as the *Bottom Line* took on water and slowly slipped under the relentless ocean water. When all traces of the boat were gone, the driver expertly backed the racing boat away from the spot, spun the boat around, and gunned the throttle.

Billy Palmer was taken away from the sinking *Bottom Line* and his dead friend, wondering where they were taking him, and how long before they killed him, too.

CHAPTER ONE

DAWN.

The sun began its daily climb into the sky, burning low and bright over the distant Atlantic Ocean horizon. It brought with it the promise of another glorious day. Autumn in New England was one of Brice Bannon's favorite times of the year. The evenings were cool, the days still relatively warm, and on his morning run, he had the beach nearly to himself.

Not that he didn't like the summers on Hampton Beach. He did. He fed off the energy, the atmosphere of the crowds: mostly young people, having fun, enjoying the sun, the surf, and the sand. But Fall was special. To Bannon, it felt like the world was taking a breather from the energetic, hot, active summer, but not quite ready to settle down for its long winter nap just yet.

Wearing a gray T-shirt with the Coast Guard seal—a pair of crossed anchors superimposed by a life ring with a shield surrounded by a line grommet—on it and blue shorts, he ran at the water's edge where the sand was wet and hard-packed. Six miles each morning. His daily routine, whenever he could, had been the same since his arrival at the Coast Guard

Training facility at Cape May, New Jersey. He ran even during the legendary winter storms and record cold that defined New Hampshire for a good part of the year.

This morning, he ran north toward Rye Beach.

He'd only gone about two miles when he first caught sight of a larger-than-usual colony of seagulls circling overhead, up where Hampton Beach became North Hampton. A large sea animal had probably washed ashore, dead, he'd surmised, until he caught sight of electric blue emergency lights flashing across the wet sand and the facades of the condos across the street from the beach.

He slowed his gait to a fast walk, looking ahead.

Where the beach grew rocky and the land hooked to the right to form a small, rocky peninsula, his way was blocked by yellow crime scene tape. It fluttered in the early morning breeze from stakes driven into the sand and out about five feet into the surf.

On the road above the rocky incline, parked along the retaining wall, were two Hampton Police cars and another one from the neighboring town of Rye. Also, in the mix were two dark sedans with flashing grille lights and an ambulance.

So much for his beached sea animal theory.

A few early morning onlookers lined the retaining wall with their cell phones out and recording. Probably they were from the row of hotels and summer rental condos along Ocean Boulevard, just before it reached Great Boars Head Avenue. At the water's edge were several uniformed cops, two EMTs, and a couple of people in civilian clothes were milling around looking down at the rocky shoreline.

Bannon pulled his earbuds from his ears and walked toward the tape where he'd spotted a young Hampton cop he knew, Stewart Willoughby.

"Stu," he called. "Hey, Stu."

The cop was hammering another stake in the sand to further cordon off the crime scene. His uniform pants were wet to his thighs and sparkly with sand. He'd drawn the short straw and had had to wade into the cold ocean water to bang in the crime scene stakes.

He looked up, pushing his hat back off his unusually high forehead.

"Oh, hey, Brice. What are you doing out here so early in the morning?"

Dressed in a sweat-damped T-shirt, shorts, and running shoes, Bannon concluded detective wasn't in the cop's immediate future. "I was about to ask you the same thing. What's going on?"

Willoughby glanced over his shoulder at the group of uniformed and plain-clothed cops behind him.

"I don't know if I'm supposed to say."

"How long have we known each other, Stu?" Bannon asked.

"Ever since you opened the Keel Haul. What's that? Five years?"

From day one, Bannon had made it a practice to be very involved with the community. He knew all the cops, of course, and made free coffee and cold drinks available to them whenever they wanted. He'd also hosted who knew how many promotion, retirement, and bereavement parties for members of the department.

"You can tell me, Stu. It's not like I'm going to put it on Facebook," Bannon said. "I promise."

Willoughby's face soured. "Who uses Facebook anymore?" Even though no one was in earshot, Willoughby leaned in closer. He lowered his voice. "A body washed up on the rocks."

The cop's voice was so low, Bannon had trouble hearing him over a strong gust of wind. Hampton Beach was a quiet resort town. A very, very quiet town after August. Certainly not the sort of place where foul play reared its ugly head often.

Had to be a boating accident or a drowning, Bannon thought. "What happened?"

"That's what we're trying to find out." The baritone voice came from behind Bannon.

Bannon turned to find himself face to face with Reggie Cole, the Hampton Police Chief for the last five years. Like Willoughby, Bannon had known Cole since the day he opened the Keel Haul's doors.

Forty-five years old, Reggie Cole was African American, as wide as he was tall, with dark skin and a bald head. He'd played one season of pro ball with the New York Giants before blowing out his knee. After that, he joined the NYPD and worked his way up through patrol and detective positions to become a Borough Investigative Chief responsible for overseeing all gang-related investigations in the Bronx.

Bannon had learned this over beers late one night, soon after they met.

But that first day, Cole came into the place and issued Bannon a stern warning about the sort of conduct he and his department would not tolerate from a gin joint on his strip. Any transgressions, and he'd have the Keel Haul locked down faster than you can say last call.

Cole had said it just like that, and he'd meant it.

Bannon made sure the Keel Haul had never been a source of concern for Cole and his department. The man hadn't said a cross word to Bannon since.

Now the two men shook hands.

Cole wore a forest green soft-shell jacket with the police department logo over the pocket, a matching green baseball cap that said Chief in big yellow letters. He held a steaming hot cup of takeout coffee in his hand. He took a sip.

Over those same beers, Cole had admitted to Bannon he'd been born and raised in the Bronx, had spent his entire life there, but after twenty years on the police force, he'd tired of the rat race that was New York City. That motivated him to pull the pin, take his pension, and 'retire' to the cushy chief's job in the quiet coastal town of Hampton, New Hampshire.

That had been before he'd policed Hampton Beach during a rough and tumble summer season. He never referred to the job as cushy again after that, though in truth the rest of the year it usually was.

"Truth be told, you being here saves me from making a phone call."

Bannon arched his eyebrow. "How so?"

Cole lifted the crime scene tape.

Bannon ducked under it like a prizefighter entering the ring.

"You got that access log, Stu?" Cole asked.

"Yes, sir."

"Mark Brice as being on scene at this time. Capacity. A consultant."

"Consulting on what exactly?" Bannon asked.

He and Cole trudged through the wet sand toward the group of people milling around a small eddy where water gently splashed in and around the rocks.

Cole sipped his coffee. "I thought I left this all back in the Bronx. Like Stu said, a body washed up this morning. A vacationer walking his dog found it. My guys are taking a statement from him now."

They neared the group.

Bannon saw the body lying face down in the sand. Water washed up around him, then eased back. He wore jeans, a T-shirt, and a dark green wool hoodie. The EMTs stood off to one side. Their services would not be needed, but no one had released them yet. The one woman in the group was taking photographs. A brunette with her hair tied back in a sloppy ponytail. Two other men Bannon hadn't seen initially were wading in the water, collecting debris floating in on the tide.

"Boating accident?"

"That's what we thought... at first."

The woman took a step back from the body. She appeared done taking photos, at least for the time being. The group turned as one as Cole and Bannon approached.

Cole pointed them out one at a time. "Officers Delarosa and Yu, you know." Hampton cops who worked for Cole. Then he pointed to the others. "Hackett, Orlando, and Reeder are from the State Police Major Crimes Unit. They're here to assist us with the crime scene stuff and any other assistance we might need."

Bannon wondered why the chief was telling him all this.

Cole squatted down and pulled the bunched-up hoodie back, giving Bannon a better view of the back of the head. One of the state police detectives shone a light at the base of the body's skull. The dark hair was matted with blood, strands pulled apart to reveal a bloody hole six inches above the base of the victim's neck.

"Definitely not an accident," Bannon said.

Cole came to his feet. "Not unless he accidentally shot himself in the back of the head. We're grabbing the debris that's drifting in, but we don't even know if it's got anything to do with our vic or not."

He looked out into the water as he drank his coffee.

Bannon eyed the items that were floating in the water and had been collected and carefully laid out on the sand: A seat cushion. A cooler. Some empty beer bottles. A half-smoked cigar. A single strip of torn fiberglass hull.

"What do you think happened?"

Cole shrugged. "If this were the Bronx, I'd say our vic here had an appointment to swim with the fishes."

"A mob hit? Here?" Not likely, Chief," Bannon said. "Have you IDed him yet?"

"Wallet was in his back pocket, along with credit cards and eleven hundred dollars in cash."

"Not a robbery then."

"Nope. Name's Alex Riggi. Age twenty-seven. Driver's license says he lives in Boston's Back Bay."

"What is it you think I can do for you, Chief?"

"I'm not sure yet. Normally, I'd figure the guy was killed here along the beach or dumped here, but with the floating debris… "

"You think there's a boat involved."

"Or all that junk's got nothing to do with this." He shrugged. "Normally, I'd call in Fish and Game. They've got a dive team for this sort of thing."

"To find a boat, if there is one," Bannon said.

"And any other evidence that might've sunk rather than floated," Cole added. "Most of the dive team's out of state at some training function. The ones left back are involved with something up at Lake Winnipesaukee. Your buddy, McMurphy, he's got a dive boat, doesn't he?"

"Yes."

"And you're both ex-Coasties, so you're qualified to dive, aren't you?"

"Sure," Bannon said. "You want to know if we'd—"

A high-pitched, hysterical scream cut him short. "Is that my boy? Oh my God! Is that my Alex?"

CHAPTER **TWO**

BANNON AND COLE TURNED toward the commotion.

Willoughby had dropped his roll of crime scene tape to the sand. He stood holding a heavy-set woman, preventing her from advancing past the tape he'd been stringing up around the crime scene. The woman was short and compact. Her short hair blew in the stiff wind as she shouted over the sound of the surf. "Let me through!"

Behind her stood a short, middle-aged, balding man wearing plaid shorts, a purple Polo shirt that didn't cover his paunch, and sandals. He wore tortoiseshell-framed sunglasses and had a worried look on his face. Bannon thought he looked like a pale turtle.

With him was a tall, thinner, and more composed woman with brown hair. Like the other two, Bannon figured her to be close to fifty, no more or less than a year on either side of it anyway. She wore dark slacks and a spring-weight suede jacket.

"You can't go in there," Willoughby said. "Ma'am. Please. You must—"

"Crap." Cole handed his coffee cup to Bannon and crossed through the wet sand to give Willoughby a hand. Bannon tagged along behind him.

"Ma'am. Ma'am. I need you to calm down." Cole raised his arm, collecting the woman's attention. "I'm Police Chief Cole."

His approach abated the woman's attempt to stampede across the crime scene and over poor Willoughby. "You're the one who called?"

"Are you Ruth Riggi?"

"Yes. Yes, I am."

"My office called, yes."

She stood on her toes and tried to look over Cole's broad shoulders. "Is that my son?" she asked. "Tell me!"

Bannon glanced back, too. From her angle, the woman would only be able to see the back of the body on the ground. She might be able to see the body had on a wet, green hoodie, but not that gunshot wound to his head.

Cole put his hands on her shoulder and gently held her. "I know this is hard."

"Your office called me. Woke my husband and me up." She glanced at the balding man behind her. "Is that—"

"We don't know yet—"

"Is it!" she shouted.

"I need you to calm down, Mrs. Riggi," Cole said. "I'm going to tell you what we know. A young man's been found on the beach. He's dead. We found your son's wallet."

The woman lost color in her face. Bannon stepped closer. He'd made death notifications during his time in the service. Her pale complexion worried him. One could never tell how a person would react to the most devastating news possible, the death of a son or a daughter.

Ruth Riggi moaned, and her legs buckled under her.

Bannon and Cole rushed forward as Willoughby, reacting quickly, and with help from the man who looked like a turtle, caught her before she slipped to the sand. They walked her over to an outcropping of rocks and sat her down there. She groaned and held her head like she was suffering from a migraine headache. What she was actually going through was much, much worse.

"Can I get you something to drink?" Willoughby asked. "Water?"

"Yes, please," the man said, answering for Ruth Riggi. He held her hand and patted it. "That would help."

They watched Willoughby retreat as the brunette woman stepped forward as well.

To them, Cole asked, "You two are?"

"Sam Riggi," the man said. He leaned down and put a supportive arm around the woman's shoulder. "I'm her husband."

"And I'm Meredith Palmer." She rubbed Mrs. Riggi's back. "They're my friends. We've known each other for most of our lives. Alex and—"

"Okay," Cole said. "I'm going to need you—"

Sam Riggi, proving to be of sturdier stock than his appearance suggested, interrupted the cop. "You need us to identify the body?"

"Yes, sir," Cole said. "But let's not get ahead of ourselves. First, I was hoping you could answer some questions about your son."

"What do you want to know?"

Bannon thought the man was curt in his response. But again, different people reacted differently to what these people were going through. Bannon didn't have children, so he could only imagine the toll of being told your son or daughter might be dead could take.

"He lives in Boston, doesn't he?" Cole asked.

"He does," Riggi said. "Yes."

"Do you have any idea why he'd be up here? On the beach?"

Meredith Palmer answered for him. "I know exactly why Alex was here," she said. "He was with my son."

"Who would that be, ma'am?" Cole asked.

"Billy. Billy Palmer. He and Alex grew up together. They're from here originally."

"Hampton Beach?" Cole asked.

"No, but New Hampshire. Amherst, specifically. The boys live in Boston now."

"Together?" Bannon asked.

"No," she said. "They each have their own apartments now."

"You think they might have been together?" Cole asked. "Last night?"

"I know they were," she said. "Billy and I spoke yesterday afternoon. He told me they were going out on the *Bottom Line*."

"The bottom line?" Cole asked.

"That's his boat. He keeps it docked at the Hampton River Marina. The slips are cheaper than in Boston."

"I'm familiar with the marina," Bannon said. "It's a little late in the season to be out boating, especially at night."

She looked Bannon up and down. "Excuse me, are you a cop?"

In his sweaty T-shirt and shorts, he hardly looked like one. "No, I'm—"

"He's consulting with us on this," Cole said, getting the interview back on track. "You were saying, the boat?"

"He wanted to take it out one last time before they took her out of the water for the winter." She looked from Bannon to Cole. "Is Billy with Alex? Have you found my son? I've tried texting and calling him ever since Ruth told me the police called. He's not picking up. Do you know... Where is my son?"

Bannon and Cole exchanged concerned glances. Good question. And here was a better one, Bannon thought. Was Billy a second victim or a suspect?

Want to keep reading?
Grab *The Yakuza Gambit* today!

ALSO BY DAVID DELEE

Brice Bannon Seacoast Adventures
Crimson Storm
Siege at Tiamat Bluff
The Yakuza Gambit
Strike of the Stingray
The Oceanic Princess
Facing the Storm

Parker Quinn Archaeological Thrillers
The Scarlet Death

Dark Justice Thrillers

Between Truth & Lies	Out of the Game
Cold Cases	With Intent
Too Far	Moral Misconduct
Stare at the Moon	Pin Money
While the City Burns	Crystal White
Takedown	Fatal Destiny

Runners

ABOUT THE AUTHOR

David DeLee is the acclaimed author behind the *Dark Justice Thrillers*, a gripping crime fiction series that brings together the bold worlds of bounty hunter Grace deHaviland, ex-DEA agent Nick Lafferty, and NYPD detectives Frank Flynn and Christine Levy. Anchored by the *Grace deHaviland Bounty Hunter* books—known for their dynamic protagonist and compelling action—DeLee's work captures the raw intensity of justice on the edge.

David also writes the high-octane *Brice Bannon Seacoast Adventure* series, a nautical action-thriller saga that captures the pulse-pounding energy of Clive Cussler, Brad Thor, and James Rollins—especially with his spin-off *Parker Quinn Archaeological Thrillers*, which blends adventure, history, and intrigue, adding a bold new layer to his ever-evolving storytelling landscape.

A former licensed private investigator and Certified Fraud Examiner with a Master's Degree in Criminal Justice, DeLee draws from real-world experience to craft authentic, edge-of-your-seat narratives that resonate with fans of crime, justice, and pulse-pounding action.

David now resides in New Hampshire, where he enjoys the lakes, the coast, and four very distinct seasons while he continues to write stories that explore the darker corners of justice.